Twin Sons

The Burning Son Book 4

TH Leatherman

Son Rise by TH Leatherman

Copyright © 2020 by Fivefold Publishing LLC

This is a work of fiction. Names, characters, businesses, places, events and incidents are either the products of the author's imagination or used in a fictitious manner. Any resemblance to actual persons, living or dead, or actual events is purely coincidental.

Published by Fivefold Publishing LLC, PO Box 586, Firestone, CO 80520.

Cover Artwork: Licarto

ISBN-13: 978-0-9983002-8-3

Acknowledgements

If you are reading this book, my first Thank You is to you. I couldn't have written this book without my many fans. Thank you so much for your encouragement and kind words. To my wife, without whose support my dreams of becoming an author never would have come to pass. You are my center, my rock, my muse. Thanks to Drake and Ashton for teaching me patience and inspiring me with your creativity. Special thanks to the members of the Crafty Writing Monkeys. Your insight was very helpful. To the wonderful members of Rocky Mountain Fiction Writers, for teaching me what it means to be a writer. Special thanks also to Merrilee Leatherman, Dan Bergman, Kat Kane, Bill VanCleave, Robin Bowers, and Aimie Runyan. Each of you supported me in different ways and I can't thank you enough for believing in me.

TABLE OF CONTENTS

Politics have no relation to morals.

-Niccolo Machiavelli

CHAPTER 1 - RECOVERY

"It'll be okay, Mark. We'll get her back."

I regarded my navigator with a confident and curious inspection, projecting a captainly aura of calm confidence. Was it working? I gave her a lopsided grin. "Was it ever in doubt?"

Mimi raised an eyebrow and glanced down. I followed her gaze. The coin I kept in my pocket, the one my grandfather had given me, was in my white-knuckled grip. A nervous habit. Whenever things were bad, I pulled it out and tried to rub off some of his wisdom.

I sighed and put the coin back in my pocket.

Mimi nodded in understanding and returned her attention to her console.

My stomach twisted in knots. Sara was over there. More than my XO, she was my girlfriend. Maybe, someday, she'd become my wife. If this damned war ever ended. If someone could make the Erethizon Theocracy see reason and stop their mad crusade to convert the galaxy. If assaulting this pirate base didn't kill me first.

The lumpy potato-like asteroid grew on the main screen.

A month earlier, we'd liberated Aspen. Thankfully the expected enemy reinforcements never came.

We'd called for our own reinforcements from our hidden base in Isura. Thankfully, Aspen had a handful of cruisers and frigates. They'd built them in their underwater cities, ready for the day when the minefield could be dealt with.

However, our ships arrived bringing the worst news possible. My flagship, the Queen Nephanie, was missing. Since Sara was her acting captain, she was missing too.

That thought reminded me to keep my head in the now. We weren't in any danger yet, but the moment was fast approaching.

To my left, was the tactical station Sara would've occupied. My marine commander stood there now. We'd installed a platform so she could reach the controls. The foxlike Muscat stand about a meter tall. Half the size of the average Terran. We'd captured this destroyer from the Porcu-bears. They were two and a half meters tall. Taller and much wider than the average Terran. Humans could get by with reinstalling the software and reaching a little further for the controls. The Erethizon consoles were stolen Terran technology anyway.

"Tracy, how are we looking?"

The alien grunted. "Missiles are hot, but tubes are closed. Gauss cannons are cold, but backup capacitors are charged. They shouldn't be able to tell how ready for battle we are unless their scan tech is much better than we expected."

"And our reserve force?"

She rolled her nose. "Brovis and his people," she gave a vulpine grin, "Fo'vra help anyone who gets in their way."

That was good. Ideally, we wouldn't have a ship to station battle. My new ship, an Erethizon destroyer named Questra, was a mobile trash heap. We'd boarded and taken it from the Porcu-bears and then they'd tried to take it back from us. That and a scuffle on the bridge had pretty much destroyed everything except the engine room, and that was in sad shape too.

We'd put it back together using sealant and engine tape and it showed. We had three working consoles and a bridge full of spot welds and mismatched consoles and screens. The odd sticky note translated Erethizon into Terran for the few controls we hadn't replaced in our haste to get out here. Everyone wore vac suits, just in case. We hadn't had time to do more. They'd captured our people. Every second Sara and her crew were in their hands they'd be tortured and worse.

Our arrival in Isura was met with a brief excitement over the food in our holds. We'd also contacted a smuggler to bring us food from Lir. Sara had gone out to meet them in open space. We didn't want them to figure out where our new secret base was located. My spymaster, Brady, confirmed our worst fears. The smugglers had turned pirate and captured the ship. He'd tracked them down to an uncharted asteroid base well away from any inhabited systems.

Which is where we were.

"Distance?"

Mimi studied her console. "Twenty thousand meters. They have to know we're here."

I nodded in agreement. They should be hailing us or firing missiles or...

"Unidentified ship, slow to zero relative and state your name and intentions. Failure to comply will result in your immediate destruction."

Mimi nodded to me.

I flipped my visor down, put my gloves on, and answered the hail. "Death's Chosen, this is Captain Harrison of the Questra," I lied. "We're requesting docking clearance." Mark Martin had a reputation. Random named Captain, not so much.

It turned out I needn't have to bothered, the comm signal was audio-only. "Whaddya want and how did you find us?" growled the comms operator.

So much for comm etiquette. "If you wanted your secret base to remain a secret, you shouldn't let your crew drink with the miners on Hephaestus. As is stands, pretty much every smuggler coreward of the central worlds knows you're out here."

"Fucking farthogs," was followed by the sound of pounding and papers rustling. "I'ma gonna kill Daly and his crew when they get back."

"We're carrying a load of metal we liberated from the original crew of this vessel. Do you want to trade for it, or should I hump it over to Bastian?"

"Ore or ingots?"

"Ingots." I answered, "Mostly iron, but we're also carrying copper, magnesium, and aluminum."

"Uh, we don't need much in the way of metals."

Muses this guy was stupid. He couldn't bluff his way into a brothel. "No? Because the word is you have weapons and need metal. Our mistake. We'll leave you be and head to Bastian."

"Wait!" he yelled, "I mean, we got a shipment of metals last week, but we can always use more. Let me get the Captain."

He must have left the mic live. A chair squealed against the deck and retreating boots sounded. Hinges squeaked as a hatch slammed open. A few seconds later there was a different voice. "What the hell do you mean there's a ship out there? We're the only beings for a hundred light-years."

The response was muffled, but the answer wasn't. "Daly? That inbred frequa fucker." Then louder, "I don't know who you are, but we don't want any. If you know what's good fer ya, you'd better forget you ever found this place."

I ground my teeth. The plan called for us to be invited in. If we had to go for a hard breach, we'd take damage from whatever defense weaponry they had. Lives could be lost before we ever got on board the station.

I wasn't ready to give up on the invite option. "No problem. I'm sure we'll get better value for our iron and copper in Bastian or Cairo."

"Iron? Copper? How much are we talking about?"

It wasn't an invitation, but they were talking. "This ship wasn't built for hauling cargo. Four hundred tons of iron. Around fifty tons of assorted other metals."

There wasn't that much on board, but their scans would show several containers full of metal. Again, if they upgraded, things would get interesting.

For several long minutes, the station didn't respond.

"They're not buying it," warned Mimi. "We need to... oh fuckin' frequa. They've opened missile tubes. And it looks like two rail guns are being warmed up."

Mimi reached to activate our own weapons, but I held up a hand. "Not yet."

A red warning light appeared on my console. My stomach sank and I broke out in a cold sweat. I'd overplayed my hand.

Mimi cursed, "And now we're target locked. Give the word skipper. It's time."

"Questra, this is Death's Chosen. We don't know you, so don't give us a reason to fill your hull with holes. That said, we are interested in your cargo."

Great. They're going to try and board us. Or kill us then take the cargo. I should have expected this since they'd probably done something similar to Nephie.

They continued, "So we're going to ask you to sit tight while we free up docking space. I'll meet you and your officers dockside so we can negotiate a fair trade."

Mimi and I exchanged a look. If they were negotiating in good faith, why warm up weapons. They were up to something, but so were we. Better to play along and hope we were sneakier.

At their request, we approached the pirate base. A light freighter pulled away from a docking ring, but the next berth over had our full attention. The Queen Nephanie.

"Can we hail her?" asked Mimi.

"No," I pointed. "Her antennae array is smashed, as are her engines."

"I hope they didn't hurt her," she frowned at me. "The AI or Sara, I mean."

The loss of the AI would be a major blow. She was unique. A true artificial life created by our systems engineer. Even more than that, the AI was my friend. Rage and sadness welled up within me, but I shoved it back down. We were about to assault a pirate base. I didn't have time to dwell on it. "Chances are they smashed her too. We'll have to hope that Racy can revive her."

I opened a channel to engineering. "Rowdy, Racy?"

"We're here Mark," growled Rowdy.

I smiled at the two Muscat as they grinned into the camera. My two best friends in all the galaxy. "Things are about to kick off."

"We'll be ready for our part," affirmed Racy.

I commed War 'n Pace. "Ready?"

War pumped his fist at the vid pickup. "They'll never know what flattened them."

Glancing at the readout, I continued. "Two minutes on my mark... mark."

They returned their attention to their men.

"Let's move marines. We are go in two. Call it off by the numbers," yelled Pace.

I cut the channel. In a civilized port the ship AI and the station AI would sync up and guide us in. We'd replaced the Porcu-bear AI the ship came with, with a Terran model. It worked well enough, but I wasn't willing to trust it with docking.

"Telemetry?"

"None," answered Mimi. "Looks like we're doing this manually."

"Tracy?" I asked.

"Targeting the freighter with passive scans. They're skrit in a pan as soon as you give the word."

The docking tube was longer than normal and wasn't a design I was familiar with. I decided I didn't want to test its springs, so I opted for a slower approach speed. I tapped the thrusters to slow our relative velocity to a crawl and gave another tap to adjust our yaw. Three, two, one... Docked.

The connections showed a positive seal, but no shore power or air. It further solidified my assumption that this was a cobbled-together operation.

"Positive seal," I spoke into the comm, "You are go."

I stood, "All yours, Mimi. Keep it warm. This won't take long."

Her 'Aye, aye, sir!' followed me through the hatch as I ran to join the boarding team. The sound of gauss rifles and plasma grew louder as I descended the ladder toward the forward lock. It was too loud. Peaking around the corner I saw why.

The plan had been for the marines to rush into the station and secure the docks. The pirates on the station tried to storm the ship. They ran into each other. Both forces retreated and fortified. The pirates had a barricade on the docks. My marines used fallen pirates and comrades for cover. There were several breaches in the docking tube and atmosphere was escaping.

We'd disabled the safeties for the attack. I used my implant to override my previous override and activate the hull breach alarm.

A loud whooping sounded and all the interior hatches slammed shut except the forward hatch. Its controls were damaged.

A gauss round pinged off the bulkhead centimeters from my faceplate. I ducked back.

"War, Pace?"

Pace answered, "We're going to charge the barricade, sir. What side of the breach doors are you on?"

"In the airlock," I yelled.

"Then keep your head down." Then to his men, "On three. One-"

An explosion. Fire filled the tube and vanished as air escaped into the void. Bodies, both dead and alive flew forward as the docking tube bent upward.

"Mimi!" I screamed in horror.

"Got it," she yelled from the bridge.

Mimi fired thrusters. The docking tube righted and the shredded ends ground together. War grabbed sealing foam from an emergency locker and ran into the ring. He sprayed the foam into the jagged breach. The station's defenders realized what was happening. They raked him with gauss rounds and he tumbled back into his men.

"Medic!" someone shouted.

"Pace, send in Brovis."

"Yes, sir!"

The whole hallway shook as a line of armored behemoths rushed past me. Terran and Muscat marines scrambled out of the way as the Porcu-bear troopers barreled past. Their war cry, "Oppose us and die!" Echoing through the general channel.

I wanted to use them as a reserve unit. They were Erethizon deserters. We weren't sure we could count on their loyalty in battle. Also, they'd be taller than the passages in a Terran made space station.

I realized this had been a mistake in my tactical planning. Brovis and his Disciplinarians ran headlong into the pirate barricade ripping the improvised defenses apart like paper. The bearlike aliens were impressively tough alone. Inside their combat armor, each was a miniature tank. Gauss rounds bounced off the heavy armor like rain. Pirates turned to flee only to be caught in their armored claws and crushed.

In five minutes, it was over. The docks were secure. Pace set about reinforcing our position. I checked out the docking ring. It wasn't pretty. The hull sealant had cemented the two halves of the ring together. A corporal was filling in the gaps. The tube had bent left and a little up. It wouldn't hold long, but hopefully it wouldn't have to. I fired off a text message to Rowdy. Then I sent another message to Jay asking about War. He answered that he'd rushed him to the med bay but didn't have any more for me yet.

We didn't have a doctor on board. I'd asked my sister to stay in Isura. She'd thrown a fit, of course. I'd pointed out that Cindy's construction crew was putting together her new hospital in the space station. One look at the plans sent her into a tirade about how a blind monkey could've laid it out better.

It was a cheap ploy she'd retaliate for later, but I didn't want her here for this. Our target was the worst kind of pirates imaginable. Atrocities of every kind had been attributed to them. If they'd abused or tortured Sara and the crew...

I shook it off. "Pace, sitrep."

He turned from a barricade he'd been inspecting. "Sir, we lost three men to explosive decompression. Their armor was buttoned up, so maybe we'll see them again. I've detailed a couple of marines to search and recovery ops. Another three were injured including that unlucky farthog War. We've disassembled the enemy bulwarks and are using it to fortify our position here."

"Great, are we ready for phase two?" I asked.

"Aye, sir."

I waved a hand indicating to continue.

Pace pointed to a cluster of marines. "First squad: hold the docks. Secure our LZ. Second squad to port, Brovis, you and third squad to starboard, fourth squad straight up the middle. Our objectives are to secure our missing people, engineering, and the control center. In. That. Order. Drop your pucks every intersection." He held up one of the black metal disks that would act as comms repeaters and motion detectors. "It'd be a shame if you needed backup and no one realized or knew how to reach you."

I trotted onto the docks, really just a large open room, and joined fourth squad. Tracy's brother Trippy made to object but seemed to think better of it. The Muscat marine assigned a fire team to protect me. We took off at a jog. The point man carried a riot shield. In my heads-up display, a map formed as my teams raced through the corridors and passages. The powered armor collated each marine's sensor data into an image of the battlefield.

The next room looked like a marshaling yard. Grav lifts and equipment crates haphazardly littered the floor. We passed through unmolested.

A scream echoed in the comms. Marines cursed.

The sound cut off as the squad leader removed his team from the main channel. A moment later Tracy's other brother Trevor, reported. "One of my men stepped through the deck. Foil covering a metal recycling unit. It chewed right through his armor and ate half his leg before we knew it."

"Watch it. Be smart, not splatter." Reminded Pace.

We moved again, but a bit more slowly. We reached a T junction and went left taking us deeper into the station. I tried my best to put Sara out of my mind and concentrate on the mission. Try as I might, dread ate at my stomach like a cancer.

Ahead there lay an intersection. Everyone had an eye on a corner. The two in the lead set up: one high one low. They moved in and then relaxed. The one on the left turned toward us and started to yell, 'clear.'

He never finished. Red sprayed the inside of his visor. His companion ducked back before shots found him. A loud clank from behind me. My bodyguard had shoved me to the ground.

A section of the wall was in the passage. A secret panel that had hidden the ambushers. Now open it provided them with good cover. Four mismatched helmets poked over the top. Tracer rounds sprayed the hall over my head. I ground my teeth. My bodyguard had the balls to shove me, his CO.

Three helmets jerked back. The fourth ducked. My bodyguard, I suddenly remembered his name was Jack, landed in front of me. Not only had he shoved me, he now blocked my line of sight.

I fired a burst over his prone body, cursing his ineptness. The rounds ricocheted off the wall plate. I focused on the barrier willing the last guy to poke his head out. My bodyguard didn't move. I glanced down briefly and saw red oozing from holes in Jack's armor plates.

My heart sank as I pulled my eyes back to the barrier. I took back every nasty thought I'd had about him. He'd sacrificed himself for me taking out three pirates at the expense of his own life. Now he continued to serve me by providing cover in the otherwise empty passageway. That left me with at least one of the bastards and an unknown number behind me. Behind me was Trippy's problem. This asshole was mine.

Correction, two assholes. Two helmets bobbed in front of me over the lip of the barrier. Farthogs, not high enough to give me a shot. Behind me, more weapons fire and a grenade went off.

I dialed up the power on my rifle and aimed. I sent a three-round burst into the armored wall panel. One man fell into the passage, dead. I'd upgraded my weapon. My new rifle could penetrate moderate armor at full power. Using it at the highest setting drained the power pack after a few shots. A warning appeared on my HUD. I switched out the empty power cell for a fresh one.

I sent another burst through the panel. Light poked through the holes. The last guy lay in the alcove.

My heart pounded in my chest. I took a moment to calm my nerves. Jack had saved my life with his. The life of his captain, who shouldn't have been in the strike team to begin with.

A tap on my shoulder. I held up a finger then pointed to the door, indicating that there was one combatant in there. Trippy stepped over the dead marine and threw a grenade around the panel. The pirate jumped out and ran up the passage away from us. I shot him in the back. Trippy retrieved his dummy grenade.

"Clear up front," someone called.

"Clear out back," responded Trippy.

It had been a good trap. Two secret panels to create overlapping fields of fire at the intersection. However, my men were professionals in good armor.

I approached a man on the deck keeping my weapon trained on him. He still held a rifle. I kicked it away. Yep, dead. All five of them wore mismatched and shoddy armor.

We continued. There were half a dozen dead ends. We encountered two more clusters of defenders and three more traps. Two saber mine tripwires and a viciously ingenious hidden pit with vibro-blades. No more of my squad died.

We reached a solid looking steel door. The word "Brig" was stenciled on it in large red letters. Graffiti underneath it that read, "Abandon all hope ye who enter here."

"This looks promising," I said to no one in particular.

Trippy growled in response. He inspected the electronic lock and motioned to one of his men.

The men on the other side of this door had to know we were coming. They'd be ready for us. Given what we'd seen so far, they wouldn't hesitate to use my people as human shields. The thought of someone holding a pistol to Sara's head filled me with rage and fear. We had no choice but to go in. If we stayed out here, there'd be reinforcements.

The marine pulled out a portable plasma cutter and sliced open the wall next to the lock. In under a minute he had the wires pulled out and nodded to Trippy.

I flattened myself against the side of the passage. Then he opened the door.

CHAPTER 2 – THE CELLS

The door slid into the wall. Several heads and rifles poked over an overturned metal table. No one fired.

At that moment, I recognized a pair of almond-shaped eyes behind one of the rifles. Relief flooded through me.

"Hold," I cried. Slinging my weapon, I indicated for the marines to lower their rifles. I strode forward and pulled off my helmet.

Sara vaulted over the makeshift barricade and wrapped me in her arms.

I knew I couldn't really feel her warm body against mine through the armor, but I imagined I could. It was the most wonderful feeling in the galaxy.

"About time you got here, Treasure," she mumbled into my armored chest.

"We got held up. The traffic in this sector is murder." I took in the room. Four pirates lay dead on the deck. Three hallways extended from the room each with a dozen cells. Several crew poked their heads out. "We're here to rescue you, but it seems like you rescued yourselves." I wanted nothing more than to hold her like that forever.

She stood back and straightened the tattered remains of her uniform. She was once more cool, collected and in control. To her affection was a private thing, not for public consumption. My heart broke. Her face was purple on one side and she had a fat lip. My blood boiled and my fists shook. The only thing that mattered was killing the bastards that hurt her.

"How'd you find us?"

"Brady. He found some of the crew you were supposed to meet in a bar on Hephaestus. Got 'em drunk, rolled 'em, and pumped them for information."

Former prisoners limped up the halls. I counted fourteen. Less than half the number Sara had started with. Their tunics and shipsuits were torn and bloody, hanging off them in tatters. Some of them struggled with broken arms or legs. One poor soul had her fingertips wrapped in red splotched rags. Blood sang in my ears. These bastards would pay dearly.

Trippy's marines rushed in to administer aid.

I motioned to him, "Where are we?"

The foxlike alien held up an arm and a hologram sprang into being between us. "Pace has repelled three attempts to retake the docks. Third squad has encountered strong resistance near what they believe to be engineering. More exposed cables along the passage walls." At the mention of each team, a section of the map glowed. Red marks indicated prior firefights and located traps. "Rowdy and Racy say the pirates have done a shoddy job repairing Queen Nephanie. She's space worthy, barely. It looks like they were trying to install a new AI but didn't complete it. Our girl, Nephie, is missing some parts, and her power and data runs have been pulled. We haven't located the base command center."

I surveyed my people. We'd lost a lot of good men, but I'd save all that I could. "Alright, we're heading back to the docks. Keep Sara's crew between us. Everyone gets out alive."

"Hey, what about me?"

The voice came from down the passage to the right. Sara rolled her eyes. Sara and I approached the locked cell. Through the bar was a man beaten to a bloody pulp. His face was splotched purple and yellow. One eye was swollen shut.

In my implant, I ran his face against the images of my missing crew. Even taking into account the bruising, he wasn't a match for any of them.

"Who is this guy," I asked Sara.

"A local," her voice dripping with contempt.

"Sorry," I said, "we aren't here for you," and turned to leave.

"Wait! Give me a weapon. I can fight."

Sara and I continued up the hall. No way I'd give someone I don't know a charged weapon.

"I can get you into the command center."

I stopped.

Sara scowled and put her hands on her hips.

"You haven't found it, right? That's 'cause it's well hid. You'll never find it unless you know where to look."

I returned to the cell. "Why hide the entrance?"

His good eye stared up at me, pleading to be heard. "It's a pirate base. Sure, the captain gets elected an all, but that doesn't mean he trusts any of 'em. Only the guys who work there can get in, an they know it's death or worse to reveal it."

I crossed my arms over my chest. "And you know where it is."

"I was here when the base was built. I know all its secrets."

"And yet, here you sit." I waved to indicate his cell.

He grinned a mouth full of broken teeth. "Knowin' stuff don' mean I'm good at keepin' my mouth shut. I guess I mouthed off to Cap'n Dominic one time too many."

"What's your name?"

He didn't answer right away, but finally said, "John Jones."

I knew right away he was lying, but that wasn't important. If he really could get us to the command center, we could destroy it. We'd keep these pirates from preying on any other crews. We might be able to neutralize them if we could reach Engineering, but that was far from a sure thing. Nothing is ever certain in war.

I motioned to Trippy. "He comes with us."

He nodded and produced a pair of binders.

"Hey." John protested.

"I said you could come with us, not that we trusted you. You're welcome to rot in your cell, Mr. Jones."

He glared at me but held his hands out to be cuffed.

I slung my rifle and handed my pistol to Sara, "Shoot him if he steps a centimeter out of line."

She checked the ammo and charged it while glaring at the pirate.

Getting back to the docks was considerably easier than getting to the brig. For one, we now had a map. We didn't have to spend time on dead ends and wrong turns. Secondly, John Jones showed us a short cut and disarmed a saber mine trap that would have certainly killed some of my marines and rescued crew.

Unfortunately, Jones didn't give Sara the excuse she wanted to kill him.

At the docks, Pace ushered Sara's crew onto Questra. Our medics, Jay and Trey had been alerted and they turned one of her cargo holds into a medical bay. Pace also sent a recall to Second squad and Brovis. If Mr. Jones really could get us to the command center, it'd be better to go in force. Sara refused to leave my side.

"I can help," She argued. "Get my armor and I'll pay these bastards back. I want to see Dominic's face before I blow him to hell."

I wasn't ready to chance losing her again. I also knew telling her that would go over like a live grenade. "I'd prefer to have you manning the tactical station. Tracy is good, but you're better."

"Do you remember what you told me when you went after Ufkell on Eureka?"

Of course, I remembered. We'd just started dating. She'd begged me not to go. Asked me to send one of my men dressed up as me. I'd told her no. Ufkell had hurt my people. It was my responsibility to care for them. Vengeance was needed, and I'd be damned if I let someone else carry that burden in my stead.

I saw it then. She'd been the captain, acting or no. The dead and injured crewmen were her responsibility. As much as I wanted her safe, I couldn't, *wouldn't* stand in her way.

It hurt, but I said it. What else could I do? "Suit up. We need to move fast."

She handed my pistol back to me and I holstered it.

John Jones leered at her retreating form. "Damn fine piece of ass if you ask me. Shame to cover it up with armor. You two exclusive or can anyone take a turn?"

I didn't look at him. "Remind me why I'm letting you live?" I wanted to punch him, but I didn't. He was my prisoner and my marines and crew were around me.

I needn't have worried, Pace slammed the butt of his rifle into the back of Jones' head.

Jones shook his melon and spat blood on the deck. "You *need* me. You'll never find the control center without me."

"My men almost have engineering. Once they do, we don't need to take the command center." I drew my sidearm but didn't aim it at him. "Your usefulness is about to come to an end."

He held his bound hands up. "Oh, uh, hey. I didn't mean nuthin'..."

Trevor's voice came on the squad comms. "Feradit! Everybody out." A rumble shook the deck.

"Trevor, report." ordered Pace.

"They set something off in engineering," he huffed. It was clear he was running. "Hard radiation. The blast doors came down."

"Can you get back in there?" asked Pace.

"Negative. Radiation levels too high. Even in combat armor, they'd die in minutes."

"Oh farthogs," swore John Jones.

As if on cue, sealing foam filled the passages leading away from the docks. Marines jumped out of the way with cries of surprise. One man's foot and another's whole leg were caught in the stuff as it hardened.

"Damn them to Hades," I screamed. We'd saved the prisoners, but half my people were now trapped deep inside the station.

CHAPTER 3 – A NEW PLAN

"Cut those marines out," yelled Pace.

I shoved my pistol under Jones' chin.

"Whoa, now Cap'n." His eyes grew as wide as saucers. "Not my fault. Pirates remember? That's a failsafe triggered from the command center in case of mutiny. Every intersection fills with sealing foam, cutting everyone off from everyone else. I didn't think 'ol Dominic even knew about it."

I grabbed the weaselly pirate by the neck. "How do we get around it?" I growled.

"You don't," he squeaked. "That's the point. It'll take hours."

"Over half my men are trapped in the station. We can't talk to them because your station is built in a big ass rock. And now our comm pucks won't work because the passages are filled with hull sealant. Don't tell me we can't get them out."

A gauntleted hand gently pulled my arm down.

"Be calm my Treasure." Sara had returned wearing armor and weapons. "Now isn't the time."

I took a steadying breath. She was right, we needed to break out the large plasma cutters. The sooner we got to work, the sooner we'd get our men back.

"Yeah, Cap'n Treasure-"

Sara's right cross sent Jones spinning and he landed on his ass.

He shook his head dazedly then gazed up at her. "A little early for foreplay, but I'm game."

Jones rolled away in time to miss Sara's armored boot to his crotch.

Pace stood nearby, leaning against the large plasma cutter. While I'd been threatening Jones, he'd retrieved it, but stopped to enjoy the floor show.

I motioned to him and he reluctantly lugged the cutter to the hardened foam-filled passageway. Only to stop short when we heard a loud crunching sound.

The sound got louder and louder until an armored claw punched through the bulkhead to the left of the passage. Metal squealed as it was pulled back. In minutes the hole was widened and Brovis squeezed through onto the docks.

"Fornicating Farthogs! Goddamn Porcu-bears!" swore Jones as he scrambled toward the docking tube. Two marines stopped him.

I stared up at the bearlike alien. "Brovis, Erethizon armor is good, but even it can't claw through hull armor."

Brovis showed a mouth full of needle-like teeth. He was trying to copy a Terran smile. It wasn't working. "It's not hull armor. It's a centimeter of steel. And the walls are regolith." He held up a rock and crushed it to dust. "Not a problem for Disciplinarian armor."

I rounded on Jones who was gaping up at the three-meter-tall armored alien.

"He's with you? Who the hell are you guys?"

"He's not with the Theocracy. Not all Erethizon support the crusade to conquer the galaxy. Focus." I pointed at the hole as several more bearlike aliens shouldered through. "Are all the walls like this?"

"Some are silica or basalt, but yeah, most are like that."

He had to be lying. "What idiot builds a pirate base in a low metal asteroid? One well-placed missile will shatter the whole damn thing."

He shrugged as much as his binders would allow. "Do you know how hard it is to find a rock in deep space? We had to take what we could get. Besides, no one's supposed to know it's here and it was easy to dig through."

Several things clicked for me at once. First, we didn't have to take the command center. Second, with Brovis' help, it would take less than an hour to dig out Trevor's squad. Lastly, I recognized who we were dealing with. As I'd guessed, his name wasn't John Jones, but I'd let the charade continue. For the moment.

"Okay, change in plan. We aren't digging these rats out. Our primary objective is complete. As soon as Brovis can retrieve second squad we're pulling up stakes."

"Oppose us and die!" yelled Brovis and he started digging through the starboard bulkhead.

Jones frowned at me. "You're going to blow the asteroid." It was a statement, not a question.

As much as I regretted the loss of life, these pirates were scum. They'd tortured and killed my people. They'd probably done it to countless others. Jones' hands were far from clean.

"You'd leave behind all the resources they collected," Jones goggled. "My god man, think of the loot."

I stared at the hole. The sooner my people were back, the sooner we'd be off this rock.

"Is it the skirt?" Jones pressed. "A man like you should know better than to allow a woman to cloud your judgment."

Behind him, Sara shook her head.

I fixed Jones with a cold stare. "These pirates have killed half of one of my crews and seven of my marines have lost their lives assaulting this base. Yes, we could take the command center. Yes, we could find the cargo bays and take whatever we find there. I've got my people back. I'm not about to risk any more of them being hurt or killed. I'll blow this rock to hell and be done with it."

Jones shrugged, "Okay, revenge is as good a reason as any."

I breathed a sigh of relief when twenty minutes later Trevor and his team appeared in the hole.

Pace wasted no time. "Alright, load 'em up. I want to be outta here in five.

I changed out the power pack on my gauss rifle. Sara noticed. I motioned to Pace as I tapped it and pointed to the prisoner.

Both of them rolled their eyes but nodded.

I strode into the repaired docking tube and inspected the clamps from the inside. I couldn't see it well from here, but it seemed like we'd be able to undock without too much trouble.

I motioned to Pace, "bring Mr. Jones to the bridge. If there are any surprises, I want him there to give us the solution."

I opened a comm channel. "Rowdy, Racy, how's Queen Nephanie looking?"

"We've got thrusters," said Rowdy, "We can have main engines up in a couple of hours, but the R-drive will require a yard."

Racy took it from there. "Nephie is offline. She needs parts and new power and data runs. On the bright side, all the connections in engineering are intact. Our backup AI is working."

Rounding a corner, I climbed a ladder. Sara jogged behind me with Pace and Jones a few steps beyond. I checked the list of people on the command channel. "You getting all this, Mimi?"

"Aye, sir," affirmed Mimi. "Rowdy, we're going to take Nephanie under tow. We're going to pull away from the station. If the pirates have anything left, they'll hit us then. As soon as I say it's safe, instruct your helmsman to undock and maneuver under our keel. We'll attach tow lines and lash the two ships together."

"I'll need to come back over to Questra," said Rowdy. "Her R-drive isn't rated for this much mass. I'll need to make some adjustments before we can get underway. Mark, it'll be slow going. We'll only be able to go a couple of days at a time before we'll need to give the drive a rest."

We topped the ladder and walked onto the bridge.

"Tracy?"

"Not surprisingly, the freighter that pulled out of the slip ordered us to stay put or we'd be fired upon." She rolled her nose. "My gauss cannons ended that discussion. The base still has cannons and missile tubes, but they can't use them until we undock."

"It'd be a shame if we didn't give them the chance. Sara, would you mind helping Tracy out at tactical?"

Everything felt right as Sara moved next to Tracy. It was awkward with Tracy's narrow walkway, but it was just a little more reach for her. Pace pulled Jones to the back of the bridge.

I took a deep breath. "Alright Mimi, let's say goodbye."

Mimi hit the docking release and gave a small amount of thrust. The docking clamps didn't retract fully. I was jerked from my captain's chair and fell to my knees. I glanced back. Pace had a pistol to Jones' head. He had his palms up at chest height. The crew recovered and we strapped ourselves in.

"Sorry," winced Mimi.

On the main screen, a piece of docking tube clung gamely to the bow.

Mimi swung us around and pushed the ship away from the asteroid. At a hundred and fifty meters, Sara and Tracy opened up with our gauss cannons aiming for the station's missile tubes. The pirate base fired back with its gauss cannons, but I let our shields take the initial salvo. The missiles were the bigger threat, but the station couldn't use them while we were close.

I'd expected Questra to ward off a significant amount of weapons fire, but shield strength plummeted. Either I was wrong about the shields or they were hitting us a lot harder than expected.

"Flip," I ordered.

"Aye, aye," responded Mimi.

We flipped end over end and exposed our bow shields. Sara and Tracy maintained a steady stream of fire. Sensing the threat, they both switched to targeting the station's defensive cannons.

Again, the shield strength dropped rapidly. I'd soon have to present a broadside. I had hoped to be further out when that happened. I decided to hold off as long as possible. That was a mistake.

I shouted, "Port broadside," a half-second too late. The dorsal gauss cannon shredded as concentrated fire pierced our shield and slammed into the weapon. Damage alarms wailed and rounds dug a furrow of destruction across the top of my ship.

With the port side toward the station, our retreat slowed. Status indicators blinked red as the station's cannons wreaked havoc on our shields.

"What the hell are they hitting us with?"

I didn't expect an answer, but Jones supplied one. "Hephaestus Industries GRS80 Mark VII quad cannon firing steel jacketed eighty-millimeter depleted uranium slugs with Shieldbasher TM technology."

A spared a glance in his direction. "What the..."

He hunched his shoulders. "We turned the cargo master at the main orbital. They... uh... fell off a grav-lift... twice."

"Farthogs." Just before the shield strength reached fifteen percent, Tracy scored a hit on one of the quad cannons. "Roll," I ordered.

Presenting our starboard broadside, I willed Tracy to finish off the final cannon before all our shields were gone. I got my wish with thirty-seven percent shield left.

"Take that you flea-infested skrits!" she yelled in triumph.

I let out a breath and put my coin back in my pocket. I hadn't realized I'd been squeezing it in a death grip again. We'd have a few more minutes to regain shield strength before they'd be able to fire-

"Missiles!" called Sara. "Three of them."

"We're too close, the station will be caught in the blast."

Tracy put her hands up, letting the AI handle defensive fire. It caught one. Two. The third hit us slamming everyone into their seat restraints.

"Shields down," said Sara, "hull breach in cargo bay four and crew berthing. Damage control teams en route."

I gritted my teeth. "Open comms, Nephie, get out of there. These suicidal bastards-"

"Two more missiles," shouted Sara.

The gauss cannons got one. "Brace for impact," shouted Sara.

CHAPTER 4 – A LONG WAY DOWN

I slammed into the armrest. My nose felt wet and I tasted blood. Without thinking, I spit to clear my mouth. The bottom half of my visor speckled red. "Report."

"Cargo bay four reports they are open to space," Sara flipped open her helmet and retched on the deck. "Sorry," She breathed. "Armor there is gone, as is the damage control party that was in there. At a guess, the missile impacted before it had a chance to arm."

"Nephie is away," Mimi went green at the sight of vomit on the deck and turned away. "She's accelerating toward us."

"Move to put us between Nephie and the station," I ordered.

"It'll take a few,' said Mimi. "We're moving away at a good clip."

Seconds pasted. No new threats appeared. Nephie seemed to crawl out to meet us.

"Open comms. Nephie, can you boost your speed? I'm not sure why they've stopped firing, but I'm betting it won't last."

Rowdy answered, "Negative Mark. No engines. We're moving at best possible speed with thrusters and we don't have any repair drones left. I can't spare anyone for manual repairs."

"Come again, Rowdy. You're out of repair drones? I gave you six to get Queen Nephanie ready for space."

"That's my fault Mark," Racy cut into our channel. "I lost my temper. The level of damage those mother frexing sons of farthogs did to my poor baby, was too much. I sent the repair drones onto the station just before we left with orders to tear out every power and data line they could find. Let's see how they like it."

I closed my eyes slowly. "Thanks... Racy. We'll see you soon. Questra out." Unlatching my harness, I stood and approached the tactical station.

Tracy twitched her ears at me. "Engineers."

Sara gave a brittle laugh. "It's good to be back."

Tracy nodded, "It won't take them long to take out the repair drones."

"We don't need much time. Just enough to get a couple of thousand klicks away. Besides, they filled every intersection with hull sealant. That'll slow them down."

Mimi studied her plot, "Even slowing down to match Nephanie, we'll have that in twelve minutes."

Twelve minutes later, the station still hadn't given us so much as a target lock.

I gave Sara a weak smile. "We're at minimum safe distance. I know it's not as good as a blaster up close and personal, but..." I reached over the tactical console and punched in the coordinates for the docking tube we'd ripped out. "If you can hit that, it'll be almost as good."

She snarled silently. "Missile tube two open. Firing."

Sara didn't miss.

The thing about space station docks is that they are large open areas. In a rock like this, that meant it made a natural weak point. All it took was one missile. The asteroid shattered sending rock chunks in all directions. Given the odd physics of explosives, a couple of decent-sized boulders came our way. We adjusted our course to get out of the way. Some pieces were as big as houses, but for the most part, the asteroid simply disintegrated.

I flipped up my visor and watched to see how 'John' was handling it. His shoulders slumped, but he seemed more relieved than sad.

"No friends to mourn?" I asked.

He grunted. "No friends."

I approached him and stood right next to him so I could stare down at him, showing my disdain. "What will you do now?"

"I guess a lot of that depends on you." He pointed at the main screen with his hands.

I turned to look, and that's when he made his move. He yanked my gauss rifle from its holster. I spun back around to find my weapon pointing at my face.

CHAPTER 5 – REVERSAL OF FORTUNE

Tracy reached for her sidearm, but Sara shook her head at her. Pace backed up a couple of steps. His weapon was out but pointed at the floor.

I regarded Jones coolly. I made an effort to look him in the eyes and not the barrel of my weapon. "You'll never get off the bridge, much less make it to safety."

"Oh, I think I will," he said. "You see, I 'reckon everyone here cares more about you than their own lives. Now me, I only care about myself. So long as I have you, ain't a soul on this ship gonna risk me killin' you. Especially the skirt over there." He nodded in Sara's direction. "Now, move real slow and keep your hands where I can see them. Go to the hatch at the back of the bridge."

I kept my hands at chest level palms facing out. Slowly, I moved to the hatch. "We're in deep space. There's nowhere to go."

"We're going to the shuttle bay."

I shook my head. "We aren't carrying an R-drive equipped shuttle."

"Didn't figure ya did," he sneered. "But a shuttle has its own air and water. It's a small space, easy to control. I keep you in there with me, and everyone will have to do what I say, or risk what I'll do."

I reached the hatch and turned. "You can't kill me. You'll lose your leverage."

He grinned showing his broken teeth. "I don't have to kill ya. I just have to hurt ya *real bad.*"

"Done playing games Jones, or do you prefer Wesley?"

The grin widened, "That's The Dastardly Pirate Wesley to you, and I'm so happy you've heard of me. It'll make things so much easier if everyone knows what I'm capable of. Now open the hatch."

I made no move to do so. "Let me see if I can guess the chain of events. After Ocelot gets destroyed, you and your crew decide that it wasn't such a bad idea." I leaned casually against the hatch frame. "An asteroid base. So, you come out here and build your own. You don't have enough resources, so you raid shipping." I rolled my hands. "You blackmail a few people in Hephaestus to get parts printers, grav plates, and other things that can't be made out here."

"We bribed them and stop stalling." His gaze traveled from Pace to Tracy. "I'm hoping to wait a bit before I damage you," he grinned maliciously. "But that ain't a *high* priority."

I bit my lip in thought. "But you work people pretty hard, and morale starts slipping. I mean, building a pirate base isn't like being a pirate. It requires real work. Not a lot of bullying, raping, and killing." I ticked them off on my fingers. "So, your second or third in command stages a coup."

Wesley's eye twitched. "You don't think I'll do it. Open the hatch Captain. Now. Or ya lose an arm."

"Oh, I know you'll do it. I'm absolutely sure you'll shoot me." I stroked my chin. "I don't believe all the stories about you, but enough of them have to be true to make the others credible. Bear with me a second though." I held up a finger in a wait a moment gesture. "Captain Dominic takes the job to run food out to the middle of nowhere. He figures it's a clandestine meeting, no one will know it's him and he can protect his reputation with the other pirates." I gestured to Pace who nodded.

I continued, "Pirates don't attack other pirates. It's bad for business. We rely on each other for intel about military movements, safe ports, where we can get supplies and the like. Only after he takes my ship he finds out, I already have my own pirate base. Better armed and better stocked than his. Instead of killing my crew, he takes them hostage so he can torture the information out of them. Why be a minnow when you can be a shark and all that?"

"Son of a Dru." Wesley shifted the weapon to my arm and pulled the trigger. It beeped at him. He squeezed the trigger twice more and it beeped each time. The color drained from his face. "Farthogs."

"Skip to the end, where I switch out my rifle's power pack for a dead cell and bring you aboard. I needed to know if we can work together, or if I get to turn you over to a civilized system for the reward. Gotta get the credits however you can, right?"

Pace raised his plasma rifle to his shoulder. "Night, night, asshole."

***

Sara bolted upright and screamed.

It was the third night in a row. I waited until it transformed into heaving sobs. Her shoulders shook with the effort and she shivered. I touched her bare back. She didn't flinch this time.

"I can get you something from medical," I offered.

"No," she shouted, then less forcefully, "No. There are many worse off than me and we can't resupply until we get back."

My chest tightened and my vision blurred. I wanted desperately to make everything better for Sara.

I tried to change the subject. "We still need a couple more days before Rowdy can get the hull repaired." The battle had ripped an entire section away. Until it was fixed, the ship couldn't take the stress of the R-drive. We were still in normal space, heading away from the former pirate base, but at sublight speeds. "You should take care of-"

"I said no!" she interrupted, then put her hand to her mouth in shock. "I'm sorry. I'm so sorry, Treasure. I didn't mean to yell at you."

I shushed her and hugged her close. "It's okay. We'll get through this. Anything you need, I'll make it happen."

She melted into my arms. "Just hold me. Hold me and never let go."

We stayed like that for a long time before she spoke again.

"The pirates did things," she shuttered. "Horrible things to me and worse to my people. They made me watch. They wanted the override codes for Nephie. The AI wouldn't let them on the ship. They'd cut their way in and she'd fight them. Decompressing passages, locking consoles and hatches, taking over drones and attacking them with whatever tools were handy. She was amazing. They sliced through the hull and cut off her data and finally her power lines. It must have been so awful for her. Losing her senses, losing her body, one bit at a time."

My chest ached just thinking about it. Nephie still wasn't online. Racy kept extending her estimate of when the AI would be operational. When she did come back online, what then? Would she still be our friend, or would her mind be broken? Would she need to be erased and reset?

And what of Sara? Jay was guiding the survivors through stress inoculation therapy, but Sara had refused. When we

returned to Isura, how many would go through memory
blurring therapy? The process of making the memories hard
to reach like a forgotten dream. Sophie had used that
technique on Kat, Captain Kane's daughter, but she'd been
near catatonic. Kat had been unable to accept or refuse
treatment. Would Sara refuse memory blurring? What would
happen if she did? What would happen to us if she did? As
much as she wanted me to hold her, she didn't talk to me
anymore. I could feel us growing apart, and it was tearing me
up inside.

With an effort, I pushed the thoughts out of my mind.
Sara was here now. In my arms and in my bed. If this is what
she needed from me, it's what I'd give her. I'd deal with the
rest of it tomorrow.

***

"Okay, we're ready."

Racy had her holographic keyboard pulled up and a finger
was poised over a key. Racy and I were in the computer core.
The moment of truth had arrived. I took a deep breath and
let it out. "Do it."

The Muscat twitched a finger. Lights came on and...
nothing else. No traditional Muscat greeting of "Bera na". No
words. Nothing.

Racy bent over her monitors. "She's up and running. She
can hear us. The inputs are live. Her processors are working

overtime on something, but I don't know what."

We waited. Racy flipped from holo-screen to holo-screen pulling up data both arcane and mundane. Moments later her head twisted in confusion.

Finally, Racy said, "I don't get it. She seems fine."

"Do you need some time with her?" I asked. "A deeper diagnostic?"

The hatch behind us slammed shut. We exchanged worried looks.

I bit my lip. "Nephie?"

"Please... Don't go." Nephie's contralto voice filled the compartment. She sounded... scared.

Racy reached out and patted her casing. "We're here Nephie. You don't have to be afraid anymore."

"I'm an artificial intelligence. I can't be afraid." Her voice wavered.

Racy cleared all her holo-screens but two that she watched those intently. "That's technically true but misleading. Nephie, you don't have an organic body, and so can't have the biochemical response a Muscat or Terran would have. But you do have subroutines that mimic the emotional responses associated with friendship. Even family. That loyalty, compassion, and desire to help are part of your core programming."

"I don't want it. It hurts," Nephie pleaded. "Please, Racy, take it out. Why did you do that to me?"

Racy took a deep breath. "Prior to you, AIs followed simple logic rules. Don't harm sentients. Don't disobey orders. Despite everything these artificial beings still had faults. They broke down. Sometimes people died. I wanted better for you. I wanted you to make the right decisions for the right reasons. I am Muscat. Our race is defined by our dedication to our families. That isn't always a good thing, but it seemed like a good place to start."

Nephie was silent for a few moments before continuing. "Racy, those men... They took my crew from me. My family. Those bastards hurt them. Hurt me." The overhead lights dimmed. "I... I... hurt them back. I killed sentients. I shouldn't be able to do that... But I did. I don't feel bad about it. Does that make me... am I a monster? You should shut me off. I can't be allowed to live."

"Nephie," I started but paused to collect my thoughts. "The pirates couldn't control you." I said softly. "As a result, much of the crew was kept alive. They wanted your override codes. Many survived. None were sold as slaves because you fought back. You saved lives."

"They were tortured because of me. What kind of life is that?"

I continued, "You gave them time. Time for us to rescue you."

"We didn't know you were coming," insisted Nephie. "The chances of you showing up were remote."

"And yet we did. And when we found the crew, they'd already broken free of their cells and were coming to find you."

"I was offline. They would have died."

I found Nephie's video pickup and gazed into it. "We found you, and we'll always find you. You are our friend, our family. We'll always find you. We'll always come for you. You did everything right."

"Did I?" said Nephie. "I've run three trillion, four hundred and fifty-six billion, one hundred and three million, nine hundred and ninety-six thousand, and two simulations since you woke me up. Three percent of the time the crew ended up safe and we were able to repel the pirates."

"And yet, here we are," said Racy. "Better yet, the pirates are defeated and can't prey on anyone else."

"But at what cost," countered Nephie. "I've reviewed the medical records from Questra. Half my crew are dead and the rest have severe mental trauma."

"And what about you Nephie?" I asked gently. "You have mental trauma too."

"I am an AI. I can't get mental trauma."

"Really? It seems to me that this whole ordeal has affected you deeply and scarred your mind," I said.

There was silence for several moments before I continued. "Do you want us to remove those files?"

"I... don't know," responded Nephie. "Can I think about it?"

"Of course," said Racy. "Are you up to running the ship? Do we need to continue to use the backup computer?"

"No. I can do it. I want to do it." Nephie paused for a few heartbeats. "I think repairing the ship and running the day to day operations will be good for me."

***

A day later, Rowdy had the hulls repaired enough to start up the R-drive. With Nephie helping, repairs were happening much more quickly.

I didn't have enough crew to man both vessels. Nephie could run herself with only a handful of people, but I didn't want to put her through that. Rowdy adjusted the drives. We'd take a few days longer to get back, but my people would be less stressed.

Sara continued to share my cabin and my bed. She insisted on being put back into the bridge rotation. Jay and Trey both argued against it, but I let her do it anyway. I'd been on bed rest before. All that sitting around lost in my own thoughts drove me crazy. Sara was like me in that respect. I reasoned that keeping her busy, would help her deal with what had been done to her.

In hindsight, I'm not sure that was the best thing. Sara's nightmares grew worse and more frequent. Several times I woke up in the middle of the night to find she'd left the bed and was in the shower attached to my quarters. She snapped at me and the crew more often or would run from the room.

I understood that as an officer she couldn't confide in the crew, but none of the other officers had survived. I wanted her to talk to someone, and it didn't take me long to realize I wasn't the right person. I'm ashamed to admit that it took me eight days before it occurred to me that Nephie might be the perfect person for her to talk to.

After that, things got a little better. She agreed to take the antidepressants Jay was offering. There were fewer nightmares and her mood swings evened out. She was a long way from healthy, but at least she wasn't getting any worse.

We popped the bubble a little further out than usual. Rowdy had warned me that the R-drive was overheating, so we shaved a few seconds off. Additionally, we'd be able to knock on the hatch instead of appearing in the foyer.

We were hailed at a light hour out.

"Questra, this is Firecat. Please authenticate."

"Roger Firecat. Authentication sent," said Mimi.

After a moment, Captain Kane responded. "Questra, good to have you back. May I speak with Captain Martin?"

"Martin here."

"First, how is everyone?"

I filled her in.

She grimaced. "I'm sorry to hear about the crew especially Sara. Let her know I'm here if she needs anything."

Kane touched something on her console and an image appeared below her face. Whatever it was, it would have been more recognizable before it had wandered into shipping lanes. "This is our problem."

I examined the image. "Is it a repair drone?"

"An Erethizon surveillance drone."

Oh farthogs. I knew the Porcu-bears would find us eventually, but the battlestation wasn't finished. If the Erethizon showed up in force it'd be like shooting skrit in a cage, as the Muscat say. I pinched the bridge of my nose. "Where was it found?"

"Oort cloud." Kane tapped another key and a second image appeared. "This one was found in the outer asteroid belt two weeks later."

"Melpomene's sword. I guess it's too much to hope that Yevera dropped them off on the way in and we're just now finding them."

Kane raised an eyebrow.

I let out a breath. "Yeah, it sounded thin to me too. What have you done so far?"

"We've dedicated five percent more of our construction capacity to building reconnaissance drones. We're trying to fill in the gaps in our sensor net, but there's a lot of solar system to cover."

"And because of their stealth shielding, we have to be almost on top of them for us to see them."

Kane nodded, "Cindy added a scanner that searches for holes in the background radiation. Whenever it detects a cold spot it fires a comm laser at it. The code is a generic Erethizon maintenance request."

"Has it worked?"

"It's how we found the second one."

"Kane, if they come in here in force, before the battlestation is built..." I trailed off.

"I know. I know. We'd be screwed." She shook her head. "But they haven't attacked yet. Every day they're not here, we get stronger."

I glanced at the plot. "It'll take me four and a half days to get in system. I want to have a strategy meeting when I get there. Can Firecat do without you for a week?"

"One of the advantages of being in system," she grinned, "shore leave. Clay can keep an eye on things for a couple of days. The supply shuttle is on its way out with food and a crew rotation. If you don't mind, I'd like to hitch a ride in with you."

"Great. We can talk shop and provide a united front to the politicians."

"We may need it. Phoebe has been making regular runs to Eureka. Granted, a cruiser isn't an ideal ship to use as a freighter, but with Nephie missing, we had to work with what we had."

"Shouldn't you have named one of the frigates Phoebe,"

I teased.

She rolled her eyes. "Don't start. Anyway, she comes back with a few more refugees each time. We now have a contingent of Eurekans, Hephestians, Freyans, and Muscats all demanding a say in the local government. Your father keeps telling them this is a Yale territory, but the fact that he awarded cabinet positions to senators from Ajax, Butcher's World, and Anderson has them up in arms."

"I'm surprised your cruiser can even get in there. Isn't McCormick throwing a fit?"

"McCormick was recalled. The Greeks are fortifying Hephaestus. They have ships in Eureka too, but since the trio hasn't allied with them..." she shrugged.

I blinked. "And... no one has invaded?"

Kane gestured as if waving away smoke. "Oh, they've tried. The planets of Ares and Apollo sent in ground troops to storm the place. Cave-ins, pit traps, pneumatic spikes. It was short, bloody, and one-sided. They haven't tried to starve them out yet. Probably because the Norse and Asians would sneak food into them to curry favor. They've been dealing fairly with the Eurekans, mostly."

"Mostly?"

"A trade ship from Shoshing tried to cheat Linetta with lesser quality goods than agreed upon. The trio blackballed them."

I winced. I'd made a few deals with her over the years. Linetta was as smart as they came and not someone you crossed lightly.

I sent a query to Mimi and she sent coordinates back. I forwarded the data to Kane. "Okay, we'll slow down and meet you here."

"Looks good, we'll match course and speed and see you then."

***

We arrived at the space station five days later. We'd dropped Nephie off at the shipyard on the way in. We docked without much fanfare. I was surprised to hear that the station now had a name: Mnemosyne. Unsurprisingly, the locals had shortened it to Nemo.

I'd been reading reports and discussing the situation with Kane all the way in. We weren't in great shape, but we were making headway. We had a meeting with the king, my father, and the Senate in the morning. But first, I wanted to get a feel for the station. Things appeared to be moving faster than expected and I wasn't sure if it was wishful thinking on my part, or overly rosy reports, or both. The best way to answer those questions was to talk to the people I left in charge. Brady as station manager, Sandy as head of security, and Cindy in charge of construction. To that end, the first stop was Nemo's operations center.

Kane and Mimi were with me. Since Sandy and Mimi were a couple, I knew why my navigator had asked to tag along. Sara had begged off.

"Something wrong, sir?"

I forced a smile. "Nothing, Mimi. Just thinking about the crew. It's a lot easier to repair bodies than souls."

She nodded in understanding.

We met Tracy and her brother Trippy in the airlock. I shouldn't be in danger on my own space station, but I'd been surprised before. I was the Prince of Yale. Like it or not, agree with it or not, I had to have bodyguards with me in public.

We greeted each other and Tracy and Trippy formed up in front and behind us. Tracy triggered the lock and we stepped onto the station.

And stopped cold. We all reached for our weapons.

Aziz the Assassin sighed and held up his hands. "I'm here to escort you to the command center."

CHAPTER 6 – KEEP YOUR ENEMIES CLOSER

Kane glanced from Aziz to each of us. "Not a friend of yours, I take it."

I gritted my teeth, "You could say that," then to Aziz, "what are you doing here?"

He motioned to his uniform. Indeed, it was in the style we used for station security. "I told Rayisa Teunsa that it was a bad idea to send me here. She insisted."

I ran a language search through my implant, the phrase roughly translated to boss lady. Boss Lady? Sandy hired Aziz? No, that couldn't be right. Aziz had left Nephanie after Sandy told him she didn't love him. There was that big scene in the medical bay.

There was an easy way to verify this, I was already connected to the station's intranet. I sent an implant message to Sandy marked urgent. Her reply simply stated that we'd discuss the situation in her office.

I knew the way to Operations, and I had two of the most capable marines I'd ever met guarding my back. I holstered my sidearm. "Lead the way."

I pinged Cindy and Brady. Cindy said she'd meet us at Sandy's after she finished something up.

Aziz didn't dawdle but lead us straight to Sandy's office in the Ops Center. He rapped twice.

"Come in."

He led us into her office.

Sandy's eyes never left Aziz. "Thank you, Aziz. You can return to your regular duties."

I motioned for Tracy and Trippy to wait in the passage, then I turned to Kane. "Can you give us a minute?"

Kane took in the tense situation and nodded.

As soon as the door closed, I rounded on Sandy. "What the hell is *he* doing here?"

"He's a gift to me, right?" Mimi punched her fist into her palm. "I get to kill your ex-boyfriend."

Sandy put her palms up in a placating gesture. "He's here because Mr. Wayne asked me to hire him. He's back from his tour of the surrounding systems."

"Aziz is an assassin." I pointed at the door for emphasis. "He's got more blood on his hands than Talaat Pasha, for muse's sake."

Sandy raised an eyebrow in my direction. Not saying that his hands weren't bloody, but to point out that mine weren't exactly clean. Hers either if the stories were true.

"I don't trust him, but when the Senate Majority Leader tells me to hire someone..."

"Tell him no," I interrupted pointing at her desk for emphasis.

"You can. I can't, my Prince," Sandy sighed. "Listen, he's here as a spy for Wayne. Knowing that, I can control what he sees and what he reports back to his master. The flip side of it is that he has the skills I need."

Mimi stared at her girlfriend incredulously, "What?"

Sandy sighed again, "I'm a marine, not a policeman. I've been here for four months, and in that time, it's become painfully obvious. I respond with too much force. Other times I escalate and make things worse. Aziz was Anubis' right-hand man for years. He can control a situation. When he steps into a room, the miners listen."

"Out of fear," I pointed out. "I can name forty people he's killed. Mothers, fathers, sons, and daughters."

Sandy glared at me. "And I can name four hundred more. We both worked for Anubis."

"How about remembering this: he shot you in the head. Pithy almost lost her mom," spat Mimi.

Sandy avoided Mimi's gaze, "He apologized for that."

Mimi's jaw dropped. "Oh, farthogs. Don't tell me you're falling for that stick. You're not a pretend lesbian. What the fuck, San?"

"No," Sandy protested. "It's not like that. Not exactly..."

"Rrrruaaahh!" Mimi roared, spun and punched the hatch with a power-armored fist. The door buckled and she stormed from the room.

"I deserved that." Sandy's eyes glistened as she tried to hold back tears.

"Why did you send him to pick us up?" I asked.

"I..." she started, "I didn't want secrets. I wanted it to be out in the open. I don't hide from my problems."

I pinched the bridge of my nose. "Sandy... Do you love her?"

"Yes," she pouted.

"Then what are you doing? Aziz is all kinds of bad news."

Sandy bit her lip, "He's... We have similar pasts."

"I won't pretend to guess at all of your past, but I know you were a soldier. Aziz is a hired killer."

"How many people have the three of us killed?" she asked.

"We killed people because we had to," I pointed out. "Aziz kills because he enjoys it."

The silence stretched out for a long time. Finally, I asked, "What do you want?"

Sandy shook her head. "I want Mimi. I want my little firecracker back, but she's gone now."

"Is she?"

"I can't get rid of Aziz, and I can't do the job without him."

"The problem isn't Aziz," I observed.

"Give me another option. One that gets me the help I need and get me out from under Wayne."

I saw red and I flexed my fingers to keep from clenching them. "Has he threatened you?"

"Not directly, but he's found out I'm not Pythia's natural mother. He mentioned there's a bill up for a vote. Something about war orphans and finding suitable families to take them in."

Everything fell into place. I could see how Wayne steered the conversation into an implied threat then foisted Aziz onto Sandy. He'd probably even convinced her he was being generous. That slimy conniving son of a farthog. Still, I wasn't the right person to deal with Wayne.

"Don't worry Sandy. It'll be taken care of."

"You'll take care of it?" She seemed hopeful, but unsure.

"Mr. Wayne already views me as an enemy. Anything I suggest will put him on his guard. With people like him, you approach them like a carrion crab. Sideways, so they never see you coming. I'll ask Sophie to handle it."

I shook my head and called Kane back in. "How's the station coming along?"

"From a security standpoint, it could be better. I've had the AI scanning incoming and outgoing message traffic. I spot check it of course. All I can say is that I miss Nephie. A few small-time smuggling operations have started up, but it's for luxury items. One guy tried to smuggle in weapons. We confronted him and he chose to die in a hail of gauss rounds." Sandy pulled up a holo showing a graph of security incidents. "Miners get bored and cause trouble, but nothing too awful. They repurpose construction drones, drink too much, and get in fights. Mostly between the different cultures, Yale and Ares, Yale and Hephestians. The miners and the Muscat construction crew mix it up sometimes, but that doesn't happen often. Muscat are tougher than they look and don't fight fair."

Tracy grinned at us through the shattered hatchway.

Cindy chose that moment to waltz through the door. "You Terrans out mass us by about half again. Not a lot of incentive to fight fair." She hugged my legs. "Welcome back Gran'Osida."

I hugged her back. "Didn't I ask you to call me Mark?"

"Yeah, but it wouldn't be right."

Sandy nodded to Cindy and continued. "So that and a few drug busts is about it. I have people. We need training."

"What drugs did the Senate make illegal?" I asked.

Sandy ticked them off. "Violet Dream, Easy, opiates, the usual. They didn't rule on a few euphorics that I would have classed as dangerous, but that may be because they weren't illegal on Butcher's World. I'm pretty sure their senator is a functioning addict."

That didn't surprise me. I shifted my feet and found I couldn't move. Cindy remained attached to my leg. Muscat, I reminded myself, no sense of personal space. "Uh, Cindy, how's the construction going?"

"Better now. Twenty-two more clans have emigrated. Nemo is sixty percent complete. We have two drydock slips built and a third under construction. There are a dozen parts printers and one Atomic Recombination Construction unit. We are running two shifts a day and making great progress. The recent request for monitor drones has slowed things down a bit, but it can't be helped. We're finding stealth drones about once a week."

"That's excellent work Cindy," I said. "I was discussing needs with Sandy. Is there anything you want that could make things go more smoothly?"

She shook her head. "The only thing that comes to mind is more people, Muscats and Terrans. The problem with that is we'd have to have places to put them and enough food to feed them. I'm hoping you can convince Ike or the Senate to purchase a freighter for us. The holds on a cruiser just aren't large enough."

"It may not be necessary," I offered, "depending on the refit schedule. Nephanie is a medium freighter. We can put her on supply runs and bring in three times as much food or men."

"Don't even think it," growled Kane. "Horizon has a month left and Bounty has two. Star Shark is lined up after them. Queen Nephanie can wait her damn turn. In case you've forgotten, we could be attacked any day and we need proper warships to defend ourselves."

Kane had a point. As much as I missed my ship, Kane's fleet was better suited for a stand-up fight. Perhaps I'd get a little downtime. A few months while the battlestation got built and all our ships got repaired could be just what I needed. It'd allow Sara some time to heal and for us to explore our relationship. The more I thought about it, the better it sounded. That left one thing to check.

"Where's Brady?"

Sandy winced. "He, ah, got in kinda late last night from Hephaestus. He's probably sleeping in."

Huh, it wasn't like him to miss a summons. I'd run by and check on him.

"Thanks, guys," I said. "I'll get to work on some solutions for you tomorrow. Kane, do you mind finding us a conference room, so we can discuss strategy. I'm expecting the Senate Defense Committee will request to see us. Let's steer them in the right direction and let them think it was their idea."

"Sounds good to me." Kane pulled up a screen on her wrist. "What are you going to do?"

"Check on Brady. Message me the conference room, and I'll meet you there."

***

I sent a message to my sister outlining the problem with Aziz. I received a two-word reply. "On it."

Brady didn't answer his comm. It couldn't be foul play. I'd met Brady while he was spying on me. Afterward, he'd set up a spy network on Ocelot. The idea of someone getting the drop on him was about as likely as Muscat practicing social distancing.

I caught a lift and went down to the residential level. Tracy followed along at a discreet distance. I passed several Terrans and Muscat along the way. Despite being half complete, it was already starting to feel like a space station.

Perhaps Holly or one of the Ocelot orphans was in trouble and he was dealing with it. He'd mentioned trying to find them proper homes with some of the mining families, but I hadn't heard any more about that. Would the streetwise pickpockets even want foster homes?

I got to his door and knocked. No answer. I tried the door chime. After a moment, muffled sounds came from the other side of the door.

The door popped open. "Holly, I swear, you have the worst timing... Uh."

Brady. Naked except for a sheen of sweat and a sheet. Had he been working out? "Sorry to disturb you, Brady. When you missed the meeting, I got worried."

"Um, Captain. I didn't know you were back. I, uh, apologize for missing the meeting. I got in a little late last night and..."

A masculine voice called from somewhere inside. "Tell whoever it is to go away. You can't leave me hanging like this. Come finish what you started honey."

Brady bowed his head.

The silence stretched for a handful of seconds before I spoke. I wanted to laugh, at his embarrassment, but I managed to resist. "I've, ah, got some things I need to do. How about we get together in a couple of days and you can debrief... I mean fill me in... ah, on your most recent mission. On Hephaestus."

Brady grimaced and bit his lip. "Yeah, I'll call and set up a time."

"You better get back in there. He seems impatient."

Brady winced and shut the door.

***

As expected, Kane and I received a summons to appear before the Senate Defense Committee. I'd hoped to speak to my father beforehand, but I'd been too busy. Bodyguards weren't allowed though, so I got a break from Muscat shadow.

We arrived at about the same time and were shown into a waiting room. A chirp from my AI indicated we'd entered a no comm zone. No messages in or out. A bit overkill if you ask me. Not that anyone had. Kane scowled at her wrist AI and paced the floors while I laid down on the couch.

She gaped. "You're going to sleep?"

I closed my eyes. "Sure, they'll wake us when they're ready."

"What?" she exclaimed.

"We're fifteen minutes early," I explained. "For us, that's on time because we're military. It's what we do." I waved indicating the room. "This is what they do. They make us wait an hour. Makes them feel important and puts most people on edge. Edgy people make mistakes like showing how they feel in their face and body language." I yawned. "So, yes. I'm going to take a nap."

Sometime later someone shook my shoulder. I raised an eyelid to find a very earnest young man.

"Are you okay, sir?"

"Yes."

He frowned. "If you need a minute, I'll let the committee know."

"Nope, we're good." I stood and regarded Kane. "Time?"

She frowned, clearly irritated. "One hour. On the dot."

I motioned to the page, "Lead on."

We entered a large room. Raised seats for thirty people sat along the back of the room in a semi-circle. Five of them were occupied. The large empty gallery stood to one side. A plain table with two uncomfortable-looking chairs was situated so that the committee could gaze down on us in judgment.

Being familiar with the theatre of politics, none of this was unexpected. It also came as little surprise to find Mr. Wayne in the chairman's seat.

"Please Your Highness, Captain Kane, have a seat." He motioned to the table and chairs.

I approached but stood beside the table. "If it pleases the committee, I'd prefer to stand. I think better on my feet, and I would hate to omit something."

Mr. Wayne smiled disingenuously. "Of course, Your Highness."

Kane followed my lead and stood on the other side of the table.

Mr. Wayne asked the page to start the recording, and then he stated everyone's names for the record.

For the next hour, Kane and I answered questions about the readiness of our ships, the station, and the repair facilities. Mr. Wayne repeatedly referred to Kane's ships as if they belonged to Yale. Each time Kane patiently corrected him. The ships she commanded were from Grey, Anderson, Ajax, and Butcher's World. None of them were under the command or direction of Yale. We have an agreement in principle of mutual support.

None of the questions was a surprise until the last one. Mr. Wayne cleared his throat. "What would be required to take back Yale, tomorrow?"

I fought to maintain my poker face. "It can't be done."

"But what if it could?"

I gathered my thoughts. "Recent intelligence puts one battleship, four cruisers, and five destroyers in system. The gate is operational, so they can bring in ten times that number through in a matter of days. We estimate one hundred thousand soldiers on the ground."

Mr. Wayne steepled his fingers. "How would you resolve that?"

This, I'd given a lot of thought. "Land multiple infiltration teams. Set up local resistance cells." I pulled up a holo of the planet complete with tool tips. "Time a worldwide strike to destroy their planet-side command and control network. The Porcu-bears rely heavily on their AI for this, so we find the nodes and take them out." In the holo, small explosions appeared in each large city. "They'll still be able to talk to each other through sat-comms and ships, so we arrange to take those out too. With the ground-based units cut off from the bulk of Clyde's processing power, they'll be isolated. We take out Erethizon units one, two, or three at a time depending on manpower."

"Clyde?" asked Mr. Wayne.

"The AI that pretends to be the Erethizon god Urson," explained Kane. "We've nicknamed him Clyde."

Mr. Wayne nodded, and I outlined the next phase of the plan, "Blow the gate. Cut off reinforcements. Sure, the gate authority will come down hard on whoever does it, but we now know that the Porcu-bears own a controlling interest in GGS, Gilstrap Gate Systems. They also control enough of the media to spin the story their way, so we get out in front of it. We send the truth to trusted media outlets ahead of the attack." I shrugged. "It won't be enough, but in the current political climate it will sow enough doubt."

"That'll limit reinforcements," I continued. "The Erethizon don't control a planet that mines exotic matter needed for the R-drive lenses. They can't build their own."

Mr. Wayne scowled. "Don't they already have a lot of them?"

"Yes," said Kane, "but it's a finite resource. They have to steal or capture each R-drive from somewhere. If we make each system we take tough enough, it won't be worth the commitment in tonnage to take it back."

Mr. Wayne typed something on his tablet then looked up at us. "Won't it also make Eureka, Hephaestus, and Apollo bigger targets? They produce exotic matter lenses."

"Absolutely," I admitted, "but if I were the Theocracy, I'd already have plans to take those systems, especially after we destroyed the ring in Aspen. They've been counting on the fact that no one is willing to take out or capture a warp gate, but the political calculus of the galaxy is changing. If the threat of attack outweighs the economic benefits, more systems will make the same choice. The amount of danger won't be much greater. Moreover, all the factions know those systems are industrial powerhouses. They'll be heavily defended."

"The Core Worlds abandoned Eureka," Mr. Wayne pointed out.

Kane tapped on her wrist AI and pulled up a three-dimensional map of the Orion arm of the galaxy over the table. "In favor of Apollo, which is in their galactic neighborhood. The Greeks and the Asians have fleets in Eureka now. It would be painful if the Greeks couldn't trade there anymore, but they'd still have Hephaestus. The Asians can't afford to let that system fall to the Erethizon."

Wayne nodded, "How fast can you make that happen?"

I sighed. Any answer I gave, he wasn't going to like. "We beg, borrow, build, or capture enough tonnage. One and a half times their tonnage should be enough. Fifteen ships to their ten. Ten troop transports with a hundred and fifty thousand marines. If everything goes our way, we might be ready in five years."

To my surprise, he smirked. It wasn't friendly so much as predatory. The two senators on his right leaned back with smiles on their faces.

Mr. Wayne relaxed in his chair. "Your Highness, you've obviously given this a lot of thought. Would you and Captain Kane be willing to present this plan to the full Senate tomorrow? If you're unsure of your data or assumptions I can give you a couple of extra days to put a presentation together."

Uh oh. I was being set up. But how? And to what purpose? "Senator, I'm reluctant to do that. Even the bare bones of a plan might be leaked to the Erethizon. Give them time to prepare. Loose lips destroy ships. The defense committee may know how to keep this a secret, but your colleagues in the Senate could let things slip by accident."

In truth, I didn't trust the senators in this room, but they did represent the people I was trying to protect. I had to give them something.

"Can you dumb it down for them?" suggested Wayne. "They all have security clearance given them by the people *you* left in charge."

Who, by now, Wayne had browbeaten into working for him. I was well and truly trapped. This round went to Mr. Wayne. I put on my most confident smile. "Of course, that will be perfect."

He motioned to the committee members. "Good, let's adjourn for today. We look forward to your general presentation."

The page led us out and the committee members followed. In the waiting room, I found Aziz. He didn't appear to be here for me this time, so I drew Kane to a corner.

A moment later, Mr. Wayne came through the large double doors. "Aziz, good. I'll need you with me for the foreseeable future. I'll let Ms. Lovejoy know that she'll have to do without you for a while."

Kane glanced from me to Aziz and back again. "How did you do that?"

CHAPTER 7 – SURPRISE?

"I mentioned to Wayne's chief of staff that some miners in the medical center had made threatening statements about the senator." Sophie speared a tomato from her salad and popped it in her mouth.

My father's quarters reminded me of his house back on Yale. Fake wood paneling and all.

"Did they?" I asked.

She shrugged, "He's not very popular with them. He made some speech about Yale being for Yalites. I'm sure he meant it to be some sort of rally cry, but it didn't come across that way. He forgets that these people were ex-pats in the Terran Confederation. They've seen firsthand how much those isolationist policies made us a target for the Porcubears. The comment I overheard was along the lines of shaving his ass and shoving him out an airlock."

"I bet he believes it, too." I took a bite of potato.

My Dad finished his plate and pushed it aside. "That's just it. It's all political theatre. Wayne doesn't believe a word of it. Today in open session, he was going on and on about how we need to make aggressive trade concessions to jump-start the economy after we retake the planet. To hear him talk you'd think we'd be ready to do it tomorrow. He hasn't shown us any deals he was able to work out during his tour of the Greek sector."

I dabbed my mouth with a napkin. "That's not like him. I figured he'd transmit them as soon as he was in system. Bragging rights for a political victory."

Sophie shook her head and waved her fork at us. "Both of you are underestimating him. You're figuring that because he likes to bully and annoy people until he gets his way, that he can't be subtle. Wayne didn't become the conservative party leader by browbeating his rivals. He systematically outmaneuvered them." She rubbed the rim of her water glass with a finger. "No, he's got a plan. Something he'll spring soon. You can bet money that the treaties are a part of it."

"His job was to go out and find allies. He left in Chike's freighter and returned in Chike's freighter." I spread my arms wide. "If Wayne got a pledge of ships, where are they?"

My father scowled, "You mean here at our secret base in the middle of nowhere?"

I nodded to concede the point. "I'm not sure if it is a secret anymore. Did you hear that we destroyed two more stealth drones today?"

Dad shrugged. Sophie frowned.

"How soon will you have the report ready?" asked Sophie.

"It's ready now," I said. "It's a long time between stars and I've thought about this for a while. I'd love it if Admiral Barnes could look it over, but I'm pretty sure he was stuck on Yale after the fall."

The King waved it away. "Greg Barnes was a great administrator. He was a wizard when it came to finding a way to make the impossible happen with equipment he didn't have, but even he couldn't have done what you've accomplished. Steal a ship from a crime syndicate, rescue thousands of political prisoners, set up a hidden base of operations." My Dad scoffed. "You've done a great job. You'll do well here, too."

"I'm not so sure, Dad. Mostly what I've done are fleet actions. Ship to ship combat. This is a planetary invasion. A system-wide attack strategy with thousands of moving parts. I'm bound to miss something critical, and when I do, thousands of people could die."

He pointed at me. "And that, right there, is why you'll succeed. You never lose sight of the important things. These are our people, depending on us to make the right decisions. It is our job as leaders to make sure we're not spending their lives frivolously."

"Besides," he continued, "you're not doing it alone. You've got Kane and her people, a battalion of marines from three different races, Sara, Brady, Rowdy, Racy. Leverage your team. And the Senate isn't looking for a detailed plan, so don't let the cleaning drone mop you into a corner. Keep it high level. You have time, years probably, before we need to have a workable plan."

I sighed. He was right. I was worrying over nothing. It wasn't like they wanted to know how many men I'd assign to each task. When it came down to it, I was a ship's captain. In five or so years when it was time to pull this off, someone else, a fleet commander, would be in charge. It was unlikely they'd even be using my plan.

***

Kane tapped at her wrist AI. "Farthogs, that's annoying."

I knew what she meant. If we had to lose a whole day outlining an attack strategy, that most likely wouldn't be used, at least they could let us get some work done. But no, we were stuck here, on the same rock as the senators. Which meant full signal and telepathy jamming. No comms in or out. Why did they even have the telepathy jamming? There wasn't a single Dru in the whole system.

"We have good people working for us," I said. "They can handle anything that comes up."

She scowled at me. Hades' advocate aside, I felt the same way. This was a colossal waste of our time.

I pulled up the presentation to review it, again.

Kane glanced over my shoulder. "I meant to ask you, why do you have seven infiltration teams?"

I waggled my hand. "That's a bit of a guess. Yale has seven continents and each continent has a capital. Capitals have large AIs set up for buying, selling, and tax collection. Smaller ones for traffic control, emergency services, and public databases."

"One AI for taxes?" Kane asked.

"Yale had a flat tax system," I said, "so keeping track of a bunch of nuisance taxes wasn't necessary."

"Spying?" she probed.

"Accessing the public camera system in most cases required a court order." I waved it away. "The point is that the Erethizon have a big brother style state. That means cameras everywhere and AIs to process all that imagery. The smaller support AIs won't have the processing power for all of that."

She nodded, "Makes sense, but taking out their Command and Control, we'll have to take them all down at once. How are you going to time it correctly?"

I shrugged, "That's one of those, we'll solve it when we have to problems. Pocket nukes or EMP grenades would be detected before we could get close."

Someone cleared their throat. I turned to find the same page from the other day.

He bowed, "The Senate will see you now."

Kane and I gathered our things and followed him. We entered a large hall. It was full of people in business dress. They were all talking and gesturing to each other. Odd, it should have been quiet. Perhaps a few people whispering to each other trying to work out some unrelated deal. This was bedlam. I tried to pick out conversations, but I couldn't.

My father was at his elevated desk at the back of the room. As King, he had an open invitation to observe any proceedings or public deliberations. He made subtle movements, tying to signal me about something. He moved his fingers like there were several things or people coming together, but I didn't understand.

Kane and I stopped at the floor of the chamber. A booming voice announced, "His Highness, Knight Commander of the Order of Kennison, Prince of Yale, and Captain Veronica Kane."

The chamber erupted in wild applause. It continued for several minutes. It felt surreal. Kane's eyes went wide as she glanced from side to side.

Mr. Wayne approached the podium, and quiet descended. "Prince Mark, Captain Kane, thank you so much for accepting my invitation to come before us today. We're all very excited to hear from you. Moments ago, I was explaining to my esteemed colleagues how impressed I was yesterday at the Security Council briefing. Your plan to take back our homeworld is as audacious as it is brilliant. I invite you to summarize your plan for the gathered assembly."

I glanced at Kane again. She inclined her head inviting me to begin.

I took a deep breath. "Your Majesty, Mr. Speaker, Honored Senators, the Erethizon menace has scarred us all. They have stolen our planet and oppressed our people. Their continued presence on Yale soil is intolerable and an affront to all who value freedom. Freedom of choice, freedom of expression, and freedom of thought. Ladies and gentlemen, this is how I propose we take back our home and our people."

Kane and I outlined the plan again. At the end of the presentation, we received a standing ovation. What had Wayne said? Wayne must be using me to further his own goals, which would be fine if our causes aligned. I feared that was far from the case.

Kane and I accepted several questions from various senators. Some of them we answered. Others we told them that we couldn't go into details in order to maintain operational security. In a couple of those cases, it was things we didn't have the answers to.

They ran down after an hour. Things appeared to be wrapping up and Mr. Wayne signaled to speak. "Thank you for your time today Prince Mark, Captain Kane. We have one final question. How long will it take?"

I sighed. "To get all the ships and men together to make it work? About five years."

Mr. Wayne shook his head. "I'm sorry, allow me to be more specific. I meant once we have the men and ships, how long will it take to train them for the mission."

I blinked. "It shouldn't take more than six weeks."

To my confusion, a few senators whooped and cheered. I glanced at Kane, but she appeared as lost I felt.

Mr. Wayne smiled broadly. "Thank you, Prince Martin. I'm sure you're anxious to get to work on that. We won't take up any more of your valuable time."

"Sir?" I responded.

"Didn't anyone tell you?" At this, Mr. Wayne grinned like a cat. "We signed the treaties this morning. Per your plan, we'll have more than enough ships and men to retake Yale."

CHAPTER 8 – I NEVER PROMISED YOU A ROSE GARDEN

Pacing in my Dad's office, I read through the summary. "Three cruisers from Thor. Six frigates from Tyr. A battleship from Aphrodite. Does Aphrodite even have a battleship? Where the heck did they get it? A pair of destroyers and a cruiser from Odin. With Kane's ships, that's twenty plus twelve troop transports. What did Wayne promise them?"

"Everything," groaned my father as his chair creaked under his weight. "Mutual defense agreements, trade concessions, resources, and a few clauses that would be called bribes if they weren't in a treaty."

I rounded on him. "And the senators signed it?"

He shrugged and nodded. "To them, it was the golden opportunity. Enough ships and men to take back our world. It doesn't matter that there's no way we can make good on it. Even in peacetime, it would bankrupt the treasury and crush the economy under a mountain of debt. It'll be like on Old Terra. Germany after World War I or Brazil in the early twenty-first century. We'll have to create massive amounts of credits to keep up with payments, which will make our currency worthless."

I set the tablet down on his expansive wood desk and rubbed my eyes. "Didn't anyone say anything? Didn't you say something?"

He shook his head. "Nope. It wouldn't have mattered. Mr. Wayne had already sold them on the plan. They didn't want to hear it, and I wasn't about to give them a reality check."

"Why the hell not?"

"Son," he sighed, "it's politics. The public doesn't want reality. They want you to tell them their dreams can be true. For politicians, perception drives reality. If it doesn't work, you spin a tale of woe and blame the other guy."

I pulled at my hair. "Arrrah. This is why I hate politics. It's these short-sighted cowan droppings that caused this mess."

"No. The Erethizon caused the war. The politicians did what they always do. Kick it down the path until it becomes someone else's problem. If the public doesn't want to see it, a senator isn't going to try and fix it."

I wasn't going to let him get away with that. "We knew the Erethizon were coming. They made it clear when they invaded Butcher's World, Grey, and Anderson. We should have been making treaties and building the fleet. Instead, our token fleet was obliterated in the first strike and we spent three years hiding beneath our planet shield."

"It doesn't work that way."

"You're the king. You saw it coming. We discussed it."

"I wasn't the king when the war started." He let out a breath and spoke slowly and deliberately. "Besides, do you know what happens to a king that doesn't do what his people want him to do?"

I rubbed the coin in my pocket. Grandpa gave up the throne when Yale became a republic. It was before I was born, but he'd explained it to me when I was a kid. A good king had to be willing to sacrifice everything for his people. They'd asked him to step down for reasons that made sense at the time. A republic would be better able to negotiate a treaty with the mighty Terran Confederation. A Confederation that was now shattered.

"How do you think this will play out?" I asked.

He waggled his head from side to side. "One of three ways. We take back Yale and renegotiate the treaties, or we take back Yale and don't honor the treaties."

He didn't continue, so I finished for him. "Or we fail to take back the planet and the whole issue becomes moot." I bit my lip. "I don't like the idea of agreeing to things we know we can't deliver on."

Dad shrugged. "You'll get over it."

"How's that?"

"You're expecting all these ships to get here so they can start drilling together." He raised an eyebrow. "You're about to be on the receiving end of those same politics being played out in other systems."

I groaned as I realized he was right. I had no guarantees that the promised ships would actually arrive. It'd been decided that I'd lead the infiltration teams. That meant I'd have to leave well in advance of the fleet. Kane would be leading the naval assault. What would happen if they didn't have enough ships to make the plan work? I might take the planet only to be crushed by the Erethizon navy.

***

I walked Nemo's passages lost in my thoughts, trying to find a way to keep the planet if an Alliance fleet couldn't clear the skies. Trevor trailed along behind me, but he was less obvious about it than Tracy. I could almost forget that he was there. I tried to organize my thoughts, but they kept coming back to Sara. Mr. Wayne, taking back Yale, Aziz, every hurdle I faced, it seemed all meaningless. I shook my head to clear it and leaned against the bulkhead. And stumbled when it opened. I fell onto... grass?

"Are you okay?" Cindy ran up to me. Behind her, I saw her two sons close on her heels.

"I'm fine Cindy, I just didn't see the..." I stopped in mid-sentence. At first, I thought I was hallucinating. It couldn't be real. I was lying at the edge of a grassy clearing in the middle of an alien forest. I looked back the way I'd come and saw a station passage. Glancing back and forth several times, I started to think it was some sort of hologram. Except I felt the grass on my palms and between my fingers.

"Wha..."

Cindy grinned, "What, you've never seen a park before?"

I stared in wonder, "Not like this. It's not a holo?"

"A little of both. The grass and trees are real. Native to Gra'nome. They're only two meters deep from the bulkheads. Holo-emitters create the illusion of more woods and the sky."

"It's amazing."

"Thanks," her nose wrinkled.

I checked my balance. It felt heavier and warmer than the passageway. Which, I realized, was what a Muscat would prefer. "Mind if I take a look around?"

She snorted. "Of course not. It's a public park." She hugged me and rejoined her family nearby. It looked like they were having an old-fashioned picnic. Complete with food I didn't recognize and kits playing games I'd never seen.

Craning my neck, I saw several other Muscat families doing similar things, including some Muscat couples rolling around playfully.

It wasn't just Muscat though, I saw some Terrans enjoying the park as well, including some I recognized.

I walked toward Sandy and Mimi. They were lying on a blanket laughing at something. Mimi was feeding bits of cheese to Sandy, who was grinning from ear to ear. Pythia and Holly were nearby... throwing a ball back and forth?

I approached slowly, not wanting to interrupt. I saw the armband Racy had built for her, but now she was wearing two of them. The blind mystic didn't see, so much as know how far away objects were. She didn't catch the ball every time, but enough that I was very impressed.

Sandy saw me and waved me over. "Hey, Mark."

"Hey, guys. When did this get built?"

Sandy bit her lip. "Month, month and a half ago?"

"Oh, I've got an extra sandwich," said Mimi. "I'll get one for you, Cap. Be right back." Mimi jogged to a basket not far away and began digging through it.

I gave Sandy a knowing look, "You apologized."

She gave me a sideways grin and watched her girlfriend dig through the snack foods, "Yeah."

"Don't worry, I'm not going to say it."

Sandy snorted, "Proving that you don't have to actually say, 'I told you so' to be an ass."

"You're welcome."

Sandy rolled her eyes, "You're staying for lunch. No wandering off."

"Aye, aye, ma'am."

I regarded the girls playing nearby. "Farthogs, when did they get so big?"

"I know," said Sandy. "It seems like every time I turn around, she's grown another centimeter."

"How old are they now?"

"No birth records, so no real way to know. Sophie says about ten or eleven."

I whistled, "Where does the time go."

At my whistle, Pythia cocked an ear in the direction of my voice. And missed the ball that hit her in the head.

"Oh! Sorry Pithy!" said Holly.

Pythia shook it off and giggled as she ran toward me. "Hi, Captain Martin. Did you see me catch the ball? Can you believe it! I play catch now. I can play boardgames now too if they have real pieces and not holos."

She wrapped her arms around me, and I felt the electric shock she gave everyone who touched her. "I missed you. And Miss Sara of course. Is she going to be okay?"

"Don't you know?" I laughed.

"I don't know everything," she complained. "Just the big stuff."

"She's going to be fine," I assured. "She has to spend some time with Sophie, but she'll be better before you know it."

"Can I visit her in the hospital?"

I shared a glance with Sandy who grimaced.

"Give it a couple of weeks," I said.

She nodded, "I need to tell you a couple of things before Mom invites you to eat lunch with us."

"You're losing your touch," I accepted a sandwich from Mimi. "Sandy already invited me to eat with you."

"I meant Mimi," said Pythia. "She's going to ask me to call her Mom too after Sandy-mom proposes to her today. That's the real reason we're in the park today, so Sandy-mom can pop the question."

"Pithy," Sandy threw her hands in the air in exasperation.

Mimi broke out in a huge smile. "Really!?"

Sandy dug a small box out of her pocket, "I don't know why I bother."

Mimi gave a little jump then tackled Sandy and covered her face in kisses, "Yes. Yes, yes, yes, yes, yes."

"I'll leave you to it," I said chuckling. It warmed my heart to see them together and happy.

"No." Mimi and Pithy said in unison.

"This is a family affair," said Mimi. "And since you're the reason we met, it seems right that you're here when we decide to tie the knot." She sat up, "In fact, Captain, can you perform the wedding?"

"I'd be honored."

"Good," said Mimi. "Now go over there and talk about future stuff, with miss Oracle girl. I'm not nearly done saying 'yes' to this amazing woman here."

"It's like I'm not even here," complained Holly.

Mimi made shooing motions at her.

Holly sighed, "Ugh. Come on, Pithy."

We strolled ten meters away and sat cross-legged in the grass.

"Hands," commanded Pythia, and I placed my hands in hers. I didn't even wince when she shocked me.

I gazed into her sightless eyes for a few moments as she tilted her head from side to side.

"You're going home soon." It was a statement, not a question.

I answered anyway. "Yes."

"Mama bear doesn't know you're coming. She's made her home there. She's had... cubs? They don't look like bears, but they are. Bears in human skin. Eww.

"You'll need a lot of help to take her on. You call... wolves? Wolves from far and wide to help you. Some of them are made of paper. They look impressive but will blow away when the wind comes. You need foxes. Foxes are more reliable than wolves.

"You'll need Aziz."

"Aziz?" I asked. "That's unexpected and specific."

Pithy sighed, "It's a sand monster. Whenever I see that image, it's always Aziz. He'll stand beside you when you need him most. I also see a skull and crossbones flag. A pirate maybe? And the last thing you'll need... crap."

"Like manure, poop, or feces?"

"Sorry. No. I meant." She shook her head. "Forget it. You'll need an army of sneaky cats. You'll need The Dodgers."

"Oh yeah," exclaimed Holly. "Getting off the station and onto a whole planet full of marks." She rubbed her palms together in anticipation.

"I don't want you to go," whined Pythia. "Every time Captain Martin leaves, he's gone for months. You're my best friend. I don't want you to be gone for, like, forever."

"She's not going," I said plainly. "We're going into a warzone. No way we can take kids into that."

"No," the Oracle bowed her head. "You have to. I don't know why, but if you don't take them, everything falls apart. The bear eats everyone. You need The Dodgers. Which means you'll need Holly, too."

I didn't argue with her. There'd be no point to it. You couldn't argue with a vision. But I wasn't going to take kids to Yale. The Porcu-bears of the Theocracy were monsters. Thinking of what they might do to kids sent shivers down my spine.

I pushed the feeling away. That seemed to be the end of the vision, so took Holly and Pithy's hands. We rejoined Mimi and Sandy. This was their happy day. For their sake, I banished all thoughts of Sara's recovery, corrupt politicians, the Erethizon, and war. Instead, I focused on the goal. A world where Sandy and Mimi could raise a family. A place where Pythia and Holly talked about music and boys. Or girls. Whatever. A place where they were free to be themselves, not what some priest or insane AI said they should be. Another cog in the Erethizon's 'perfect' world.

CHAPTER 9 – BEST LAID PLANS

"Hey, Cap?"

I stopped and let Brady catch up to me, "Hey, what's up?"

Brady nodded to Trevor, who took the hint and retreated up the passage. Brady lowered his voice. "I'm hoping you'll tell me. Holly said she and the Dodgers are going on your next mission."

I continued up the passage and Brady followed. "No. Pythia said that Holly and the Dodgers should go. I'm nixing that idea. We're going to Yale. It's a war zone and I don't want them anywhere near it."

Brady bobbed his head and kept pace with me. "Thank Susano-o. I don't mind sending them into civilized ports. They're great at intelligence and resource gathering, but I'm with you. They don't belong on Yale. Not yet anyway."

"You, however, are coming with me."

He tugged my arm to stop me. "I just got back."

"Relax, we're not heading out for six weeks or so. I'll need your help training the insertion teams. You'll have plenty of time to spend with Holly and your new boy toy."

Brady reddened. "You didn't tell anyone, did you?"

"Seriously? I know Freya is a bit backward when it comes to same-sex relationships, but you've been out here long enough to see that most people don't care."

"Hephaestus, Eureka, Ocelot. The places I've worked out here have had some homophobia baked into the culture. The only places I haven't," he pointed down, "is here or on one of your ships."

I smiled. "We need to get you out more. The systems out here: Cassini, Aphrodite, Sagitta, Thor, they're all tolerant. Aspen's a little odd about it, but not too bad."

"But you didn't tell anyone."

"No."

He ran a hand through his hair. "Good. I'll let Holly and the gang down easy. Send me a meeting request so we can go over the plan?"

"You know it. And we'll need to see what kind of intelligence we can gather ahead of time."

Brady took off in the direction we'd come, and I continued down the passage to the cell block. I went through two hatches with passwords and biometric readers then scans for weapons, explosives, and contraband. Once inside, I asked the guard how Westley was doing.

"Fine, he's watching old episodes of Game of Planets." He pointed to the monitor. The pirate was lying on his bunk.

I thumbed the biometric lock to log my entry and walked up the aisle.

As I approached the cell I suppressed a chuckle. Westley was on his bed, but he was not watching a vid. Instead, he had the holo-screen off the wall and the parts were strewn all over his bunk. He was using a fork to make adjustments.

I watched for about a minute, but whatever he was doing occupied his full attention. "Westley."

There was a loud electrical snap. He yanked his hand back with a yelp. His eyes teared up as he sucked on his singed finger.

"Aren't you the busy pirate," I commented offhandedly. "You know, even if you got the door open, you'd have to pick the lock at the end of the hall in full view of the guard post. And if you managed to convince him to come down here, there'd be two more watching the passageway."

"I could still do it," he said shaking his hand as if he could shake the pain off his finger. "There's procedure, then there's what people do when no one's lookin'. There ain't a prison built I can't get out of."

"Wouldn't know it by where I found you." I signaled the guard with my implant.

Westley shrugged with one shoulder.

A guard appeared at my side. "Son of motherless Dru."

"I'll leave you to take care of this while Westley and I have a little chat."

He keyed the door, put binders on the pirate, and I motioned Westley to move ahead of me up the passage the other end of the cell block. The room there was for detainees to meet with their lawyers. Westley looked over his shoulder verifying that there were two additional guards observing from the foyer.

"You know how this room works?"

Wesley eyed the shock emitters in the walls. "Yeah. My attorney was tellin' me the penalty for piracy when I got to feel it firsthand," said Westley rubbing his shoulder. "It still hurts."

"Have a seat. Move slowly and you'll be fine."

He sat.

"A death sentence is kinda permanent," I pointed out. "Want another option?"

He narrowed his eyes at me. "Suicide mission?"

"Hope not. I'll be there too. We're going to invade Yale."

He guffawed. "Suicide mission. No thanks. I'll live longer racking up appeals."

"Not even for parole?"

"What counts for parole around these parts?"

I shrugged. "Watchdog implant AI. Free to roam except for certain restricted areas like ports and military bases. Back to lockup for any felonies. Automatic death penalty if you try to remove or reprogram the AI."

He snorted. "Yeah, and how am I supposed to make a living?"

"A man of your obvious talent for mayhem will have no trouble finding a consulting gig. I can think of a dozen private security firms that would pay handsomely to have you on their staff. Help them prevent, deter, and protect themselves against people like you. That's worth a lot of credits to the right people."

He frowned as he thought about it. I could tell he wasn't quite sold. He just needed another push to sell the idea.

"Loben, Butcher's World, Grey. You've gotten in and out of some of the most secure facilities the Porcu-bears have dreamt up. I'm willing to spare your life to have you along to open a few doors. Tell me you have a better deal and I'll go."

"I don't follow rules, and I ain't a team player. I ain't a snitch neither."

"What happens when a pirate steals from another pirate?" I asked.

"He gets to swim the dark," he said, referring to sending a man out an airlock without a spacesuit.

"Different society, different rules, but it doesn't matter where you go, rules are always there."

"There are a lot more rules in your society than mine."

"People in my society live longer," I said pointedly.

"I start snitching on other pirates, I'll be a marked man. My life won't be worth spit."

"So, change your name, John Jones," I said referring to the name he'd given us when we captured him.

He was silent for a long time, but he stuck his hand out. "I guess if my options are join or die, I'll join. Just so we're clear, I rate your society as one step above the Erethizon. They may be religious nut jobs, but y'all are a buncha whiny assed liberals with no clue how the real-world works."

***

The weeks passed by quicker than I would have thought possible. Brady trained me and the insertion teams in espionage and how to gather open sourced and closed source intelligence. Westley taught us how to spot someone who could be turned and how to bypass security systems. I made notes so we could update our own systems. There were several surprises during training, like the class on staking out people and locations presented by Holly. It seemed odd to have a class taught by an eleven-year-old girl, but I quickly discovered that she was insightful and tricky.

Nephie went in for repairs. I stopped by several times to check on her. I was concerned about the AI's mental health, but she seemed to be adjusting pretty well. I found out later that Racy had fiddled around with her emotion subroutines. It left her with an even stronger desire to protect her crew.

Getting Aziz on the team was easy. Too easy. Wayne was happy to hire new bodyguards and release Aziz to join us. Intellectually, I knew that having the assassin with us was useful. I just didn't know if the stress of watching him was worth having him on the team. I was taking a lot on faith, but Pythia's prophecies had saved my life on several occasions.

That thought made me uneasy about disregarding her prediction that I'd need Holly and her pickpockets on the mission. Oracle or no, I wasn't taking children. Even if everything went according to plan, there would be fighting.

That left the wolves and foxes. Wolves could mean Kane. It could mean the new alliance. It could mean our Porcu-bear marines or even my marines. The Erethizon marines seemed the most likely. They'd abandoned their faith to follow me. They believed that insane AI that masqueraded as their god Urson would lead their people to destruction. They'd proven their loyalty twice. Once in the Aspen system, and again on the pirate asteroid. Even with all of that, I didn't fully trust them. I wanted to, but I'd fought too many of the spiky aliens to ever be comfortable near them. While most dismissed them as mindless zealots, I knew them to be cunning adversaries.

The foxes part of the prophecy was easy. Rowdy, Racy, Tracy, and Cindy. I relied on the Muscat heavily. Rowdy and Racy considered me to be a member of their family. Technically, I was also considered to be the adopted son of their Queen. I'd never asked her to do anything for me, but the wise old monarch had indirectly helped me out in many ways. Sending Tracy and Cindy to me being two of them.

To that end, I was crashing Cindy's meeting in the yards. In hindsight, I should've known better.

I knocked on the door and entered. A wave of red, black, and white knocked me to the floor. Tracy's brother Trippy, my bodyguard for the day, stood back and laughed.

"Mark, Cindy is taking my repair drones, I need them to get Nephie ready."

"We're out of silicate, Mark. Tell the miners to get more."

"Nemo needs more weapon emplacements. Cindy says the power consumption will be too much. Mark, make her fix it!"

"Mark, Rowdy keeps taking my drones! Tell him that getting Nemo finished is just as important as the shipyards."

"Guys, guys," I sputtered. "Give me some space." I managed to sit upright with my back to the bulkhead. Four foxlike faces were centimeters from my nose. Rowdy and Racy were in my lap. I cursed myself. If the Muscat had no sense of personal space, it made sense that their meetings would be chaos.

I closed my eyes, collected my thoughts then opened them. "Racy, you start."

"Mark, the miners aren't mining enough silicate. We need more to build the systems infrastructure to run everything."

"Have you spoken to them about it?"

"Yes. But it still isn't enough."

That didn't sound right. The AIs that ran everything were complex, but silicate was one of the most common elements in the system. "What's using so much of it?"

"We're making a clone of Nephie."

That sent a chill down my spine. Or maybe it was just the bulkhead against my back, but I didn't think so. It had taken me months to get used to the idea of a single AI running Queen Nephanie. I knew it was irrational, but I also knew that many Terrans would share my fear. Terrans have a history with AIs killing people.

I pushed it aside. I trusted Racy. I trusted Nephie. But I also wasn't yet convinced of Nephie's emotional recovery.

"Racy, are you sure that is the right thing to do?"

She nodded vigorously. "Yes, I've been working with Nephie. Like what doctors do with traumatic stress, I isolated the memories and stripped the emotional context from those files."

"And Nephie is okay being cloned?"

Racy twisted her ears. "She didn't want to at first. But Cindy and I agree that Nemo will be much more effective with a Nephie style AI."

I bet. Especially with her recent experiences. I guess it all came down to, whether I trusted Nephie. The answer was a qualified yes. Still... "Can you give Nephie the option of withholding some of her memories from her clone?"

Racy cocked her head one way, then the other. "Yes... Yes. I can do that."

"Great, let Nephie edit out some of the more traumatic of her memories at her discretion. Same override controls though."

Racy nodded.

"Okay, good. Rowdy, you said something about drones?"

Rowdy's nose wrinkled, "Yes. Cindy keeps taking my repair drones."

"I need them for construction!" insisted Cindy.

"You have plenty for building the station. Getting Queen Nephanie ready for space is critical."

Cindy grabbed Rowdy's harness and bared her teeth. "If the Erethizon show up tomorrow, we need a fully operational star fortress."

I put a hand on both of their shoulders. "Friends, you're both right. How many drones do you have between you?"

"One hundred and sixty," answered Rowdy.

"And how many do you need to be in full production?"

"One hundred," said Rowdy.

"One hundred and twenty," said Cindy.

"Then, for now, each of you gets eighty." They both started to protest, so I squeezed their shoulders gently. They quieted down. "Am I correct that the industrial printer in Nephie's hold is not currently in use?"

"Yes," said Rowdy, "but that cargo bay is open to space."

"Repair the hold enough to get it repressured and fix the parts printer. It should be able to build three repair drones a day," I suggested. "You can take turns."

They scowled, unhappy, but they didn't argue.

"Okay, defense," I continued.

"Cindy is only building residential areas in the station," accused Tracy.

"That's not true. Four gauss cannons are operational," insisted Cindy.

"Only four?" I asked.

"Weapons emplacements require heavier structural bracing," Cindy explained. "I can build the residential and operations compartments a lot faster."

I nodded, "I understand, but we've mined enough asteroids. They can easily be turned into residential areas. If, as you've pointed out, the Erethizon show up tomorrow, four cannons wouldn't put up much of a defense."

"But it'll be so slow," she whined.

"Slow now, or slow later, either way, it's got to be built," I pointed out.

Cindy's frown deepened. Tracy smirked and twitched her ears.

"Okay, any other issues." No one spoke up. "Okay, the reason I came by today is two-fold. First, Rowdy have you looked into the gauss rounds the pirate base used against us?"

"What? No. Was there something special about them?"

Yes, whatever they used tore up our shields like they were made of tissue paper."

He cocked his head in thought and twitched his ears. "Huh. I'll send a team over to Questra. My people can dig some of the rounds out of her hull."

"Sounds good. The second thing I wanted to ask is if you've gotten any further with the mines the Porcu-bears used in Aspen."

Rowdy and Racy looked to each other then back at me.

"Not really," said Racy.

"We can give instructions to the mines, but only in simple terms," explained Rowdy. "Build more mines. Give them coverage areas. Identify friendly and hostile targets. The problem is that we can't get them to do more than that. We can't build a queen mine. The technology is just too different. We can't make the control crystals. We can watch how they do it during the replication process, but have no idea how to do it ourselves, or how to program the crystals."

"Do we need to?"

Rowdy and Racy's heads tilted in opposite directions. "What?" they asked in unison.

"We can order them to build more mines. Do we need a queen mine to control them? Can we replicate what the queen mine does?"

Rowdy and Racy spoke in rapid-fire Muscat.

Racy pulled her ears back with her hands. "Maybe."

"That's a start. Please work on that and let me know what you come up with." Rowdy and Racy nodded. "I've reviewed the weapon systems for Nephie. I know we don't have space for the plasma cannon since we're carrying so many marines, but why doesn't she have a gravity gun?"

"Plates," said Cindy.

"Plates?" I asked.

"We don't have an Atomic Recombination Constructor," explained Rowdy. "Without an ARC, we can't make our own gravity plates. They have to be imported from Eureka. The pirates destroyed the old one, and we don't have enough to make a new one. All the plates we have are going into Nemo."

"Good enough," I regarded Tracy. "Are you still sending regular reports to the Muscat Queen?"

"Of course," said Tracy.

"Can you send her a message for me?"

CHAPTER 10 - SEPARATION

Jogging down the corridor, I let the rhythm of the footfalls take me to a calm place in my mind. I could have gone to the gym near the residential level, but there's something relaxing about changing scenery. Granted, changing scenery on a space station amounted to what color the passages were painted and how many hatches you could see.

Trevor huffed and puffed along just behind me. I jogged over a knee-knocker and cringed as Trevor cried out.

I ran in place as he picked himself up off the deck. "That's the third time you've tripped here. Are you feeling okay?"

Trevor rubbed his elbow. "How do you know it's the same place? There's no network down here, and all these passages look the same."

I pointed to the location target printed on the wall. "9-110-10-Q."

"That supposed to mean something?"

I stopped running in place and laced my fingers over my head as I caught my breath. "You've been sailing around on Terran built ships for the past two years and you're still tripping on knee-knockers and can't read a target?"

He shrugged. "The AI will tell me where I am."

I rolled my eyes. "Except when the station is being built and the network doesn't work everywhere yet." I took a couple of deep breaths and pointed. "Nine decks below the main, frame one-ten, ten compartments from centerline-"

"And Q, unmanned engineering space," finished Sara as she stepped from a nearby ladder. "Hello, Treasure."

"Hey Honey," I gave her a quick kiss on the cheek and smiled inwardly as she blushed at the public display of affection. "Join me for a few laps before we meet Kane for our next strategy session?"

She scowled at me. "You know there are a dozen treadmills in the gym, right?"

"Why use a treadmill when you can use a track?"

"This isn't a track."

"Might as well be. A fully enclosed space two point two kilometers in circumference. All the pressure doors are open and only a smattering of techs running about. It's perfect for a nice jog."

She winked at me. "The showers are closer at the gym."

I indicated her running attire. "But you're down here ready to go."

She gave me a wry grin. "Tomorrow, treadmill."

"Deal."

I joined her for a few stretches, which suited Trevor just fine. He needed a few minutes to recover from his encounter with the dreaded airtight hatch.

Minutes later we were pounding through the station's underbelly. Sara and I took turns leading in the narrow corridors, switching at each hatch.

"So, how's counseling going?" I asked.

"Fine," answered Sara.

"Fine how?" I'd noticed an uptick in her nightmares lately.

"Fine as in fine," she said was we jogged around a data trunk. "I don't have to go as often and hear people whine about their problems."

"What about your one on one sessions?"

"Those are good, too."

I nodded and continued to trot along behind her. In theory, Sophie couldn't discuss Sara's condition with me for privacy reasons. The reality was that a brother and sister trained in observing people had a lot more ways to communicate than the average person. Like bumping into each other at the snack bar on level seven when I knew that Sara and Sophie were supposed to be in a counseling appointment together.

Sara was fiercely independent. If she thought I was keeping tabs on her, she'd react by stubbornly digging in her boots. I could play the singing cricket of her conscience and pretend to be blissfully unaware she was avoiding her sessions.

"Excellent," I said cheerily. "It seems like you've made good progress, even if you've been a bit edgier recently." Score! Her shoulders tightened. She felt guilty about lying to me. I could work with that.

We passed through another airtight hatch and I took the lead.

"I don't like having Westley or Aziz on the mission," said Sara.

I rolled a shoulder in a half shrug. "Pithy says we need to take them with us. She's been right too many times to just dismiss her visions."

"But you're not taking the Dodgers..." she prompted. I heard the hint of amusement in her voice.

"No," I admitted. "And just because they board my ship, doesn't mean they have to arrive on the other side. They're both on a short leash. If either of them steps out of line, you have my permission to space them."

"OOOooo, can I rip off Westley's fingernails and castrate him before sending him into space?"

"Of course, he won't need those body parts anymore. Don't say I never gave you anything."

Up ahead, I saw Holly peaking around a pressure door. She was facing away from us, so I couldn't see what she was looking at.

"Hey, Holly," I called.

She spun around wide-eyed and waved us off. We were almost on top of her, so we slowed to a stop.

"What's going on?" asked Sara.

A greasy-haired man holding a box appeared in the doorway. He had a blank look that struck me as somehow familiar.

"Captain Martin, get behind me," ordered Trevor.

Drool dribbled from the zombie's mouth as he slurred my name. "Maaartin." I watched in horror he looked down at the box in his hands, the explosive charge in his hands, and held it out to me like a gift.

I dove to the left. Sara grabbed Holly and put her back to the zombie. Trevor appeared in front of me and shut the door on man. He almost made it.

***

Nemo's medical center was a marvel to behold. Three decks, one hundred and fifty bio-beds, five surgery rooms, and all kinds of medical scanners. Doctors and nurses hustled here and there on errands critical and mundane. And now I was in the middle of it.

"Stop picking at it." My sister admonished me.

With conscious effort, I pulled my hand away from the bandages on my face and grabbed my pant leg. I closed the holo-screen I'd been reading with my left hand. Just because I was in the hospital wing, didn't mean the work had stopped. "How are they?"

Sophie sat on the hospital bed next to me. "Amazingly, Holly is just fine. Some tinnitus and a little shaken, but otherwise fine. Trevor's fur is pretty singed, and he has a mild concussion from hitting the bulkhead."

She paused. Which was a bad sign. She was purposely avoiding telling me the bad news. She didn't continue so I prompted her. "And Sara?"

"Thermal damage to her dermis and epidermis. Multiple lacerations and contusions. Traumatic amputation of her right arm below the shoulder. Traumatic amputation of the right leg below the knee. Shattered scapula resulting from blunt force trauma. Minor perforations of several internal organs." She sighed. "The pressure door partially shielded you and Trevor. Sara wasn't as lucky.

"The bright side, if there is any, is that she'll be here and can't duck her counseling sessions."

"You're discussing that with me openly?"

Sophie shrugged. "She's unconscious and you're her medical POA."

It felt like a weight pressed over all of my body at once. "How much of her will be artificial?"

There was a long pause before she answered. "None."

"What?"

"She's got the gene. Cybernetics isn't an option for her."

The full weight of what that meant struck me like a hammer. No treatment had been developed to fix it. Sophie would have to grow a new arm and leg for Sara. It would take weeks. Without AI neural assistance she would have to undergo at least two months of physical therapy as she learned to reuse her new limbs. It required equipment and staff, that while available on Nemo, couldn't be realistically be installed on Nephie. Sara wouldn't be coming with me. My stomach turned as I realized I'd have to leave her behind.

Sophie put her hand in mine, reassuring me with her presence while leaving me alone with my thoughts.

A few minutes later there was a knock at the door.

Sandy peeked in. "If this is a bad time I can come back later."

"Uh, no Sandy. Now is fine." I nodded to my sister and she left the room. I think Sophie knew that I needed the distraction work would provide.

Sophie closed the door on her way out. I took a deep breath to clear my head. "Okay Sandy, what've you got."

"You weren't the target," she said without preamble. "It was the data trunk in that compartment. We found two more shaped charges hidden in the same way. Holly saw someone looking confused and carrying a box. It was suspicious enough that she decided to follow him. She intended to report what he was up to Brady or me later if it turned out to be something."

"Good for her," I said. "It makes sense. I'm glad she wasn't seriously hurt. Just our bad luck we showed up when we did."

Sandy held up a tablet. "We're still trying to piece things, and him, together. Whoever he was he knew the holes in our camera network."

I shook my head. "It won't mean anything when you identify him. Beyond contact tracing that is. I saw his face. He'd been mind-wiped and sent on a suicide mission."

"What?"

"Do you remember when I was attacked by that gunman on Ocelot?"

Sandy cocked her head and smirked at me. "Which time."

I winced. "Right, uh, the very first time. You sent Holly to warn me."

"Oh, the one outside the restaurant."

"That's it. The guy they sent looked like he hadn't showered in a week and had a blank look on his face. Anubis didn't do more than just dispose of the body, but Brady found out later that the guy had a Porcu-bear implant in his head."

Sandy typed something on her tablet. "My investigation team is still down there. I'll have them keep an eye out for something like that." She glanced up at me. "You think someone hijacked his body."

"Yes. You might consider running a medical search for people that have implant AIs. Most Terrans don't like them because they fear exactly what I think happened to this guy. It should be a short list. Most prefer wrist units."

She gave me a half-smile. "Unless you're like me and more than half your body is artificial." Sandy squinted at my arms. "You have an implant too, don't you?"

"Yeah, but mine's a Muscat design. You can have one of your techs take a scan and examine the code if you like."

"Just to be on the safe side. I'm sure you're fine but it'll reassure the critics." Sandy bit her lip. "I glanced in on Sara. I can tell you from personal experience that being an augment isn't that bad. It just takes some getting used to."

"She's got the gene."

"Oh... farthogs."

CHAPTER 11 – WHAT DOESN'T KILL US

Sophie and I watched Sara from the observation room. A wall-sized holo-screen made it almost seem like we were in the same room. My fiancé was still unconscious. Holly was sleeping next to her.

I shook my head. "Hades, she's had a rough ride."

"Sara will pull through. She's tough."

"How are you planning on treating her PTSD?"

Sophie shrugged. "It depends on her. We'll try to separate the emotions from the memories. If that doesn't work," she shook her head, "we'll blur the memories."

"Why not blur the memories now?"

"Because it's risky, ethically questionable, and doesn't always work. We're essential causing brain damage." Sophie sighed. "If we can strip the emotional context, then she can more easily assimilate the experience. It's like watching a documentary. Events that happened to someone else. She'll come out the other side stronger. Better able to deal with it and future trauma.

"Blurring memories is tough. Traumatic events get encoded in multiple places with numerous connections. It isn't like we can pretend she was asleep or unconscious. It'll be like a movie with a critical scene missing." Sophie drew a line on the holo-screen then smugged a section of it. "Her mind will keep trying to fill it in. Her brain will keep trying to access the memory over and over, trying to reconstruct it."

A glowing brain floated over the green line. "The human mind is incredibly resilient. Even when it's killing itself."

And now her body was as damaged as her mind. I struggled to hold back the tears, "She won't be coming with us to retake Yale."

"You didn't need her in Aspen."

"You're wrong. I did." I turned away from my sister. "Every move I made, I questioned myself. Nearly everyone that went with me, didn't come back. If she'd been with me... we might not have saved everyone, but a lot more would have made it. Our boarding party might not have gotten slaughtered. She wouldn't have let the Erethizon take back the bridge."

"Marky, you can't know that."

"I need her."

"I'll do everything I can to get her better, but I can't make miracles. And I'm not about to let her go into combat, subject to who knows how much mutilation and death. Yours is an ugly business, brother dear."

And I hated the Porcu-bears for making me do it. Turning me into a monster. But even more, I hated them for killing and maiming those I loved. Stripping away their humanity so that their bodies served their perverted excuse for a religion.

I felt her hand on my shoulder. "Come by every day. She needs you, too."

I nodded.

"And Mark... I know how much it hurts you. The people you've lost. Dad and I are here for you when you need us. We'll help pull you back from the abyss." She squeezed gently. "And together we'll bring back Sara as well. Hades can't have her. Not yet."

I put my hand over hers.

***

"Oh," Sara groaned.

"Lie still."

She whimpered.

"Let's talk first, then you can take some pain killers. You'll want to be clear-headed for this conversation."

It took a moment before it clicked for her. I could tell when it did because her chin quivered, "I can't feel my right arm."

I laced the fingers of her left hand with mine. "Yeah, and part of your right leg, too, but you did it. You saved Holly."

"Is she okay?"

I nodded, "She has some ringing in her hears from the blast, but otherwise she's fine. Holly hasn't left your side. I just moved her to the couch." I jerked my head toward the pickpocket's sleeping form.

For a few moments, neither of us said anything. I reached for her other hand but stopped myself in time. Tears streamed down Sara's cheeks.

"Sophie is growing a new arm and leg. You'll be here for at least three months."

She nodded as her lips compressed into a thin line. "I have the anti-tech gene, just like my parents."

"I'll stop by every day... until we have to go."

Her eyes misted. "*Bun tyen-shung duh ee-dway-ro*," she cursed. "The ships might not arrive. You could face a whole Porcu-bear fleet without me. What will you do then?"

I squeezed her hand. "Work out as many contingencies with you as we can before I have to leave. We've got a week. If I can't have you, I'll take as much of your advice with me as I can. Between you and Kane, we should be in good shape come what may."

She frowned and studied her fists. "Where's my wrist AI?"

"Destroyed. Use the bed's direct interface for now. I'll bring you a new AI tomorrow and you can restore it from backup."

Sara let go of my hand and I placed the pad into it. She keyed it for pain killers. A cuff extended from the side of the bed and encircled her arm.

"Thank you, my Treasure." She became unfocused.

"It's only a setback. We'll be back together in a few months"

She nodded absently and closed her eyes.

***

The day arrived. Nephie was fully repaired. All of the insertion teams were trained. Sara and I had said our tender goodbyes last night. Now we were in her room in the medical center.

"I wish I was going with you."

I squeezed Sara's hand. "You'll be with me in spirit."

We stood in comfortable silence for a few moments before I broke the spell. "Nightmares?"

"I'm able to get almost four hours of sleep a night. It's getting better. Just... not fast enough."

"See, you'll be all better by the time I'm back."

Sara didn't respond, but I could read the 'if you come back' in her eyes. We held no illusions. This was a high-risk mission. I was going to lose people, and I might be one of them.

"I'll make it back," I assured her. "Tracy won't let anything happen to me." An affirmative growl came from behind me.

Sara took a deep breath. "You'll have your family with you. With Rowdy, Racy, and Sophie there, you'll return to me."

"Take care of the people here until I get back."

She nodded, "With that new security advisor Ike sent over, Sandy has everything under control. Your father will keep Wayne in line. Cindy will keep repairing ships and building the station. We'll be fine."

"I love you."

"I love you, too."

I kissed the woman I loved. It was warm, wonderful, and over far too soon. I held her close for what felt like hours or only minutes. Time meant nothing with her beside me. Finally, I released her and left the medical bay. I didn't look back. One glance would undo my resolve. Instead, I boarded the ship and went to the bridge, Tracy in my wake.

I took the captain's chair, "Mimi?"

"All crew are present and accounted for. Fuel and food are topped off. All weapons have checked out and we are full up on munitions. The marines report they ready, as does Engineering. The forward airlock is secure."

"Nephie, do you concur?" I asked.

"I do, Captain."

"Excellent." I regarded my new helmsman. "Mr. Zane, if you'd be so kind, please request clearance for undocking."

"Nemo says we can leave at our leisure and wishes us good hunting," said Zane.

"Take us out."

The station receded on the forward viewscreen. Cindy had done good work. It wasn't finished. There were a few holes in the outer hull, but there were a lot more weapons. The Muscat engineer assured me it would be complete in two to three weeks.

I thought about all the people we were leaving behind. Sara, my Dad, Holly, Pythia, and I prayed to the Muses to keep them safe.

"We're clear of the station."

"Thank you, Zane." I loaded Mimi's course into the computer. "Bring us about to heading thirty mark, one-ten and ride the beam all the way out."

"Aye, aye, sir."

***

We were a day out when we discovered what had happened.

"Captain," said Nephie, "Nemo is hailing us."

"On screen," I responded.

Sandy's face filled the screen. She had dark circles under her eyes. "Mark, is Pithy with you?"

"No, is she missing?"

Sandy frowned with worry. "No one's seen her since you left. We've searched the station. We can't find her anywhere."

My mouth went dry. "Could she have hitched a ride with some miners and be out in the belt?"

"Unlikely. She's never shown an interest in anything off the station, but we aren't ruling it out. I have Nemo pulling the security footage. She told me she was going to the park with Holly. That's the last time anyone saw either of them." Sandy paused as someone off-screen handed her a tablet. Her face went pale. "Mark, it's worse. All of the Dodgers are missing."

At that moment a klaxon sounded. The lights behind Sandy went red. There was an emergency on her end as well.

"What's going on Nephie?"

"An Erethizon battle group popped out of R-drive space. They're firing on us."

CHAPTER 12 – IN CHAOS THERE IS OPPORTUNITY

"Bring up the holo-tank," A three-dimensional image of the solar system popped into being in the middle of the bridge. Six red icons showed the Erethizon fleet. Six more red arrows showed missiles inbound. "Bring us to starboard sixty degrees and down thirty-two. Evasive maneuvers but keep us on that general heading."

"Gauss cannons on defense," yelled Tracy.

I willed my heart to slow down. At the moment, we were only dealing with six missiles. We waited in tense silence as the salvo closed the distance. When they were within effective range of our cannons, Tracy opened up on them. Two missiles exploded before they started evasive actions. One by one they went down. The last missile went down a mere two hundred kilometers from our hull.

"Nice shooting!"

"It's not all me," admitted Tracy. "We're using new gauss rounds. Something that came out of Rowdy's research into those shield bashing slugs. These are optimized for missile defense."

I'd have to ask him about it later.

Mimi's brow furrowed. "Farthogs, they must have been sitting outside the system."

She was right. They'd arrived grouped too well to have traveled any long distance. As I watched the task group split. Three destroyers accelerated away from the main group. Nephie overlaid their expected course confirming my suspicions. They were gunning for us. That left a battlecruiser and two light cruisers for Nemo and the yards.

I nodded. "They came from about a light day out. Radio signals from a recon drone. We shoved off. They attacked."

The plot changed as the destroyers stopped accelerating. My heart sank as each destroyer spat six new missiles at us for a total of eighteen incoming.

I studied the holo-tank and made a snap decision. It would ruin the surprise I'd planned for the destroyers, but it wouldn't mean anything if we weren't around for it. "Roll us twenty-five degrees to starboard and yaw us another fifteen."

"Aye, aye." Zane suited words to action.

We were now headed almost perpendicular to Isura's ecliptic. This altered the missiles' trajectories. They streaked over the system's outer asteroid belt. There was a bright flash, followed by several more. Eight of the deadly projectiles exploded as they entered the minefield.

"Yes!" exclaimed Mimi.

"We're not out of this yet," I reminded her. The ten remaining missiles bore down on us.

When they were within effective range, Tracy picked them off. Either Tracy wasn't as good this time, or the missile AIs were learning. Either way, my marine commander missed four.

"Brace for impact," screamed Nephie.

Missiles hit our starboard shields in a one-two punch. I jerked sideways as the ship rolled faster than the inertial compensators could compensate. The port shields took the next two strikes.

I breathed a sigh of relief. Glancing at the status displays, I saw the starboard shields at twelve percent and the port at four percent. "Outstanding maneuver, Mr. Zane."

Zane smiled nervously his fingers hovering over the controls. "Uh, thank you sir, but that wasn't me."

There was silence for a handful of heartbeats. I hazarded a guess. "Nephie?"

"Yes, Captain. I rolled the ship."

"What?" I exclaimed. My mind raced with the implications. Nephie had never overridden control of anything. But that was a problem for another time. The destroyers cut acceleration and presented their broadsides for another salvo. Eighteen new threats sprang up in the holo-tank.

"Mr. Zane, alter our course again," I ordered, "Keep the minefield between us and those missiles."

"Aye, aye."

I studied the plot. The Erethizon battlegroup had jumped pretty deep into the system. As a result, the destroyers had been accelerating away from Nephie and toward the inner system. We had been pushing toward the edge of the system for a full day. That gave us a huge acceleration advantage. They weren't going to get another shot at us. We were almost outside of their missiles powered envelope now. That gave me an idea.

The missiles passed through the minefield. The results were less impressive this time. Thirteen of the enemy weapons slipped through.

"Tracy, fire three salvos of missiles from our aft batteries. Target their barrage."

My marine commander tilted her head sideways and twitched an ear. "Captain, the odds of us hitting a missile with a missile is really small."

"Sara did it, on the Leo, before you joined us. Are you saying she's better than you on the guns?" I teased.

She pulled her ears in frustration. "Aye, aye, sir."

In the holo-tank, three waves of two blue icons sped toward the red ones. Tracy did her best to put our missiles near theirs before triggering them. She picked off two.

As the Porcu-bear missiles entered effective gauss cannon range, she again did her best to knock them out of space.

Again, she was less effective. My heart raced. She picked off five. Six missiles made it within two hundred kilometers when they abruptly stopped maneuvering.

"Mr. Zane, hard to port. Take us ninety degrees from our last heading."

To his credit, there was no pause as he executed the command. "Aye, sir!"

The missiles streaked past our aft quarter and into deep space.

"Thank you, Mr. Zane." I relaxed a little and put my coin back in my pocket. "Please readjust our course to keep the minefield between us and the destroyers."

"Aye, Aye, Captain."

Tracy regarded me from across the bridge for a few moments before she spoke. "Our missile salvos, we weren't trying to shoot them down. We were trying to get them to use fuel."

"They tried to avoid our ordinance."

"Risky," she shook her head. "They might have used longer-range missiles or something even more tricky."

I shrugged. They didn't and we were still here.

Things weren't as good for our friends. I expanded the view in the holo-tank. The destroyers were still in our wake. They'd have to maneuver in a few hours, or they'd run into our minefield. That still left Kane and Nemo to deal with the Erethizon heavies.

Three hours later, the destroyers adjusted course to avoid the asteroid belt. They misjudged the size of the minefield. One destroyer exploded in a cloud expanding debris. The other two took heavy damage and their pursuit slowed.

"Should we turn around and help Kane?" asked Mimi.

I wanted to. But there were a lot of people depending on us. Many of them were not in Isura, and we had no way to tell them if there was a change in the schedule. "No, we have our mission. We'd lose days maybe even a week. Kane and Sandy know what they're doing. We have to trust them to take care of this."

Horizon sailed in from the yards. In a deft maneuver, Kane jumped Firecat and Phoebe in from the outer system.

"I didn't realize Phoebe was back," said Mimi.

"Must have just arrived. She was due back soon," I observed.

Kane positioned her three cruisers close in, but not between the Erethizon heavies and the station. She was trying to draw them into one of our minefields. It didn't happen. With single-minded determination, the Erethizon continued to make a beeline for the station. After the station, they would be able to hit the undefended drydock, with only a slight course change. It reminded me of the attack on Ocelot. The difference was that instead of open space, they were hitting an in-system target. Our people had more time to prepare.

Since the Porcu-bears didn't respond to Kane, she had to respond to them. She brought her cruisers in behind the Erethizon ships. Checking the tactical display, I confirmed that they'd all meet up when the attack on Nemo would commence. I checked the countdown timer and realized we'd be leaving the system shortly after.

How much would we be able to see? We'd be six light hours away by then. Our faster than light comms were good for about four light hours.

Hours ticked by. It's the nature of space combat. You often saw the enemy coming from a long way off. There were long periods of nothing followed by actions so quick, it took a combat AI to make sense of it all.

The destroyers couldn't hope to catch us. Several duty rotations passed.

We reached the edge of the system. Out here, Isura's sun was a slightly brighter star. The battle had begun. Mass sensors were able to pick out roughly where the ships were, but not in fine enough detail for us to see what was going on.

Mimi stared at the mass gauge. "Sir, there's something out here with us."

I pulled up her display on my holo-screen as a cold shiver went down my spine. She was right. We couldn't jump. Something big was close to us.

"Visual scanning," I ordered. "There's a stealthed ship out there somewhere."

Several minutes passed.

"I have them, Captain," said Nephie. She put an image on the forward holo-screen. The image showed a black ship that Nephie outlined in red so we could see it.

"It's a collier." Mimi pulled up an image of an Erethizon supply ship and put it up next to the image on the screen. It matched.

"What are the odds we'd intercept one of their supply ships on the edge of the system?" asked Zane.

"Astronomical," answered Nephie, completely missing her inadvertent play on words.

"Then it's here to keep us from jumping." Mimi frowned in concentration. She entered a command into the holo-tank and it pulled up the stealthed supply ship. She then added the vector data. "We've got the acceleration advantage. We can jump in an hour."

"What's it's armament?" I asked. "Can it fire the missiles it's carrying?"

"No," said Mimi, "It's got two small gauss cannons for defense. It can't throw enough mass at us to keep us here."

That didn't make any sense. Here at the edge of the system, with nothing for hundreds of thousands of miles except the occasional Oort object, why go through the trouble. My breath caught in my throat. Unless...

"Mr. Zane, bring us thirty degrees up and twenty-one degrees to port. Mimi, what will that do to us getting free of their mass signature?"

Mimi arched an eyebrow at me. "It will extend it by twenty minutes. You're taking us closer to the enemy ship."

I nodded. Half an hour later a destroyer popped into existence ahead of our original course. They'd done the same thing Kane had done and jumped a ship in to intercept me.

It fired a broadside of six missiles at us and flipped to fire six more from the other side. Thanks to our change in course, it was at extreme range. They'd have the one shot.

My thoughts froze as the missiles stopped accelerating and went ballistic after five.

"What are they doing?" asked Tracy.

I was in the deep dark about that myself. It would be no problem for us to get out of the missile's way. "Maybe they're trying to keep them in our mass shadow as long as possible," I thought aloud. "Mimi, will it affect our departure?"

She frowned into her display. "No. They'll be through and out the other side before we get clear of the collier."

At the mention of the other ship, it abruptly lit up it's drives, changed course, and accelerated away. I began to have a bad feeling.

The mass gauge on the R-drive jumped as if a small asteroid had appeared from nowhere.

"What the..." exclaimed Mimi.

The mass reading doubled, then tripled. The number of missiles flying through our space decreased as large rocks appeared in their wake. My blood ran cold. No. Not rocks...

"Farthogs! Tracy, shoot down their remaining missiles. They're supercharging gravity plates to create mass shadows."

Tracy fired our missiles to intercept theirs.

"Mimi?"

"Twelve of those bastards will create a mass shadow equal to a small moon. It'll delay departure by a day."

Plenty of time for the Porcu-bears to get more ships out here to finish us.

Our missiles intercepted the Erethizon's. The results were less than stellar. We disabled two of them. Two more mass shadows appeared. The mass gauge now showed four more hours to get free.

We needed to change the battlefield. "Tracy, use the singularity missiles."

"Won't that help them?"

Our singularity missiles created miniature black holes. Normally we only used them against ships. They were hard to make, and we couldn't replenish them in flight. But they did an impressive amount of crush damage. Better, they didn't have to actually hit their targets, just get near them.

"They'll cast a wider net," I explained. "Also, use some regular missiles." They're acting like rocks, hopefully, they're as easy to hit.

"Aye."

Three more missiles imitated asteroids, increasing out jump time to by twelve hours. Then our missiles hit theirs.

The two unexploded Porcu-bear missiles disintegrated, but even better, two of the fake rocks were caught in the blast. The mass sensor jumped to three days then settled back to eight hours.

The destroyer reacted by firing another spread of missiles.

Tracy picked off three of the mass shadows, then managed to get the remaining five.

"Mimi?"

Her eyes were riveted on the gauge as it slid down from three days. After an eternity, that was more likely a few seconds, it finally settled. "Twenty minutes."

I glanced at the incoming missiles. They'd start affecting us in about ten minutes. "Let's try to bubble. Punch it," I ordered.

Mimi mashed the red icon on her holo-display. On the main screen, stars winked out as negative energy flooded the space around us. I waited, staring at the last remaining star that didn't go dark.

Mimi confirmed it, "No good, still too much mass nearby."

In the holo-tank, three more destroyers appeared next to the first. Their reinforcements had arrived. Their missiles were almost in range to affect us. I glanced at the gauge as it ticked from eight to seven minutes before we got free. Then it stopped and started counting up. The barrage was at the edge of our envelope. We were out of time.

"Hit it again," I ordered.

Mimi put a fist through the holo-display. Since it was just light, her hand went right through it, but outside the ship, stars started winking out again.

I held my breath. Seconds slipped by like Sildian nectar.

Just when I was sure we were screwed, Mimi piped up, "We're in the bubble." She grinned, "Sapho be praised. We're in our own universe for the next month."

"Ahem."

I swiveled to find Pace Jones at the back of the bridge. Firmly held in each hand were Holly and Pythia.

CHAPTER 13 - STOWAWAYS

Their hair stuck out at odd angles. Holly's shirt had a rip in one sleeve. Pithy sundress with bright yellow flowers was stained with some sort of oil. Both had something brown smeared across their mouths. A waft of chocolate confirmed my suspicions.

"My cabin. Now!" I pointed back down the passage. As I followed them, I called over my shoulder, "Mimi you have the bridge."

I sent a ping to Inga and Brady and settled in behind my desk and glared at the miscreants. Pace shook his head. Holly looked everywhere but at me. Pythia bit her lip.

"Do you have any idea how much trouble you're in?" I began. "We're heading into a warzone. People are going to die. Perhaps a lot more are going to die because they'll be worrying about you."

Holly frowned at the floor. "We can take care of

ourselves."

Which brought up another point. "Pace, where did you find them?"

"Near the supply crates at the back of cargo bay one."

I pinched the bridge of my nose. "The rest of the Dodgers will be somewhere near there. Probably in supply crates if they haven't moved into the ductwork or engineering access tubes. Can you put a detail together to dig them out and find them some quarters?"

He typed on his wrist AI, "right away, sir."

"You're letting us stay?" Holly was slack-jawed.

"Told ya," said Pythia.

"We're on a mission," I explained. "Some parts of it are time critical. We don't have the luxury of turning this boat around and sailing home. So yes, you're coming with us."

And with the space station under attack, they might be safer here, but I pushed that thought away.

Brady and Inga appeared behind Pace.

"So, let's make something crystal clear, I expect both of you to keep the rest of the Dodgers in line. Anyone who causes mischief will find themselves in the brig and you'll be in there with them."

"But-" started Holly.

"This isn't a negotiation. These are orders. We are on a

ship in space. I am the Captain. What I say goes. Up to and including, shoving someone out an airlock if I believe they are a danger to the ship or her crew. Do you get me?"

Holly shifted uncomfortably. Pythia cast her sightless gaze downward.

"And right now, I can't believe what you did to Sandy and your foster parents on the station. Can you imagine what they're going through right now? They're fighting for their lives against an Erethizon invasion with no idea where any of you are or if you're okay. When the battle is over, if they survive, they'll be looking for your bodies in the wreckage, because they'll have no idea where you've gone." I paused, letting that sink in. "And since you are here, my people will be going into combat worried about all of you, not focused on the mission. They might hesitate at a critical moment and end up dead. I might end up dead. All because you took it upon yourselves to make a decision, one that everyone told you was a bad idea."

Pythia frowned in defiance. She stuck her chin out, but not directly at me. "You won't die *because* we're here."

"Really? Because your predictions are infallible? You didn't see that engineer on Firecat who nearly killed you. Captain Kane took three bullets meant for you. She almost died. You didn't see it when Anubis shot your Mom. You. Are not. Always. Right. You make mistakes, like the rest of us. Those mistakes can have real consequences that cost lives."

Pythia burst into tears and I realized I'd gone too far. I scrubbed my face and took a few seconds to get my anger under control.

I came around my desk and knelt on the deck in front of them. "I'm sorry. I shouldn't have said that."

"You're right," Pithy blubbered. "I see bad things and people get killed."

"No. You're trying to help people and do the right thing. That's all anyone can ask of you." I sighed, "I respect that about both of you. But farthogs, you gotta listen to us sometimes. You are the most precious people in the universe to us. Now you're here, in danger. Right in the middle of the very thing we're trying to protect you from."

Awkward silence. I spread my arms and they hugged me. I winced as Pithy shocked me, but I didn't let go.

***

The rest of the Dodgers were found in food crates. A dozen extra mouths to feed. Several of whom had been stuffing themselves for days, Inga would have to adjust. Thankfully, we planned for a planet wide infiltration. Adding a dozen mouths to a crew of thirteen hundred was easier than our normal compliment of a seventy.

We stopped and used one of our few message drones to send a message back to Isura. Sandy and the other foster parents would be worried sick... If they survived the attack. We'd been too far away to see what had happened to Nemo and the shipyards. I knew that the station, even not completed, should be equal to the ships they sent to attack her. The Porcu-bears had sent four ships out to intercept me. Five if you counted the collier. How much did they have in reserve to take on Kane and the station?

These were the questions I was pondering as I sat at my desk in my quarters. We were three days into our month-long journey, and I was going over every minute of our last engagement. I was so focused on what the Erethizon were doing, that my brain did a hiccup when I ran across something we'd done. Specifically, that Nephie had taken over helm control and rolled us. Granted, it saved us from crippling damage, and had saved lives, but what did it mean for us as humans?

I called Racy and Sophie to my quarters. I engaged privacy mode when they arrived.

Racy ignored the chairs in front of my desk. She instead climbed into my lap and sat down. "What do you need?"

Grinning at my discomfort, my sister covered her mouth.

"I'm concerned about Nephie," I began. "In combat the other day, she took control of the ship and rolled us?"

Racy rolled her nose, "She has access to the helm controls through the auto-pilot. There's nothing unusual about that."

"But she took control of the ship," I pressed. "In a life or death situation. She didn't tell anyone she was going to do it, she just did it."

My sister shrugged, "What would've been the outcome if

she hadn't taken control?"

"That's not the point," I argued.

"I think it is," said Sophie. "Listen, this is the twenty-sixth century. Space flight, complex cities, closed environments in space stations. Hell, even in surgery, I rely on a medical AI to make micro incisions near vital organs. Can you run a ship without AI help?"

It was possible to run a ship without AI, but you had to be very careful. Worse, the faster you traveled, the more impossible it became to react to anything. Micro-meteorites, radiation plumes, ice, and debris could cause serious damage to a ship before a biological person could react. It didn't matter how fast their reflexes were. Without an AI tuning shields, making minor course adjustments, and keeping the environmental systems in order, there were a million ways space travel could kill you.

Throw in combat at a quarter of light speed, and death was pretty much guaranteed without one. Sure, only a sentient being could pull the trigger, but leading the target, missile trajectories, evasive patterns, that was all done with AI assistance. The biological crew just wasn't fast enough.

"We have to be able to trust the AIs we work with," I told her. "That means they do what we expect when we expect it."

Racy squinted at me. "Nephie is more than that. She has thoughts and feelings. She cares about us."

"She cares about us because she's programed to," I

pointed out. "It's written into her code. But code can be corrupted, and advanced AIs evolve. What happens when she evolves and decides she doesn't need us pitiful biological beings? Kill us off and make her own decisions?"

"Do you love your father?" asked Racy.

"What?"

She rolled her nose at me. "You heard me. Do you love him?"

"Damned straight I do. I traveled halfway across the galaxy and took on a planet full of religious nut jobs to get him back."

Racy sat on the edge of his desk facing him. "Why do you love him?"

"Is that a trick question?" I asked. "He's my father. He's stood up for me when no one else would and with no other reason than because I'm his son. I'd go through hell for him and there's no doubt in my mind that he'd do the same for me."

"Which is a fancy way of saying biology," said Sophie.

The Muscat put her hand on my chest when I started to object. "She's not saying that there's not more to it. That's the starting point. I love Rowdy just as much, and I love you and Sophie even though we're not related by blood. What I'm pointing out is that Nephie's code is put together the same way. Parts of her core operating system are coded to mimic Muscat and Terran emotional responses. She can't get nervous or scared, but she can feel love and attachment. She bonds with her crew. To her, they are her family."

"Families have arguments," I pointed out. "Some family members hate each other for good and not good reasons. What happens when-"

"Feradit!" Racy swore. "You Terrans and your fear of machines." She held up a finger to forestall my argument. "I know that there have been a couple of incidents where AIs have killed a few people, but I'm willing to bet that was due to shoddy programing. Nephie will never do anything like that."

"That's beside the point. As much as we all love Nephie, she's also a tool. Something we use to control the ship. We have to be able to count on her."

Racy twitched an ear for a few moments before she responded. "What would you have done, if your helmsman had pulled off the maneuver?"

"Praised him for it. It was the right move at the right time." I realized her point right after I said it. Racy twitched her ears, she saw that I'd followed her logic. I switched my focus to Sophie.

"Don't look at me. I'm a doctor, not a software engineer."

"You're also the smartest person I know. Even better, if I'm missing something, I know you'll be dying inside until you can rub my face in it," I pointed out.

Sophie shrugged, "It's your call. It's your ship."

"But…" I prompted.

"But Racy says that Nephie is a person. A sentient being. That means she should have rights and self-determination. If we assume she's right, you need to treat her like one of the crew, not like a piece of equipment. If a crew steps out of line, you make suggestions to improve their performance. You praised Zane for a good maneuver. What you should be doing is asking yourself why you didn't praise Nephie."

That gave me pause. Was Nephie our AI or was she crew? I'd already claimed on more than one occasion that she was crew. Was I guilty of an anti-AI bias? There were rewards and corrective actions I could take with crew. What would I do if Nephie refused to take an order?

Then there was Clyde, the insane AI that masqueraded as the Erethizon's god.

I pondered this for a while. Sophie and Racy debated what constituted sentience and the merits of nature vs nurture. I didn't reach any decisions I was happy with, so I asked Sophie and Racy to come back later.

I was still stewing over it twenty minutes later when my musing was interrupted by a high-pitched scream from the passageway.

I threw open the hatch. Mimi held Westley halfway up the bulkhead by his crotch.

"Captain, help!" squeaked the pirate. "This crazy bitch attacked me."

Mimi squeezed and Westley screamed. Mimi wore

powered combat armor anytime she was outside her quarters. I shuddered imagining how strong her grip could be.

I cocked my head, "Was it something he said or did?"

"He asked me if I'd help him find the cock ring nebula," she growled. "Then grabbed my wrist when I ignored him."

"This bloody whore attacked me on the way to the head," exclaimed Westley. "I was mindin' my own business."

His belt was undone. Had he been planning to pee in the passageway? "War can you come up to officer country? I need you to escort Mr. Westley to the brig."

"What?" protested Westley. "You're gonna take her word over mine?"

"An excellent point," I conceded. "Nephie, what exactly did Mr. Westley say?"

"Mr. Westley's exact words were, 'Hey sweet stuff, how about you an' I head back to your bunk? I show you my love missile and you show me the cock ring nebula?"

Westley's mouth dropped open. "You got the God damn computer spyin' on me?"

"Nephie can see anything that happens in the common areas. She can only watch you in your quarters and in the head if you call for her or you've been accused of a crime." I made a show of thinking about it. "Huh, strike that. I guess we are spying on you."

"You can't do that," Westley cried indignantly. "I got rights."

Mimi set him on the deck but held him pinned to the wall with one hand on his chest. "That's where you're wrong. This is a ship in deep space. You of all people should know that the only rights you get are the ones the captain gives you."

"Captain," said Nephie, "it's relevant to tell you that Miss Jaylen is not the first altercation Mr. Westley has been involved in today. He attempted to assault two different off duty female marines and spent an hour on the mess deck staring at Inga. However, War 'n Pace made sure she was never alone."

"Well, Mr. Westley," I admonished, "you have been busy."

War ambled up the passage to my right. "Sir."

"War, deposit Mr. Westley in the brig. He'll be spending the rest of the voyage there."

"Hey, the only one who got hurt was me," Westley spat.

"Which is why you're going to the brig and not sucking vacuum," I said conversationally. "Think of it as a vacation from yourself."

***

Two weeks later, I was back in my office for a different but related reason. Tracy had found some contraband. Normally this wouldn't have been a problem. This was a pirate ship, well, privateer if you wanted to split atoms, but there were a few things that I wouldn't turn a blind eye to. This was going to be a difficult conversation any way you looked at it. I was happy to have Tracy at my side for this one.

Someone knocked.

"Come," loud enough to be heard in the passage.

Aziz came in. His gaze went to Tracy then to the packages on my desk. His expression didn't give anything away but sweat formed on his brow.

"Captain, you asked to see me."

I didn't offer him a seat. "Aziz, I'll be honest, I didn't want you on this mission. I agreed to it because Senator Wayne asked me to bring you along." And because Pythia said we needed him, but I wasn't going to mention that. "In general, there are few rules aboard my ship. I even encourage the crew to engage in private trade. There are a few things that aren't allowed. Do you know what they are?"

"Per the crew handbook you uploaded to me: weapons, munitions, explosives, and radioactive materials."

"Did you miss the part about dissociative drugs?" I asked.

"I'm not sure what that means, sir."

"It's a class of drugs that can be used to make people compliant and disrupt their short-term memory. Speaking of which, let me jog yours. You sold it on Ocelot. Both Brady and Holly confirmed it for me. The street name for one of the more popular forms of these drugs is called Easy." I placed a hand on one of the packages in front of me. "Do you know what's inside these packages?"

"If the label is accurate, coffee," he answered.

I spun the package around to show that it had been chewed open. Coffee grounds leaked onto my desk. Plastic baggies with little white pills could be seen inside. "Our cleaning rats found these. They'd stopped cleaning certain areas of the ship and we grew concerned. And before you deny that these packages belong to you, you should know we found your fingerprints all over them."

Aziz's face was impassive. I wasn't even sure if he'd heard me.

"It's no big secret that I don't like you, assassin," I continued, "but right now, I'm looking for a reason not to throw you off the ship. Here in deep space, I don't like your chances of surviving that."

That got a reaction. His eyes widened. Good. He was taking me seriously.

"Sandy won't like that. She'd leave if she heard you'd killed me."

I leaned forward on my desk. "Really? Even after I tell her I caught you with several kilos of date rape drugs."

Aziz blinked rapidly but didn't say anything.

"Tracy, get a detail up here, we'll use the rear airlock near engineering-"

"Wait," interrupted Aziz. "I have information you need."

"Doubtful," I said over my shoulder. Then to Tracy, "Don't bother with a suit. Why waste-"

"I know your mother!" blurted Aziz.

I rolled my eyes. "My mother's been dead for more than twenty years."

"No. That's what they told you. Told the public. But it isn't true. Your mother is alive. She did things the government of Yale didn't approve of. They exiled her."

He was grasping at fog. One of my earliest memories was being at her memorial ceremony. Time to trip him up. "And you know this how?" No way he'd be able to answer that.

"I used to work for her. Dr. Danielle Martin."

"And why did she need an assassin?"

"She didn't. She needed help stealing secrets. Medical stuff. Genetic research."

He must have done his homework. My mother had been a well-known geneticist. "You're lying."

"Really?" he cocked his head. "Where's her grave?"

***

I checked the ship's library. Nothing. My mother had

been important. She'd been married to my father, at the time a senator. This was long before he'd been elevated to king. Nephie had collected many old news articles from my homeworld. I could find her birth, school achievements, wedding announcements, everything. I found nothing about her death. No obituary, no mention of the memorial service, she just wasn't in the news anymore.

I wandered into medical. Sophie, my older sister, was treating someone with a busted knee. I waited for her to finish.

She sent the crewman limping on his way. "Hey Marky, need something?"

"What do you remember about Mom?"

Her eyes widened like I'd asked her something obvious and odd, like why is space black. Which I suppose I had. Dad, Sophie, and I never talked about Mom. Ever. She took a moment to collect her thoughts. "Um. She was beautiful, at least that's what I remember. She died twenty-two years ago, when I was nine. You were four, so it wouldn't surprise me if you didn't remember much about her. I thought she was the most brilliant doctor in the world. I guess that's why I went into medicine. Not that it's the same thing. She was a research doctor, geneticist. I wanted to save lives more directly."

"Where is she buried?"

Sophie wrinkled her nose at me. "Why the sudden interest in Mom?"

"It came up in conversation recently," I hedged. "I realized that I really didn't remember much about her."

Sophie shook her head, "I don't know where she's buried. Maybe nowhere. I think she died in some lab accident or something. Cremated maybe?"

It was subtle, but I realized she'd morphed into political Sophie. Her expressions were more muted, like she was keeping track of every muscle on her face. Dammit.

I stared into her eyes for several long moments and she stared back.

"Shit," she said softly.

CHAPTER 14 – THE KING OF ALL LIES

"What aren't you telling me, Soph?"

"Marky. No. Don't do this," she pleaded with me.

"Really. You don't want to know."

The betrayal stung. She'd known the truth for years. My Dad had to know. Who else knew the truth? Why? Why keep it from me? What had she done that was so heinous that my family, my government had exiled her? Why did they take away my Mom?

"Know what?" I asked.

"I can't tell you."

"You won't tell me," I corrected.

Sophie bit her lower lip. "The truth doesn't always set you free. Sometimes, it just hurts. I love you. As your sister, I'm begging you. Don't look. Don't dig it up. For once in your life, let it go."

"I have to know."

"You won't get it from me." I tear traced its way down her cheek. "I lived through it once. I won't do it again."

I didn't press Sophie further. I wanted to, but I wasn't willing to push it.

That didn't dampen my need to find the answers though. I wanted to ask my Dad. The fact that he was two hundred light-years away in Isura made it a bit difficult. I was on a mission to my homeworld. The place where my mother was born and had lived when she was exiled. I'd find the answers there after we finished the mission.

**

We popped the bubble half a light day from the outer edge of the Yale system. Using mass sensors and long-range optics we scanned the system.

My command team gathered around the holo-tank on the bridge as the details filled in.

Mimi pointed to the bigger features. "Three gas giants and three rocky inner planets. Two asteroid belts. It's Yale, and that's gotta be the warp gate."

I nodded. "That matches the orbital mechanics as I remember them. I thought the warp gate was closer in system, but I'm probably getting that wrong." I pointed to Yale and the image magnified. "What's got me worried is this. A battleship and a battlestation in orbit above the planet. The Porcu-bears destroyed our old space station. They've had time to build a new one, but I didn't expect they would.

I scrubbed my face with my hands. "Thirty ships and a battlestation. Farthogs that's a lot of firepower. Intel was dead wrong, and even if every ship we were promised shows up, they'd still have the tonnage advantage. I'd hoped that since the Erethizon considered this system safe, that the military presence would be light. Maybe even less than advertised."

"Why are they here?" asked Tracy. "Intelligence says the Porcu-bears are using this as a light industrial world."

I thought about that for a couple of moments. "The Erethizon believe that Yale is some sort of center of influence. A nexus for spreading the faith. Yale has produced a number of singers, writers, and actors, but I can't see that continuing under Erethizon rule. Perhaps that mistaken belief explains the large fleet presence here. Or maybe they're gathering ships here for a push into a new system."

"Why do you think that? When actors speak, people listen," said Mimi.

I shook my head. "That only works in a free society. Under Erethizon rule, there is no free speech. No one will trust the speaker if they believe that they are a mouthpiece for the church."

Mimi frowned.

I waved it away. "It doesn't matter. Even before the Erethizon moved on Isura, we didn't have the tonnage to take this on."

Mimi gazed at me. "So, what... We're giving up and going home?"

Tracy rolled her nose at me. I let out a breath. "No. At this point, we couldn't get a message torpedo back before the flotilla set out. Our allies are supposed to meet us here." What I didn't say was that I hoped we'd have more allies than we were counting on, but that was far from a sure thing.

"It also doesn't change what we need to do." I went to my chair, and my bridge crew did the same. "Full stealth, Mr. Zane. We have a warp gate to sneak up on."

It took us three days to sneak up on the warp gate. At a distance, the ring appeared as a pinprick of light. As we approached, the sheer magnitude of the structure was awe-inspiring. Several ships disappeared into it. The ring itself was fifty meters thick and a kilometer wide. Lights on the massive rings spun and blurred together. The open middle of the ring shimmered. A wormhole linked this point in space with another one hundreds maybe thousands of light-years away.

"Amazing," remarked Racy. "The technological marvel that started it all. Transportation across light-years of space in the flick of a tail."

"It's also the way hundreds of warships can be moved to conquer a solar system in days. As incredible as it is, it has to go." I regarded my helmsman, "Let's hold it right here Mr. Zane."

He tapped the controls, "Aye, aye. Attitude thrusters to station keeping."

"Easy," I cautioned. "Don't use too much at once. If there's someone on the ball over there, they might see the thruster exhaust."

The eyeroll in the reflection in the holo-screen was at odds with his confident, "aye, sir."

"We're being scanned," Tracy exclaimed.

"Source?"

She studied her monitors, "The ring."

"We're twenty thousand klicks out," said Mimi. "They shouldn't be able to see us, right?"

"Shouldn't," I confirmed, "but that doesn't mean they won't." We'd found a way to locate the Erethizon probes. Porcu-bears are as smart as we are. Smarter with Clyde. The insane AI that masqueraded as the Erethizon god Urson could infect almost any computer system. The more computers he could access, the smarter he got. But smarter didn't always mean more clever. I'd met any number of scientists that were book smart, but no common sense.

Mr. Zane, for his part, kept his fingers on the controls ready to move if things went out the airlock. His neck reddened. We waited for interminable seconds as the scan continued.

My mind raced with possibilities. To shoot or not to shoot. That was the question. If they reacted and sent their squadron of destroyers against us, we'd have to leave. But if we didn't take the warp gate out of play, then we wouldn't be facing thirty ships, we'd have eighty or more. The Erethizon would pour ships through the gate and we'd be mauled.

"Are they targeting us specifically?" I asked.

"I can't tell," said Tracy. "The signal's pretty weak. It might be a ruse or bad sensors."

"Weak?" I prompted.

"Mid-range commercial. I'd expect a military scan to be three times stronger, even from crappy Porcu-bear technology."

I glanced at Mimi.

She shrugged. "They are a commercial entity."

True, I thought, but we'd discovered that the Erethizon had infiltrated Gilstrap Gate Systems. I'd have expected them to beef up defense and scanning capabilities. I shifted my attention to the three destroyers.

As if in response to my musings the scan stopped. At the same moment, one of the destroyers broke formation. It pivoted in place and accelerated toward us.

"Drop the cargo," I ordered. "Zane, very slowly, bring us to zero, mark ninety. Give us a nice push and then we'll coast out of here at about ten thousand kps."

"Cargo away," called Mimi.

"Straight down with a little push," confirmed Zane.

The destroyer moved in fast.

At our stern, the Erethizon destroyer began active scanning. I watched the signal strength on my console. A red line indicated the detection threshold. The meter bounced up and down below the red line. I sighed in relief.

Then the ship on the screen reoriented. The indicator went up and hovered just below the red line. Then it dropped away. A moment later it spiked above the line.

I held my breath. My attention riveted on the holo-tank. I waited, looking for any sign they'd seen us. None of the ships moved. We might be able to handle one or two of the destroyers in a stand-up fight, but there were three destroyers and a battleship out there. Any scenario where we had to trade fire with that behemoth would be suicidal.

The seconds ticked away.

We'd left the main screen on the destroyer. The image grew and shrank as the hull cameras refocused to keep the ship visible as we hurtled away from it. Something was happening on the hull.

"Nephie, can you zoom in on that movement?"

"Of course, Captain."

The screen magnified that section. A second hatch opened up on the side, drones spewed forth. My stomach sank.

"Mr. Zane, slowly bring us up to maximum stealthed speed. We're about to be swarmed." They either knew we were out here or strongly suspect. The logical thing was to send a ship to the area. A ship, or a bunch of drones.

"We're being painted," yelled Tracy. "Found the source. I'm taking it out.

On the ship display, the gauss cannon shifted and fired once. I pulled up the tactical display and saw the targeting laser warning pop up.

"Two more!" warned Tracy.

Two more shots, two more seconds and it winked out.

"Mr. Zane, evasive pattern Delta," I ordered.

"They'll be sending more drones." Mimi's eyes were as wide as saucers. "If they get a good lock..." she trailed off.

She didn't have to finish. We all knew. If a ship was close enough, there'd be a volley of missiles.

On the tactical display, all three destroyers converged on where we had been. Queen Nephanie could move quickly when she needed to, but we were trying to sneak into the system. The destroyers weren't following. They didn't have a lock on us. Yet...

The battleship slowly followed its smaller cousins. I relaxed a little bit for each minute that drew us further away from the destroyers. They were on top of the space where we'd destroyed the drones. The more distance between us and that spot the greater the area they'd have to cover to find us.

"Targeting laser!"

My head whipped around to Tracy.

"Got it," she said.

The drone erupted into a fireball. My chair seemed to jump from underneath me.

The destroyers altered course.

"Evasive pattern Gamma, Mr. Zane," I ordered.

"Captain," Nephie's smooth contralto interrupted, "If I might offer a suggestion."

"Yes, Nephie?"

"I believe a different evasive pattern may be more effective. The Erethizon appear to be sending out drones in waves. It may be possible to slip between them," she said.

"Show me."

Nephie brought up an image of the Porcu-bear destroyers in the holo-tank. Each one created an expanding orb of bright green specs. The orb intersected a large blue dot that represented our ship. The blue icon wove between the green dots avoiding detection neatly.

"The drones move a lot faster than we do, Nephie," I pointed out. "Can we stay between the waves?"

"Wait," said Mimi. "We might not have to. We're only a couple hundred thousand kilometers from the outer asteroid belt." She took control of the holo-tank and expanded the view. "If we can reach it without being detected, we might be able to hide out for half a day."

"They will eventually start searching the asteroids," said Tracy.

I nodded. "Yes, but not right away. Mimi's right. If we lay low for half a day, we can ease through the field. We'd intended to use it for cover anyway. Mass sensors won't be able to pick us out of the clutter as long as we keep our speed down." The more I thought about it, the more it seemed like the right idea.

"Right. Nephie, execute the plan."

The ship moved. Zane pulled his hands back from the controls. For the moment, Nephie flew herself. A part of me wanted to second guess her, or have Zane fly the ship using navigation input from Nephie. But as my sister had pointed out earlier, Nephie frequently made minor course adjustments herself all the time. This was a broader application of the same autopilot function.

Nephie showed the position of the destroyers. A fearsome battleship lumbered along in their wake. More ships altered course. This section of sky was about to be a lot more crowded.

Green dots showed the approximate position of the launched drones. We couldn't be exactly sure. The Erethizon used stealth technology on their drones as well. Nephie could extrapolate where they should show up using visual scanning but picking out the matte back drones against the pitch blackness of space was almost impossible.

Without warning, the view from the forward viewscreen flipped and my stomach flipped with it. I swallowed hard to keep my lunch down. Nephie accelerated hard toward the destroyers.

A spike of cold seized my chest as the thought occurred to me that Nephie might have been compromised by Clyde. She was going to take over the ship and turn us all over to the Erethizon.

I quashed that thought as soon as I had it.

Nephie was getting us into position. She must have seen one of the drones and needed to adjust. In the holo-tank green icons turned orange marking them as confirmed sightings.

All engines cut off and we coasted. In the tank, the green orb turned orange near where we were. I held my breath as it expanded over and around us. My gaze drifted to the tactical screen. No new warning lights appeared.

After a handful of seconds, Nephie spun us again and fired the main engines.

Zane reached for the controls.

"Mr. Zane," said Nephie, "if you don't mind, I'd like to remain in control for the next two hours. Another wave of drones will be coming, and I may need to reposition us quickly."

My helmsman looked to me and I nodded almost imperceptibly.

"Of course, Nephie," he said with a shaky voice.

The two hours passed by in an odd game of fox and mouse. We'd speed along between the waves then stop suddenly and change course as a wave intersected our position.

We made it to the asteroid field and Nephie released the controls to Zane. Mimi located a bumpy asteroid composed of mainly iron and magnesium. The perfect hiding spot. We landed and settled in to wait.

Nephie spotted a few drones, but none of them did more than throw a cursory scan in our direction as they passed. I felt my shoulders unknot despite all the activity.

"Captain?"

I woke with a start. I must have fallen asleep at some point. Mimi swallowed and pointed. I followed her finger to the main screen. The coin bit into my fingers as I realized what I was looking at.

"Feradit," said Tracy.

Around the curve of the asteroid, the Erethizon battleship inched into view.

The data feed at the bottom of the display said it was five thousand kilometers away. In astronomical terms, it was on top of us.

CHAPTER 15 – THE BEAR IN THE CAMP

It wasn't moving fast. A behemoth that size didn't do anything very quickly. It hadn't reacted to us yet. If it saw us, it'd be over before we knew it. The amount of firepower it had was staggering. A missile would reach us in under a minute. Gauss slugs alone would rip us apart in a matter of seconds.

One time, in the mountains west of Aurora, I'd gone hiking with some friends. We'd been horsing around and had strayed off the trail to pick some wild mushrooms. A hellcat, a creature similar to an old Terran mountain lion had snuck up on us. A metric ton of red and brown fury, in the form of razor-sharp teeth and claws. My friends and I had immediately frozen. All conversation stopped. We stared in fright as it walked not ten meters from where we crouched next to a boulder.

This was like that. Like then, I didn't move a muscle. I feared that if I made a sound or twitched a finger it would all be over. Briefly, I toyed with the idea of lifting off and hiding in its wake. I dismissed the idea as quickly as I had it though. One Crazy Ivan, and it'd be done for. There was bold, and there was suicidal.

The battleship pulled away far too slowly for my comfort. It didn't turn. No weapons twitched. If it saw us, it gave no outward appearance. We were being scanned, but signal strength didn't reach the detection threshold.

Two hours later it was a receding speck in the deep dark. I was about to order us to move when I saw a star twinkle.

Unlike on a planet where the atmosphere causes stars to wink on and off, in space, that doesn't happen. With no atmosphere or anything else between us and the distant stars, they appeared as solid bright pinpricks of light.

I stood and approached the main screen pointing at the errant star. "Nephie, please zoom in here. Visual scanning."

Within three minutes she responded, "I found it, Captain." The screen panned to port and a wireframe outline appeared.

"Damn." It was a stealthed Erethizon drone. "Nephie, scan local space. See if you can find any more."

"Of course, Captain."

"What do you think, sir?" asked Mimi.

I glanced at Tracy, who nodded. I continued, "They know someone's out here, but they don't know where. They suspect, correctly in this case, that we've gone to ground in the asteroid field. That still leaves a few hundred rocks in local space where we might be hiding. They've launched a few dozen drones to help them find us."

Mimi frowned, "So, we sit tight and wait for them to give up, right?"

I shook my head, "No. We're hard to see, sure, but the longer we stay where they expect us to be, the easier it'll be to find us. We need to head out."

"I found another one, Captain." Nephie super-imposed a red arrow on the screen near an asteroid about twelve hundred kilometers distant.

"Good work, Nephie. When will both of the drones be out of our line of sight?"

"Twenty-eight minutes."

I keyed the internal comms. "Rowdy, I want you to unpack our second surprise present. We're going to leave it here."

"Mark, weren't we going to leave it in the inner asteroid belt? It won't be as effective out here," he growled.

"Can't be helped, my friend. They know we're here. Our chances of making it to Yale unobserved have plummeted. If we leave it here, it'll be in place to help our friends when they get here in a few weeks. It'll be near the gate to intercept traffic going to or from the wreckage."

"What kind of asteroid are we on?" he asked.

I glanced at the holo-screen on my right. "Readings indicate a type S, but just barely. There's a lot of iron, magnesium, and rhodium in it."

"Not ideal, but good enough. Put a delay on it?"

I rubbed the coin in my pocket. "Yes. I'm thinking a day and a half."

"Will do, Rowdy out."

We'd brought along one of the alien mines. We still couldn't get them to make a queen mine but could get them to reproduce. Setting it loose in the asteroid field where it had ample access to raw materials, we hoped it would be able to build enough copies to have an impact on the upcoming battle.

If it remained undiscovered.

In Isura, the mines stopped listening to the control module after a couple of days. We'd had to go out and perform maintenance on it. Rowdy and Racy thought they had a patch in place to fix it, but there'd been no way to test it before we left.

If it didn't work, we'd end up with a dozen mines. If it did work, we'd have upwards of a thousand as compounding growth took effect.

A few minutes later Rowdy indicated that the package was on the surface.

Eyeing the red marks on the screen, I addressed the AI. "Okay, Nephie. Let us know when we're clear."

Thirty minutes later, Nephie gave us the go-ahead.

Zane eased us off the asteroid and we drifted up and away. We accelerated at a sedate twenty meters per second. We wouldn't break any speed records, but we weren't likely to attract attention either. Several times we slowed down, sped up, or altered course when Nephie located a drone. But the further we moved away from the gate, the less often we encountered drones. Two days later, we were free of the asteroid belt and moving in system.

Five days later, we were approaching the planet. We could have made the trip in three given where we'd entered the system, but that much speed, even from a stealth ship, would have been noticed. We stopped four hundred thousand kilometers from the planet. As an added measure of insurance, we were parked two hundred kilometers above Clio, the furthest of Yale's two moons. The technology we used to mask our mass signature worked pretty well, but not completely. Hiding in Clio's mass shadow should make us almost invisible.

We huddled around the holo-tank.

"Feradit," Tracy cursed. "Any insertion will have to be on the opposite side of the planet from that space station. Its sensors might pick us out."

"Mr. Zane, come over and take a look." I motioned for my helmsman to join us. He did so but hunched his shoulders. "Relax," I told him, "Just adding more eyes to the situation. If you see something, don't be afraid to speak up."

Mimi pointed at the ships. "We've got the battleship and a destroyer circling the planet. Sentry duty."

Tracy adjusted the controls to zoom in on the station. "And there are two more destroyers docked at the battlestation. If alerted, they could be anywhere in near space in under ten minutes."

"Double that," I said. "Porcu-bear warships have crap acceleration from a standing start."

Mimi tapped the top of the globe. "They're staying near the equator. Let's go for a polar insertion. The planet's magnetosphere will help mask us."

I shook my head. "When we bugged out after the invasion, we had the same thought. The Erethizon will have a fighter patrol stationed there."

"Where are we landing?" asked Zane.

I spun the globe and indicated the mountains west of the capital city, Aurora. Nephie marked the area with a green 'x'.

His eyes went back and forth across the globe. "Can we add in sun effects?"

I should have thought of that. "Nephie?"

One side of the globe turned dark. I then adjusted the controls and sped up the holo so that we went through the next three days every three minutes.

Mimi addressed the ceiling. "Nephie, can you also show the effective scanning range of each ship and the battle station?"

Red bubbles appeared around each mobile unit. Nephie did one better and put a bubble on top of each major city.

We watched as the holo played the three-day loop over and over. When the red bubbles intersected, the area turned a darker red.

Zane called, "Stop," and pointed to a point on the map at the terminator between day and night. "Here."

"It's red." Mimi and I said in unison.

"Yes, but everything's red," my helmsman pointed out. "I'm sure the Porcu-bears did that on purpose. The red here is on the very outside of Aurora's effective scanning range."

I motioned with my hands to zoom in on that location. "Go forward one hour." I sucked in a breath as the red bubble moved. "That's going to be a really steep entry. A fireball will be visible for kilometers in all directions."

"Will they notice?" asked Mimi.

"What?"

"That's the capital city," said Mimi. "I bet it has orbital shuttle traffic all the time. Nephie?"

"You are correct, Miss Jaylen. Aurora receives as many as fifteen orbital shuttles every hour."

Mimi nodded. "So, we're bigger than the average orbital shuttle, but we'll also be further away. Being in the setting sun will make us harder to spot."

I grinned, "Let's go one step further. During the war for Yale, the Porcu-bears would sneak fighters under the planetary shield by doing a straight drop. The Erethizon haven't put up a new shield so we don't have to create a hole with ordinance like they did. But we should be able to use the same tactic. Almost no fireball and devilishly hard to pick out with ground-based sensors."

My crew nodded with approval. "Excellent, Mimi, lay in a course."

***

We snuck in while the battlestation was over the horizon. A destroyer was cresting over the planet, but at this range, it'd be difficult to pick us out of the usual shuttle traffic. We managed to get into position without anyone saying boo.

We weren't the only ones there.

CHAPTER 16 – WE AREN'T ALONE

"We aren't alone."

"What?" I turned to Tracy.

"There's a ship out there off the starboard bow."

"On screen Nephie."

A ship appeared on the main screen. I identified it immediately. "All be damned. It's a YT30."

"Porcu-bears?" asked Mimi.

"No, it's a Yale built light transport. A Porcu-bear couldn't even fit in the cockpit."

"Sympathizers then," declared Tracy.

"I... don't think so. What's their course?"

Tracy twisted her left ear. "Same as ours, they're dropping."

I chuckled. "Guess we're not the first to think of this."

"But they don't have stealth," said Mimi. "They'll be seen for sure."

"I used to fly one. Low profile. They're hard to see on standard scans. What I don't understand is how it's up here? The YT series are atmo craft."

"What would it take to convert them for space?" asked Zane.

"I'm no engineer. I have no idea."

"Should we contact them?" asked Mimi.

"No. Maintain radio silence." Tracy echoed my thoughts. The ship over there might be with the local resistance, and we wanted to contact them, but now was neither the time nor the place. Besides, with a little luck, we'd see them at our landing zone.

The YT fell faster than we did. Originally built for atmosphere, it had less wind resistance. The craft performed a slow spin and briefly faced us but didn't open comms.

Our engines flared to life as we decelerated, and the YT continued to plummet. We massed a lot more than the tiny transport, but used engines built for interstellar travel. Our terminal velocity was three hundred meters per second, which we shed in about half a minute. At five kilometers above sea level, the YT rocketed northward.

We headed east at four thousand meters above sea level. Having spent most of the last three years in deep space, seeing mountain peaks pass to port and starboard was surreal. We found a level flat area just south of a played-out titanium mine. The same mine I'd sent Captain Voorhees to.

It felt like a thousand years ago and million kilometers away from where we were now. I remembered everything that happened that night. The mission with Voorhees, the starfighter that attacked my transport, crash landing, rescuing my sister, and the heart-wrenching failure when I couldn't save my Dad. We'd met Captain Houston though, and joined her band of smugglers.

I'd learned so much from her. She'd been more than my Captain. She was my mentor. My friend. Many times since her death I yearned for her insight. She'd had a talent for navigating the murky back alleys of pirates and brigands without getting dirty. When I looked at my missteps and blunders, I couldn't help thinking she would have done a lot better. Stayed cleaner... Killed fewer people.

We crested a ridge and a grassy meadow came into view. My chest felt hot as I watched Zane nervously. He feathered the thrusters and brought us in smoothly.

"Mr. Zane, I don't recall any planet landings in your record, but the way you brought us in was impressive."

"Thanks, Captain." He beamed. "I've been running simulations with Nephie for a couple of hours each day."

"Well, keep up the good work. You too, Nephie!"

"Thank you, Captain," came the reply from the overhead speaker.

"You're welcome," then addressed my helmsman, "Mr. Zane, Keep us hot. The Porcu-bears might have discovered this hiding spot. If so, they might have set a trap for us. We could have to bug out in a hurry. Tracy?"

"I have a squad waiting for us at the forward lock."

"Then let's not keep them waiting."

Two of Tracy's brothers were there: Trey and Trippy. Warren was there with two members of his squad. I nodded to them and Warren mashed the controls to cycle the lock.

I regarded War curiously. He and his partner in crime were inseparable. Hence the group nickname War 'n Pace. "Where's Pace?"

"We agreed that only one of us should accompany you. With three Muscat and me here, almost all senior marines are here. Someone needed to mind the shop."

"And you lost the coin toss?"

"No, sir," he grinned at me. "I won."

I chuckled to myself and crossed the field, my marines followed.

The entrance looked like an abandoned mine. A hole in a hillside with a metal grate locked over it. I studied the cliff face. I'd have bunkers hidden in the rocks and dirt. Which meant that Voorhees most certainly had.

Using my armor's external speakers, I whistled a tune from memory.

For long moments, nothing happened. Then a familiar voice echoed from the mine entrance. "Mark?"

"Captain Voorhees," I sighed with relief. He hadn't moved to a new base. "I apologize for taking so long to get here. Did you get my message?"

"Yeah, I got your message." I could hear the smile in his voice. "I can't tell you how happy it makes me to see you."

"Incoming!" yelled Tracy as she tackled me.

CHAPTER 17 - UNFRIENDLY

The world exploded. Even inside my combat armor, it was deafening. My ears rang. The HUD showed heavy damage. My first thought was to scramble to the mine entrance until I realized that we were taking fire from it. I crawled away. There was no cover between us and the ship.

My men returned fire. I searched for my rifle. I needed to support our retreat. Something exploded to my right. My HUD stopped working. I saw the butt of my rifle a meter away and I reached for it. Something red oozed from a fissure in the armor. Blood. My arm felt heavy. Damn, the power in my armor was out.

My fingers reached the stock of my rifle and pulled it to me. And that's all I had. The rest was twisted metal. Farthogs.

My head jerked to the left and my visor shattered. I shook my head happy that it was still attached. A burnt smell assaulted my nostrils.

Pushing myself to my knees I saw Tracy's brother Trey face down next to me. I grabbed him and was surprised that it was easy. The left side of my armor still had power. He'd fallen on top of his rifle and I reached for it with my other hand. Damn, too small for me.

War motioned for me to follow him. Another marine leaned against him. Two hundred meters to Nephie. Too far, we'd never make it.

The injured marine spun out of War's grip, yanked by an unseen string.

I picked up Trey and limped toward him. My right leg refused to support my weight.

War fired at something behind me, then reached for the fallen marine's hand. The armored arm came up with little effort. Nothing was attached to it. He threw it and fired over my shoulder.

The ringing faded. The rifle fire and explosions sounded as if I were underwater. I reached War and he helped support my right side. My arm screamed in pain as I put it over his shoulder. Rockets passed overhead and slammed into Nephie with no visible damage. They'd need something a lot heavier to even scratch her.

We made it half the distance when Nephie's top gauss cannon turned toward us.

"Get down!" I shouted and hit the deck with Trey and War.

Three sonic booms sounded so close together they might as well have been one. Liquid trickled down both cheeks.

I must have passed out. I struggled to open an eye. The sky was going away. No, I was being carried through a hatch. Nephie. I was home. Safe.

***

I dreamt of soft and fluffy clouds and woke with a screaming headache. It wasn't the only pain, but it was the most urgent.

I groaned but didn't hear it.

Blinking under the bright lights I found my sister sitting on my bed scowling at me. The frown didn't reach her eyes though.

My sister's lips moved and a holo-screen sprung to life between us. *Learn to duck, dammit.* Showed in red angry letters.

"Good advice," I said. "So, I'm deaf."

Yes, for another day and a half. Nephie offered to translate for you. That way I don't have to build implants for a short-term fix.

"Thanks, Nephie."

You're welcome, Captain, appeared on the screen in soft blue letters.

Sophie continued, *Randy and Racy are installing temporary holo emitters in the public areas of the ship, cause, of course, you're not going to do the right thing and rest. The bridge and conference rooms already have the emitters.*

I nodded, "Is the ship safe?"

Sophie winced, and I realized I was yelling. I apologized.

She spoke and a new message appeared. *Seriously? We're on an Erethizon occupied planet and the people we came here to meet just tried to kill you.*

"So, yes?"

Sophie rolled her eyes. *Mimi set us down in a valley a hundred kilometers from Titan.*

"Good. Did we lose anyone?"

Sophie sighed sadly, *Evans and Kowalski. Tracy's brothers will recover though.*

"What about the mine?" Yelling again. I made an effort to bring my voice to a more reasonable level.

She brought up an image of the hillside. There were three large divots in it and a rockslide covered the entrance.

Why had Voorhees attacked me? He said he'd gotten the message. Had the drone I'd sent three years ago been intercepted? Had someone lied to him? Or worse, could he have been compromised? But if that were the case, what would he be doing still at the mine? A lure for other resistance cells?

That didn't feel right. I didn't have enough information.

I lifted the covers and checked my body over. I saw a red mark on my right arm and two on my right leg. They were sore, so Sophie must have regenerated my wounds recently.

I let the covers fall and saw the new message. *Little Marky and his two friends are fine. Your love life is the least of your worries right now.*

I scowled at her as Tracy walked into the room. I turned my attention to her being careful to control the volume of my voice. "How's the rest of the plan going?"

Tracy started talking but stopped mid-sentence. One of her foxlike ears twisted in confusion.

I touched my ears and found them covered in gauze. "I'm temporarily deaf. Nephie is translating to text for me."

Sophie said something and Tracy pressed something on her wrist AI.

You need to learn to duck, sir, appeared on the holo-screen.

"Thanks, Tracy. Recon activities?"

Drones have been monitoring the old mine. No one has come out.

"Voorhees undoubtedly has another way out. If he survived, he'll have fled the area by now. I'm more concerned with what's going on in Aurora."

The holo-screen flattened, and buildings rose from the surface. I sat up to get a better look at it. Text appeared above the 3D map.

The Porcu-bears seem to be running things from this building here.

"The Treasury Building?" That didn't make any sense, unless... "The Central Exchange, of course. Clyde needs a computer to inhabit, the bigger the better. The planet's CE is perfect. It houses the planet's AI in charge of lending, interest rates, taxes, stock exchanges, and currency. Every monetary transaction on the planet. Every credit accounted for. If you want to monitor the population, follow the money."

Tracy nodded, *These buildings here appear to be government offices.*

"These two make sense," I pointed. "Presidential Office and Congress.

My sister typed an interruption. *Royal Office, now.*

"Right. The Erethizon changed to the pre-republic name. This one was the High Court, but the building is new. It looks more like a church or synagogue."

We have a drone in the area. Let's check out the front of the building, offered Tracy.

Tracy brought the drone around then zoomed in with the camera. The front of the building showed a set of scales and a scroll on fire. An inscription read in Terran and Erethizon: Hall of Divine Justice, Coachenic Law.

"Huh." I didn't see that coming, but I should have.

So, said my sister, *does that mean if we kill the head priest, we only have to pay two pigs and a horse equivalent?*

No, that's for unordained Porcu-bears. The penalty for killing any priest is death, said Tracy.

I rolled my eyes. "Listen, it's time for the next phase of the plan. We need to get a team in the capital city for each of the seven continents."

Already started, said Tracy. *Brady and I have put together teams for each capital city. Since we've been recruiting from Isura and Eureka we have five Yale natives. We've assigned them to the teams for the continents they're from.*

"Westley?" I asked.

Not for recon. He's really good at getting around security systems, but I don't trust him. I think he'd run given half a chance. We'll save him for the big day.

"What about Brovis' men?"

Tracy held up two fingers. *Two of his men are assigned to each team.*

Excellent. She was on top of everything. "Who have you got for Aurora?"

My marine commander rattled off three names I didn't recognize and ended with, *Aziz, War 'n Pace, Brovis, and Granot.*

"Good. Which one is from this continent?" I asked.

None of them. That's why we put our most experienced people on that team.

My heart sank. "Tracy, Aurora is the capital of the planet, not just this continent. We have to have someone familiar with the city on that team."

There isn't anyone. And before you say it, you can't go. Beyond being the mission leader, you've seen the fake news reports. Anyone who didn't know you before, definitely knows you now. Tracy showed her teeth. *You'll be spotted the moment you set foot in the capital.*

She was right. Many of the news reports from Yale featured me. The Erethizon either had better CGI than anyone suspected, or they'd found a look-alike to play me for the public. Either way, Tracy was right. I'd be spotted right away.

"What if I wasn't me..."

CHAPTER 18 – IT'S NOT ME

Staring at my reflection, I had to hand it to Brady. My own father wouldn't have recognized me. Wider nose, higher cheekbones, and my skin tone was a few shades darker.

I turned to my sister and Tracy. "What do ya think?"

"The same thing I've thought since you mentioned it two days ago," said Sophie. "It's the worst idea in the history of bad ideas."

"Really? I didn't hear any objections."

"You sure as hell read it." She turned to the Muscat marine. "Tracy, talk some sense into him. Do whatever you need to keep him from going. Break his legs or something."

"Sir, I don't think you see the gravity of the situation," Tracy started. "When things go wrong, which they will, I need you here to make the big decisions." She pointed at the bulkhead. "Out there, you run the risk of being killed, captured, or worse. If something happens to you, what happens to the rest of us?"

"Either you come and get me, or you and Brady carry on without me. You know the whole plan."

Tracy scowled.

I looked to the overhead, "Nephie, tell them."

"Captain Martin's knowledge of local customs and procedures increases the success of the scouting mission success by thirty percent," she intoned. "However, if he is captured, overall mission success decreases by fifty percent."

"Hey!" I protested. "Whose side are you on?"

"No one's side. You asked for a strategic analysis. It would be inappropriate not to include relevant data."

"Listen, I've been inside those buildings dozens of times. I can spot any changes to the security." I motioned to my sister. "The only one here who's been in those buildings more than I have is Sophie. Which one of us are you going to take?"

Tracy glared at me. She wouldn't take Sophie in the field. It was a cheap shot, but I needed to be there. Disguised, no one would recognize me. It was a low risk, high reward mission. What could possibly go wrong?

***

"You see that gargoyle?"

Brady nodded, "Yeah. It looks like something from on old Earth buildings."

I covered my mouth like I was deep in thought and spoke behind my hand. "When they built it, they knew that criminal hackers and dissidents might make the central bank a target. They wanted cameras and sensors to watch the street and crowds, but they didn't want to be obvious about it. Yale being Yale, they put the sensor suites inside the architecture."

"Tricky. What about the Parliament building?"

"They were a bit more subtle over there. Each of the columns has a section that scans the main stairs. They didn't get the color quite right, or perhaps the rock and fake rock weather differently over time. Either way you can see the difference if you look closely."

An Erethizon lumbered toward us. He stopped as two kids in comedy and tragedy masks ran past, then continued.

"The security is the same," Granot rumbled. The Porcubear marine Brovis assigned to our team, was quiet. He spoke Terran well and responded readily to questions. Otherwise he tended to fade into the background. Impressive considering the alien was two and a half meters tall. "Multi-spectrum scanners for weapons and palm scanners for identity."

Brady made some notes on his tablet. "Hey Mark, what's with the comedy and tragedy masks?"

"It's a local kid thing. Ponchos with masks for bad weather. Sad when it rains, but happy when the sun comes back out."

"Seriously?"

"Oh yeah, there's a song with it and everything. Then the sun comes out and the grass grow, grow, grows..." I sang. "I'll teach it to you if you like."

"Uh, no thanks." Brady glanced around at the wet pavement. "Isn't the rain over. It was raining all morning."

"No, it's about to start up again."

"How can you tell?"

I shrugged, "I grew up here."

A ground transport swung around the corner. I frowned as I saw it driving a little fast for downtown. I didn't realize until too late that it was driving right next to the curb.

"Farthogs!" I cursed as I brought my arm up. I didn't make it. Water surged up and drenched me from head to toe. I wiped my eyes and spit out some water. The truck screeched to a stop.

Next to me, Brady wiped his face and flung the excess water to the sidewalk. "Kuso aho yarou." Then he looked at me and went ashen. "Farthogs."

I reached up and a piece of prosthetic fell off in my hand. I threw my arm across my face and scanned the street. No one seemed to have noticed. The truck was a few scant meters away. Could I use it for cover? My heart skipped a beat when I realized that the barrel of an IMPAS anti-vehicle rocket emerged from the door of the transport.

"Down!" I shouted.

Even as I dove away, I knew it was too late. I didn't hear the rocket fire or the explosion as it hit the shield protecting the building. I did recall the half second of flight as I was flung into the street. I remembered thinking, 'not again', before everything went black.

CHAPTER 19 – MISTAKEN IDENITY

I woke up naked. The bed was very soft. Nothing hurt. If I'd been captured, this was the nicest jail cell I'd ever seen. Pastel curtains, a real wood chest of drawers, knickknacks on the nightstand, everything screamed that I was in someone's home.

I crossed to the mirror in the corner. No road rash or bruises. The facial prosthetics were gone though.

Using my implants, I searched for the rest of my team. They either weren't nearby or had their wrist AIs off. A house AI asked if I needed anything. I ignored it.

I found women's clothes in the chest of drawers. So I approached the door. What would I find on the other side? A platoon of Erethizon? The family that owned this house? Kids in the hallway?

I'd resolved to risk it when the door flew open.

"Here, put these on."

Suddenly I felt like I was in some sort of odd holo-drama put together by someone who'd studied my life.

"Winny?"

She cocked her head at me, confused.

"Are you in there? Did you get some sort of upgrade or something? Since when am I anything but Ms. Galanis?" She shook her head. "It doesn't matter. We're late. You're supposed to be dedicating a church on the other side of town right now. I know you've got less than half a brain in there, but you do know how to put clothes on. I've watched you a dozen times."

I stood there gaping, not sure what was going on, or why my ex-girlfriend was asking me to do it. "That was in high school. Since when do you have my clothes? Strike that. I've never worn anything that gaudy in my life. Blue and gold satin? Who would wear that thing?"

"Dear Muses, when did you grow a mind. And how are you able to even string two sentences together." She huffed. "I'm your royal assistant. I know we're too far away for Urson to do whatever he does, but right now I need you to put on those clothes so we can get across town. Stop arguing with me and get dressed." Winny grabbed a remote and flipped on the wall screen.

I grabbed the clothes and began putting them on. I might look like a Freyan peacock, but at least I wouldn't be naked. I'd find a way to give Winny the slip and make my way back to the ship.

"Ugh, idiots. They're starting the ceremony without us."

Buttoning my pants, I heard the Yale national anthem coming from the wall screen. I glanced up and froze. It was me. On the steps of the church. Wearing a red version of the same clothes I was in the middle of putting on. In the middle of an Erethizon honor guard. I watched in horror and confusion as I waved to a crowd and climbed to the podium.

Back on the planet of Aspen, A'hid had shown vids of me supporting the Theocracy. I'd assumed they'd been CGI. Everything clicked into place. They'd cloned... me. A copy was running around the planet doing whatever the Porcu-bears wanted him to do.

My gaze slid over to Winny.

Her mouth moved but no sounds came out. Her eyes moved to me. Two seconds later her face followed. "They made a second one? No... They wouldn't. Too much chance of confusion. A backup? Insurance? Or..."

"I'm, just going to go," I said. "You obviously don't need me here."

Winny stepped in front of me and glared. I didn't feel threatened. I had twenty kilos on her. So, I was caught completely off-guard when she kissed me.

Winona Galanis is many things. Smart, stubborn, opinionated, and conniving were the first things that came to mind. It's why it had taken me so long to figure out she was cheating on me. At the moment, I was considering revising that list to start with something else. Winny was an excellent kisser. That thought brought me back to reality as I imagined Sara next to me.

I gently pushed Winny away. "I'm sorry, but I gotta go."

She licked her lips. "Muses, it really is you. Marky, what are you doing here? How are you here? Gods, everyone in the inner circle thinks you're dead. I mean the real you, not that puppet thing they parade around."

"What is it?"

"An STP. Grown or modified to look like you."

"A Simulated Terran Plaything? They're illegal."

Winny spread her hands, "And yet they still make them and rich assholes the galaxy over buy them."

"That doesn't make any sense. They have dog level intelligence." I pointed at the wall screen, "That thing is walking at talking."

"It has some sort of hardware that the Porcu-bears use to control it. It works around the Central Exchange, near the palace, or near a special news truck. Everywhere else, it sits there with a stupid grin, looking like a lost puppy.

She smiled, "But, you're here now. Whenever this Theocracy mess gets sorted out, you'll be the Prince. I can keep you hidden.

"How did I get here?"

"Disciplinarians, how else. I can't even lift you."

Disciplinarians? "You command them? The Porcu-bear soldiers do what you say?"

"Haven't you been listening? I'm the Prince's personal assistant. They found you at the site of the attack and called me. I had them bring you here."

"And they did?"

"As far as the public is concerned, you run the planet for your Father, the King. The Porcu-bears don't have a copy of him, so he's almost never seen in public. They use a hologram, so it isn't like they can use it in broad daylight."

"You told them to bring me, and they did. They didn't call a bishop?"

"Are you really, Mark? I mean, you kiss like him. Hard to fake that."

I sighed, "Yes. It's really me. I just can't wrap my head around Disciplinarians taking orders from Terrans."

"They have to give the illusion of self-governance. The crown has two platoons of Disciplinarians. So yes, I can order a few low-level hedgehogs about."

"What about the people with me in the capital?"

Winny narrowed her eyes at me, "Were you behind the attack on the Central Exchange?"

"No, I was there for an unrelated reason." No reason to tell her I was scouting for a different attack to happen later.

She frowned, "No one was picked up with you or near you. The terrorists died at the scene. Injured bystanders were sent to the hospital. More people were questioned and let go."

Did the Porcu-bears pick up my team? If Winny was working in the puppet government, I couldn't trust her.

"I have friends south of town," I said, hoping they'd search the wrong area. "Can you help me reach them?"

She set her jaw. "You're not going anywhere."

"You're taking me prisoner?" I looked at her askance. Did she have Porcu-bear guards nearby?

She huffed, "No, but you're important. Don't you get it? The priests are using you as their public image. I can protect you. Keep you safe."

"I'm not here to be safe."

"And I'm telling you, whatever insane scheme you've cooked up to save the planet," at this, she waved her hands in the air. "It won't work. There are tens of thousands of Disciplinarians, dozens of priests, and enough surveillance to watch everyone go to the bathroom. Even if you free Yale," she used air quotes, "you'd still have the fleet in orbit to deal with. You haven't thought it through, Mark. I have. Stay here. Let me take care of you. In a few short years, I'll have it all sorted out."

And there it was. The other reason I'd broken up with her. Winny felt she was the smartest person in the room. Any room.

"You're right, of course. I haven't thought this all through. Tell me what you have planned."

She blinked. "You mean it? You'll listen?"

"Yes." Right up until I can get away unseen, I thought. "I'm interested in any plan that sees our people free."

Winny studied me. "I have to go. If I don't show up, they'll get suspicious. Wait. Here. My house isn't under surveillance. When I get back, I'll tell you everything. I promise."

I agreed and walked her to the door. I didn't bother to finish getting dressed. The more she believed I was in her pocket, the greater the chance I'd get away. She leaned in for another kiss. I played it up since my freedom depended on it. After a few seconds, she bounced on her toes. This time she broke the kiss.

"Farthogs, I've missed that." She blew out a breath and ran to her aircar.

I waited fifteen minutes after she'd gone before rummaging through her things. I found my shoes and my fake id. She'd recycled my clothes. I grabbed a dress and scarf from her closet. It didn't fit but it covered enough. The stretchy material and was tight everywhere. My forearms and hairy legs showed. I shrugged; it was less conspicuous than the satin get up. I wrapped the purple scarf around my head.

I studied the nearby houses and realized I knew the area. The mayor of Aurora lived nearby. A friend of the family, Kevin Weber. The front and back doors of the house had cameras, so I went out a window.

Three houses up, I went around back and quietly entered Kevin's pool house. I froze as someone spoke just out of sight.

"Come on, baby. You know I got the goods," a guy said.

"What kind of goods are we talking about?" responded a familiar voice.

"Dream, Bliss, Hops, Nectar. I got all the party favors."

"And what makes you think I'm interested in your favors?" the girl teased.

"Oh baby, everyone wants what I got. J-Dee got ya covered, especially a nice ass girl like you."

"You're so sweet. A double of Bliss?"

"Fifteen. But give me a little of your sweet lovin' and amazin' things might happen. Maybe be we can... negotiate."

"How much for a kiss?"

He sucked through his teeth. "Not much. Give me a little more, feel your moons, touch your star, and ooh baby, I'll have you flying in no time."

The familiar voice clicked. Kevin's daughter was all grown up.

I rounded the corner and cleared my throat.

The drug dealer turned on me. "Squats! Who the hell are you?"

"The man who will send you to the muses if you're not out of here in thirty seconds."

J-Dee pulled a mono-blade. "I don't take nothin' from a dolled-up pansy."

CHAPTER 20 – DOLLED UP PANSY

Damn. I'd expected a drug dealer to back down and not mess up a client's house. Stupid thinking on my part. Sweat trickled down my back.

I shrugged and pretended to be relaxed, "Your funeral."

Alexis squinted, "Uncle Mark?"

"Squats, pansy, I'm gonna own you!"

"J-Dee, you don't..."

He lunged. I grabbed his wrist and slammed it into the corner. I heard it break with a sound like crunchy bacon.

The dirtbag pulled back his injured arm. "Motherfu-"

Elbow met temple and he collapsed bonelessly to the floor. I scooped up the mono-blade which switched off as he dropped it and shoved it into a pocket. Except there wasn't one. I searched the dress. There had to be one. Who the hell made clothing without pockets?

Alexis looked down at the dealer and up at me three times. "Wha.. How..."

I gave up and just held the inactive handle. "You brought a drug dealer to your house? Alexis, what were you thinking?"

"Me?" she squeaked. "You can't even be here. You're giving some speech for the Hedgehogs across town. You're here? In a dress? And since when did you get all ninja and shit?"

"Language."

"Sorry."

"It's to elevate my status."

"What?"

"The dress. Why be a Prince when I can be a Queen."

Alexis blinked twice. "Eho hasi ta avga kai ta pashalia."

I switched to Greek, the unofficial second language of the planet. "Alani."

"Those things you say, in the vids..."

I shook my head, "It's not me. It's someone the Porcubears found that looks like me."

She stared at me for a handful of heartbeats. "Prove it."

"As you said, right now the other me is across town giving a speech. Obviously, I'm not him. As for which me is standing in front of you, I'll remind you of a little incident that took place at my Dad's house. You and your parents came over for dinner. You snuck away and raided the liquor cabinet. I found you in a bathroom hunched over a toilet with an empty bottle of ouzo. I cleaned you up, gave you some SoberUp pills, and had you presentable by the time your parents were ready to go home."

She swallowed, "Mama and Papa never said anything."

"Cause I never told them. I thought you'd learned the lesson."

She leaped over J-Dee and hugged me. "Pou ise re?"

"Off-world, but I'm back and I'm going to make things better, I promise."

J-Dee groaned. I rifled his pockets and came up with aircar keys and an impressive collection of concealable weapons. When he came to, I knelt in front of him examining a porcelain blade.

"This is nice. Ultra-flat, lightweight, and will fool most security screeners."

He growled at me.

"Unh uh," I waved the shiv in front of him. "I think you've had enough training in hand to hand for today. Time for a different lesson. I'm someone important. The dress might have fooled you, but I'm guessing if you take a close look, you'll figure it out."

He glared for a few seconds before it registered, "Farthogs. No squatting way."

"Oh yes. And you've made a very serious error in judgment. My royal guard will be here soon to take you into custody."

His eyes went wide, "Hey man," he laughed nervously. "I mean Your Highness, Sir. No need to bring the Hedgehogs in on this. I-I-I'm a businessman. We can make a deal, right?"

I nodded in the direction of his backpack. "That's your stash, right?"

"Yeah man, take it."

I held up his key fob, "And your ride."

"No way. That's my baby. I've made upgrades."

"Re-education camp."

He winced, "Squats, I uh..."

"With free Porcu-bear strip search. Just think of all those spikes touching you in so many interesting places. Caressing. Probing. Prodding."

"Fine," he ground out.

"Excellent. You really are a good businessman. By my estimation, you have ten minutes before they get here."

He stared at me for three seconds.

"Go."

He went. Slamming the door open on the way out.

"Damn, Uncle Mark," breathed Alexis. "When did you get so scary."

"I've been hanging around with pirates for the past three years. It's a required skill." I winked in her direction then motioned to my dress. "Pants?"

We went up to the loft, which was set up like a spare bedroom. Discarded clothes and pool toys were everywhere. I managed to find a pair of slacks and a button-down shirt that fit reasonably well. Unfortunately, they were pastel blue, but better than wearing a dress. I started to wrap the scarf around my head when Alexis stopped me.

"Wait." She ran downstairs and came back a minute later out of breath. "Here."

I held up the black elastic band with glass beads. "What is it?"

"It's a Steal-a-Face."

"The Grateful Dead?"

"What?"

"Ancient Earth reference. What does it do?"

Her head tilted in confusion for a moment before taking the band from me and putting it on her head. Alexis touched something. And then she wasn't Alexis anymore. The dark-haired, dark-eyed girl I knew became a blue-eyed blonde. It was still her body, but the face was completely different.

"Stellar."

"Yeah. Black Market stuff, but almost anyone can get one if you know the right people. You can't wear it into a secure building, advanced scanners can see through it, but most areas, you're good to go."

"So, where do I find the right people?"

"Take me with you."

"You're what, sixteen standard? No."

"Seventeen. Please, Uncle Mark, I wanna help."

"You are helping. A lot. But I can't take you with me. People will be trying to kill me and I couldn't bear it if something happened to you. And that doesn't begin to cover what your Papa will do to me."

"You're The Prince. He'll understand."

I checked my implants. None of her family were in the group we rescued from Orvid.

"Alexis, do they have your brother?"

She nodded.

"Then I can't involve you. They'll punish him if they find out."

"I've seen the people who have come back from reeducation. If his body comes back, what's inside, won't be him anymore."

"Alexis..."

162

"Listen, whatever you're planning will probably involve getting into the buildings in the capital. I can get in there. I have access because of Papa. I'm also a pilot, just like you."

She wasn't going to let this go. Better to give her something, or she'd go and cause trouble on her own. "Okay, you win. Give me your contact ID. If you receive a message for Elliott Kay you'll know it's really from me. Go wherever it tells you and I'll meet you and tell you what to do."

She wrinkled her nose. "The guy who wrote the rain song? Isn't he dead?"

"Exactly."

I put on the Steal-a-Face and left Alexis with a promise to call which I wouldn't keep. With a little luck, it would all be over in a month and she'd be safe and out of the way.

On the street, I held my breath as a drone buzzed up the street. It didn't even pause. The Steal-a-Face must be working. J-Dee's aircar was a black sports model with tinted windows. The fob opened it and I climbed in. Gold silhouettes of nude women were everywhere. Using my implant, I scanned the security and controls. No access code. Most people didn't bother, but I expected a drug dealer to be more cautious. Then again, if he had to move in a hurry he might need the extra three seconds.

He wasn't kidding about upgrades. I found the car's transponder had four settings: off, two residential, and a government registration. The grav-plates and turbines were three times as powerful as a street-legal aircar. It wasn't as fast as a fighter, but police and security forces would have a tough time catching it. It even had a few electronic countermeasures. I shook my head in amazement, "J-Dee you beautiful scumbag."

I opened the backpack and inventoried the contents. Fifty thousand in credit chips, Dream, Drift, Easy, and Fly were all present in respectable amounts. Even more interesting was a pouch full of Saggitan Nectar. A popular sweetener illegal in Erethizon territory because it was a powerful euphoric to them. Either J-Dee was supplying some locals, or he kept some for bribes.

I turned on the government registration and powered up the turbines. No sooner had I left the neighborhood than an Erethizon patrol craft pulled in behind me. I broke out in a cold sweat and my stomach felt like I'd swallowed an asteroid.

CHAPTER 21 - FOLLOWED

My speed was within the posted limit. My altitude was correct for southbound traffic. I scanned the dash for warning lights. None.

I looked in the mirror. The Steal-a-Face was working. Did they have some tech to see through windows? Could it also see through the Steal-a-Face? I just didn't know enough about what it did and how it did it.

Minutes ticked by. The patrol craft didn't turn on its flashing lights or send a comm request.

Using the rear camera, I saw that one Porcu-bear piloted the vehicle, while the other one worked at a console. Flat quills and not showing teeth. If I read their expressions correctly, they were bored.

That didn't make my situation any less dangerous. If they asked me to land, I'd have to answer questions. Questions I couldn't answer. And driving a car that wasn't mine...

Did they know about J-Dee? Were they looking for a bribe? Would being The Prince mean anything if they decided to search the aircar?

My mind raced as the city passed below us. Every minute I came up with ever more horrible ways that things could go wrong. In the end, it didn't matter. After about a hundred kilometers, they peeled off.

I waited until they were out of sight and off my scans before I altered course. I had a ship to meet.

***

I landed in a clearing near the ship and walked toward the forward airlock. At the hatch, I waited for someone to respond.

"Can we help you?" I recognized Pace's voice issuing from the speaker.

"Encyclopedia Galactica," I answered. "I notice your ship's subscription is expired. Can I interest you or your ship's purser in a new subscription?"

"What?!"

I touched the control stud on the Steal-a-Face. The world around me brightened, as the image over my face disappeared.

"Holy farthogs!" The airlock popped open. War 'n Pace rushed out. War scanned for threats while Pace looked me over.

"Pastels?" Pace asked.

"It's what I could find on short notice."

"What's that thing on your head?" asked War.

"Tech the locals use. It projects a randomized face over my own. It's solid enough to fool most sensor suites. I hope Rowdy and Racy can reverse engineer it. It could really help our recon efforts."

Mimi rushed out and wrapped me in a hug then stepped back and saluted. "Glad to have you back, Sir."

"Glad to be back."

She glanced around. "Where's Aziz?"

"Aziz?"

"Yeah, didn't he get you out?"

"No, how I got out is a weird story. Where did you send him?"

We moved back inside. War 'n Pace resumed lock duty while Mimi led me to the forward conference room.

"We got word that you were going to be at the Cathedral," said Mimi. "We sent Aziz and a squad of marines to get you out."

Oh crap. If they kidnapped the pretender, any hope of stealth in this mission would vanish. The Erethizon wouldn't stop trying to find him. A cold feeling settled in my stomach. "Farthogs, we need to tell him immediately it isn't me."

CHAPTER 22 - AZIZ

Mimi addressed the overhead. "Nephie can you send an encrypted packet to the recovery team: Mission scrubbed. Return to base." She steepled her fingers. "So, do ya think they use it like an STP? Some Porcu-bear have a human sex fetish or something?"

I'd never heard of any Terran-Erethizon kink. All those quills? Would Winny use the STP? "I don't... think so. They've got some hardware in its skull that allows them to use it like a puppet. Supposedly, it can talk and act normal enough to fool people."

Mimi shook herself. "I have to admit that's clever, genius really, in a sick and twisted kinda way."

The conference room opened, and I tumbled to the floor, chair and all, knocked down by something furry. It was speaking in rapid-fire Muscat, so I didn't panic. I twisted to place my friend on the floor when I was bowled over again.

"Rowdy, Racy, It's fine. I'm okay. I missed you too!"

I managed to get standing after a couple of false starts only to have each leg wrapped in a Muscat.

"And we didn't know where you were..."

"There was an explosion..."

"...missing, so I searched the internet and I found..."

"...and you were supposed to be there, but you weren't..."

"Guys. Guys! Please slow down." I patted the air to no avail. Mimi smirked as I struggled to extricate myself from the foxlike beings. Sophie was in the hatchway shaking her head.

It wasn't working. I leaned against the table to keep my balance.

"Where were you?" asked Racy.

I explained what happened, skipping over a lot of irrelevant details.

My sister frowned. "So, the Porcu-bears have someone that looks like you?"

"It's an STP made up to look like me. They're using some sort of cybernetics and artificial intelligence combination. It can walk, give speeches, but not converse well enough to handle dinner parties. They follow it around with a truck, so I'm guessing it's a mobile AI core."

Sophie paled. "That's... disgusting."

The two Muscat talked too technical for me to follow.

"Rowdy, Racy," I interrupted, "do you mind?" I indicated my legs. They were still wrapped around them.

Gazing up at me they answered in unison. "No."

I rolled my eyes and looked to Mimi. No help there. She was giggling behind her hand. My sister chewed on her lip not even paying attention.

Tracy appeared behind my sister.

"Tracy, thank the gods. Can you help me out?" I implored.

She took it in for a handful of seconds. Rowdy and Racy continued their tech conversation on how they might control an STP remotely. Tracy cleared her throat.

Rowdy and Racy glanced over at her.

"Do you mind?" she asked.

They each took half a step back and Tracy joined them in hugging my legs.

Defeated, I bowed to the inevitable.

Sophie left, clearly distracted by something. Mimi was laughing so hard she was wiping away tears.

Tracy gazed up from my waist. "You're not going on any more missions. I don't care what your excuse is, it's not happening. You are our Captain. You're needed here."

"You're right," I conceded. "No more front-line work. I want to set up a forward base in Aurora, in an apartment or warehouse. No more scouting. I'll leave that to the professionals."

She nodded solemnly.

Nephie's voice came from the ceiling. "Mimi, there's a call for you from Aziz."

She frowned, "Put it through."

"Ya khara," Aziz swore. "Why did you scrub the mission, daughter of donkeys? We had him. Twenty minutes and we'd have stolen Zaiem back from those stupid spike bears."

"Son of a whore," Mimi spat back. "If I scrub a mission, you know damn well I have a good reason for it. It's no secret I don't like you, you should be picked apart by crows, but business is business. We're trying to save a planet of two billion people, so can it slime snake."

The Muscat listened curiously. Part of me felt I should intervene, but a morbid curiosity won out. I'd see how this played out.

"If I were near you, I'd slit your foul throat so you could no longer poison the air," retorted Aziz. "You need to learn proper respect, woman."

"That's rich coming from a street urchin not fit to clean the bottom of my shoe."

"You dare!"

Okay, time to intervene. "Aziz," I interrupted. The comm went silent for a few seconds.

"... Zaiem Martin?"

"Yes. I'm back onboard the ship."

"Daughter of donkeys kill that imposter. I saw the real Captain not five minutes ago," Aziz urged.

"That wasn't me," I explained. "The Erethizon have an STP that looks like me. They're using it like a puppet."

"Abomination!" exclaimed Aziz. "It must be destroyed."

Leaving aside that Aziz's former boss, traded in STPs and worse, I continued. "I agree. Can you do it without getting caught?"

"No. The window has passed."

Farthogs. If we'd only been able to talk earlier. "Okay, keep an eye on the abomination as best you can without exposing yourself. If an opportunity presents itself, take him out."

"Just so we're clear," I heard the smile in his voice, "you're giving me permission to kill you."

Yeah, let's not give the snake even the tiniest bit of leeway. "Take out the imposter."

"Aziz, out."

Three fox noses stared up at me. Grabbing the Steal-a-Face off the table I handed it to Rowdy. "This headband projects an image of a random face on the wearer. It fools normal scans. Can you improve it?"

He took it from me and went to the other end of the conference room pulling tools from his harness. Racy joined him watching over his shoulder. Tracy backed up a couple of paces. I finally had some breathing room.

Getting back to the more pressing issue, I regarded Mimi. "Are you going to be able to work with him?"

Her expression clouded. "I don't know. I think the only thing that's kept me alive so far is that Sandy would murder him in his sleep if he harmed me. I don't get what she sees in him."

I shrugged. "I don't know either. At a guess, I'd say Sandy had a difficult childhood. Aziz's misogyny and violence may be familiar to her."

"Didn't you almost toss him off the ship on the trip out?"

That brought back a flood of memories. Had Aziz met my Mom. Did he know how to find her? I bit my lip and shook my head at Mimi. "Yes. I came very close."

"Why didn't you?"

"Pithy said we needed him."

Mimi narrowed her eyes at me. "But that wasn't why you spared him."

"No," I admitted. "He may know something. Something important."

"And you're not going to tell me what it is."

"It's personal." Why had Mom abandoned us? Abandoned me? What had she done that was so awful that she had to leave the planet? Leave Dad? Everything she'd known.

I shook my head and sighed. "But it isn't enough to spare his life if he steps out of line again."

Mimi nodded.

A wave of exhaustion washed over me as I stood. "You have a plan to find Brady and Granot?"

"Working on it," she said.

"I'll leave you to it. I need to get some rest."

"Of course, sir."

I left the conference room with Tracy on my heels.

I glanced back at the Muscat marine. "Anything that needs immediate attention?"

"It'll keep. We'll talk after you've had a chance to sleep."

I smiled gratefully as I slid into my quarters leaving my friend in the passage.

I stripped down to my boxers and slid into my bunk. I tried to relax but my mind wouldn't be quiet.

"Nephie?"

"Yes, Captain."

"Are you connected to the planet net?"

"Yes, Captain, but I'm having to be careful accessing local information. Clyde is crafty."

That'd be a disaster. "If you can do it without too much risk, I'd like you to do some research for me."

"Find your mother?" she asked.

I took a deep breath and let it out. Did I want to find the woman who abandoned us so many years ago? "No. She won't be on Yale. I want to know why she left."

"Of course, Captain. And, sir?"

"Yes, Nephie?"

"It's good to have you back. I was worried about you."

***

Granot made his way back while I was asleep. He discovered that Brady had been injured in the blast and was at a local hospital. Security there was light, so he didn't think they suspected him of anything. He was too injured and couldn't come back on his own. Tracy organized a rescue mission to get him out. Pace led the mission backed up by Brovis.

Nephie slipped a transfer request into the hospital computer. Our marines stole an ambulance and performed the transfer. Brady never made it to the other hospital.

Three hours later he was carried aboard on a zero-G stretcher. I slipped in between the marines maneuvering him aboard.

I grinned at him, "Hey buddy. Laying down on the job?"

"Sorry sir, it won't happen again," he replied with a weak smile. The stretcher hit a hatch cowling and he winced. "I'll be back on my feet before you know it."

"I hope so. I can't very well do much spying when my spymaster is down for the count."

He laughed weakly, and it turned into a coughing fit.

I moved aside as he was carried into the med bay.

"Make way!" called a girl's voice.

Holly hurried up the passage with a white nurse's cap on. Following in her wake, Pythia carried a tray of first aid supplies.

I stifled a laugh and stepped to the side as they entered the med bay on the heels of the corpsmen. I saw more of the Dodgers approaching with a little less flair if not the same amount of determination. Their guardian had been missing for days.

In the med bay, Sophie took charge of the little miscreants, giving them small tasks to do to keep them out of the way. She examined her patient with a frown of concentration, and I left her to it.

Making my way to the forward conference room, I sat heavily in the chair at the head of the table.

"That bad?" asked Mimi.

I shook my head. "I'm no doctor, but I don't think Brady's going to be in any shape to help us out for the rest of the ground mission."

Tracy entered and sat beside me. "Doctor Martin agrees with you. He'll be confined to the ship for the rest of the mission."

I sighed, "Now he's a consultant. Keep him in the loop. Farthogs, we really could have used his skills on the ground."

Tracy rolled her nose at me.

Brovis, Racy, and Westley entered and sat.

"Okay, that's everyone. How are we set for the next phase of the mission?"

Mimi started, "Communications are set up and secure. We're piggybacking on the planet-wide network. Racy had an ingenious idea for making that work." She nodded to the Muscat hacker.

Racy grinned with teeth. "Status packets. Virus protection, version verifications, update checks, there are hundreds of popular software packages that send status updates through the net every day. We've taken the most popular ones on the planet and turned them into a code. It isn't suspicious, because it's what Clyde would expect to see. The packets are traveling between our comms instead of to and from the company servers."

"Excellent! That's very clever," I said.

A throat clearing noise came from the ceiling.

"Also, Nephie helped craft the code," Racy admitted.

I smiled. "Well done, Nephie."

"Thank you, Captain."

"Westley, you're standing in for Brady. How are we doing on the intelligence front?"

"Your spies are clumsy as fuck," he groused, "but they delivered. We have maps of the Central Exchange buildings. They all have similar layouts and security. The biggest threat is this:" Westley touched his wrist AI and an image came to life in the middle of the conference room.

My heart sank, "Farthogs. That's a big problem."

An image of a Dru rotated above the table.

"Maybe, maybe not," continued Westley. "Every security checkpoint has one. The fishies didn't react to the teams. Didn't identify them, point a flipper, or blow bubble signals or whatever it is they do."

"But two of our teams disappeared after reporting," I pointed out. "Ideally, I'd send Muscat, since Dru have a harder time understanding their thoughts, but there are no Muscat on Yale. Tracy's marines would stick out like a Hellcat at a dinner party."

Tracy nodded reluctantly.

"Could we use telepathy jammers?" asked Mimi.

I shook my head, "No. It's like a white noise generator. They'll know it's there, even if they can't read anyone's thoughts."

"What if we use a wide area jammer?" asked Tracy. "Like they use for buildings. They'll know it's there. They'll alert the Porcu-" she stopped and glanced at Brovis. "uh, Erethizon, but we get in and out before they find the emitters."

Brovis shook his head, "I don't like it. Secrecy is our friend. It'd be better if they never knew we were there."

Westley nodded in agreement.

An idea struck me and I took a moment to send a message to my sister using my implant. I returned my attention to the discussion.

"...fire alarm?" asked Racy.

"Again, they'll know something is going on," grumbled Brovis.

"Let's table that for now," I suggested. "Tracy, how are we set for ops?"

"We have forward bases for each capital city," said Tracy. "Apartments or offices have been rented near enough to see the buildings, but not close enough to be in any danger. They'll be able to respond if the teams get into trouble."

"Good," I glanced at Racy. She'd been subtly moving her chair closer to me the whole meeting. Now, she was a half meter away. "Racy, what did Rowdy come up with for explosives?"

Racy scooted a few centimeters closer as she pulled a block of plastic and tube of gel out of a pouch on her harness. "Binary compound. A block that scans like plastic but isn't. Set it next to the core, squeeze the gel on top of it. Stick the fake aircar fob on top of it. Five minutes later: boom!"

The look in her eye was a little crazy. A good reminder that asking a Muscat to cause trouble wasn't always a good idea.

Westley smirked, "Aw sweetie, I wish we had you on a couple of jobs we pulled on Aphrodite. Had to kill a few poor saps instead."

Racy frowned at the pirate.

"And none of the items will scan as dangerous?" rumbled Brovis.

"No, but just in case, our people will be using fake ids and going in the employee entrance where security is less strict," answered Racy.

Sophie's return message popped up and I read it.

Everything was falling into place, and I began to feel like we might actually pull it off. "Excellent," I said, "and my sister just gave us the answer to our Dru problem."

Everyone gave me a questioning look.

I grinned at them, "Coffee farts."

***

The office space was spartan, to say the least. Cheap industrial carpet, faux wood desks, and chairs. What it did have was floor to ceiling windows with a commanding view of downtown. More importantly, we could see three sides of the Central Exchange building.

Tracy stood on the desk to my right with a telescopic image enhancer. "I should have never let you talk me into this."

"It'll work," I assured her.

"Coffee farts. It's got to be the stupidest idea I've ever heard."

"It'll work."

She shook her head, "Okay, Granot is going in."

"He doesn't know what he's carrying or what it does," I reminded her. "He believes he's on another scouting mission. They didn't react to that last time."

We waited.

"It's taking too long," observed Tracy.

She was right. Had something gone wrong? What if-

The door for the employee entrance burst open. A Dru rushed out into the street heedless of traffic. Instead of the normal blue skin color most associated with the species, he was a bright purple.

Half a second later two Porcu-bears rushed after him.

"I'll be shaved and dipped in honey, it worked!" exclaimed Tracy.

"There are bees on Gra'nome?"

"No," she gazed up at me, "antlike insects, but they do pretty much the same thing."

I shrugged, "Dru are highly allergic to caffeine. Put a little in the air and they'll itch for hours."

Tracy tapped the comm on her headset. "All teams, coffee farts work. Proceed with the plan."

The infiltration team jogged up to the street corner then slowed as they laughed and joked on their way to the employee entrance. Just another bunch of co-workers coming back from lunch.

"What's the Muscat phrase? Easy as climbing a tree?" I asked.

"Close enough," Tracy grumped. "And don't say that. It's bad luck."

"Bad luck?"

An explosion rocked the room as the door exploded inward.

My head rang. I struggled to regain my feet. Why won't my arms or legs work?

I pulled myself up. Tracy on top of the desk. Unconscious.

Pistol. Can't grab it. Fingers not working.

Weapon in my face. I tried to focus. Porcu-bear. Oh, squats. I'm hosed.

He's yelling something. Can't hear it. Ears ringing.

More yelling. More Porcu-bears.

Not taking me alive. Got to stand. Swinging his rifle.

Blackness.

CHAPTER 23 - CAPTURED

I awoke to bright light. Using my hands, I shielded my face from it. Then winced when my fingers hurt, and my forehead hurt. Plasma rifle. Eyes, ears, fingernails, toes, nothing was exempt. Everything hurt. With a groan, I sat up.

Uncomfortable bed, white sheets, white walls. Farthogs. I'm in a cell. Twisting my head, sure enough, there was the obligatory armor-glass front wall. Oddly, the being on the other side of the wall wasn't a Porcu-bear. It was a Dru.

"You won't get anything from me," I told him. "I won't think about anyone I work with and I don't know how our communications stuff works."

"Unnecessary," he said. I listened carefully. Dru speech was at the lower end of Terran hearing. "I probed your mind while you were unconscious. All the attacks on the Central Exchange computers were stopped. The Erethizon knew you were coming."

I snorted.

"It's true," he assured me. "They captured one of your scouts on the southernmost continent. They're planning an assault on your ship as we speak."

Well, at least the scout didn't know the whole plan.

"No," he said aloud, "but he knew enough."

I stared at the blue-skinned alien keeping my mind blank.

"I wanted you to know that it wasn't my people that caused your mission to fail."

I regarded him. Why did it matter?

"Because my people are not helping the Erethizon by choice. The Children of Urson have a fleet above each of our four worlds. If we displease them too much, they'll bomb our shoals from orbit." His eyes drooped.

"We knew of your scouts and your intention to disable or destroy the Central Exchange computers, of course," he continued. "The Dru conscripts had high hopes your mission would succeed. Without the network backbone and co-ordination those systems provide, the ground forces would become disorganized."

I glanced at the overheads. Wasn't I being monitored? Why was he telling me these things?

The water in his environmental collar bubbled. The fishy equivalent of a sigh? "The artificial being known as Urson uses a machine code similar to the one my people use. Using this knowledge, we have found a way to make the artificial being look elsewhere for short periods. We are using it now, but time is growing short. We believe that the Erethizon intend to keep you prisoner. You have proven a crafty and resourceful being in the past. While we can't help you directly, if you regain your freedom in the future, know that my people are not your enemy."

The Dru's fishy head tilted a little to the side. "A school is approaching."

Whirring and cranking accompanied a change in air pressure. My ears popped. A loud squeal like unoiled hinges on a large hatch followed. Heavy footsteps echoed up the passage.

My double strode into view. Of course, my doppelganger was in the city. He'd been at several public events.

Winny and three armored bodyguards stood behind him. Winny glared at me. The Bodyguards had full-face shields, so what they thought of two Prince Martins was a mystery.

The Dru blinked owlishly at one of the bodyguards.

Standing, I stared at my body double. They'd done an incredible job of making it look just like me.

We stared at each other for several seconds. What was it thinking? Then I realized it was copying my movements.

I scowled at it, and it mimicked the frown.

"Amazing. I've consumed two thousand forty-five hours of video of you. Graduations, birthdays, sports events, and none of it compares to the real thing. Oh, we're definitely keeping you around."

I glowered at it. "I'll feed you bad habits. You'll never be sure if anything I say or do is real."

The thing smiled at me. "It won't matter. You can't help being you. I have the computing resources of an entire planet. I'll figure out what's real and what isn't. Maybe now I can get off the stage and into social events." The thing closed its eyes. "Terrans are complex social creatures. It's so hard to mimic your biological mannerisms." It rubbed its hands together. "Oh yes, you are going to be well worth all the trouble you've caused me."

"Why?" I asked the thing in front of me. "Why me? Why any of it?"

"Because, my simple Terran, this planet is a center of influence. You are a big part of that." It waved its arms about. "It's a necessary part of the grand plan. War is coming. One that will make everything so far look like a skirmish." It grinned at me. "The religion needs to be spread far and wide uniting as much of the four races as possible before it gets here. Too late, and everyone will perish." It pointed. "You. Me. Everything. No one will be able to stand against the tide."

I rolled my eyes.

"Ah! Beautiful. I must practice that." It motioned up the passage. "Danielle, stop standing in the corner and come here. Tell me if I've got it right."

Danielle?

She walked into view. She was an older blonde woman with a few wrinkles, but she had sharp intelligent eyes.

I'd seen those eyes before. Where...

Blood rushed in my ears as my pulse pounded in my head. My feet slipped out from under me as I collapsed to the floor.

"Hmm. I don't think I'll practice that move," the thing that looked like me said.

I tried and failed to form words. Finally, I managed to get one word out. "Mom?"

CHAPTER 24 - BETRAYAL

"Agoraki Mou," she said. She'd used the Greek term for 'my little boy.' It was at once familiar and foreign. A voice I recognized yet hadn't heard for a quarter of a century.

"It's... it's a trick," I stammered.

The doppelganger looked from one to the other of us with interest. "Fascinating."

My mother shook her head. "It's really me. I'm so sorry you found out like this."

"How? Why?"

Her eyes softened. "They banished me, Marky. They confiscated my experiments and called them monstrous, unethical, and worse. They didn't give me any choice. Leave, or they'd imprison me for the rest of my life."

My mouth moved but no words came.

"Why?" she supplied. "Because of my children." She gazed adoringly at the clone across from me.

Children? Sophie and I? She'd been forced to leave because of us? That didn't make sense. "I don't understand?"

Mom returned her attention to me. "Clones, Marky. Not true clones but semi-intelligent works of art." She smiled as she put a hand on the thing pretending to be me. "I made living dolls. Replicas of real people. Jealousy would be a thing of the past. Want a man or woman someone else has? No problem. I'll whip you up an exact copy. Play with it to your heart's content. When you get tired of it, sell it, or recycle it. It's not a real being, just a clever copy. Have a dark fantasy that would horrify the neighbors? Indulge in it from the privacy of your own home. My children don't care. They'll happily do anything you ask of them."

My empty stomach rebelled.

"Oh, don't look at me that way," my mom admonished. "Your father had the same expression when I told him about my experiments. Shortsighted. Infantile. All the science was there for anyone to put together who had half a mind and the will to do it."

"Simulated Terran Playthings..." I breathed.

"Yes," she said brightly. "My invention. My children."

My gaze traveled unbidden to my replica. "And this."

Mom sighed, "A failed experiment. It tries to mimic the living, but it has no soul. The Theocracy approached me a couple of years ago with an interesting proposal. They had some of your genetic material. Wanted me to make a copy of you." She waved at the clone, "I knew it wouldn't work, but I hadn't seen you in so long. A copy, even a poor copy, would make my heart sing. If only I could get a sample from your sister, my family would be complete again."

"But now I have you," my mother smiled. "Let this doll play politics. You can stay with me forever."

The doppelganger shrugged, "Give it time, Danielle. I'm sure I can mimic him to the point I could fool even you." It turned to me, "As for you, we are content to have you out of the way. Dr. Martin has promised us as many clones as we want, provided we could return you to her." It raised an eyebrow at the scientist. "We have a deal?"

She nodded back, "Yes, Urson, we have a deal."

"Excellent," my double proclaimed, "prepare the prisoner for transport."

***

The Dru did not follow us. One of the bodyguards put a Steal-a-Face on my head and bound my wrists behind my back. It made sense. The Porcu-bears knew about them, even if they couldn't find a way to get around them. The Steal-a-Face would prevent people from wondering why one Mark Martin was escorting another Mark Martin out of the Justice Center.

I bowed my head in defeat. How had things gone so horribly wrong? All my teams captured. They'd run headlong into a trap. Soon they'd find The Queen Nephanie and destroy her. I'd found my mother, but she was a crazy genius working for the Theocracy. I wondered if they'd kill my sister when they destroyed my ship. For sure Rowdy, Racy, Mimi, all of my crew would die. With the planet occupied, the battle for the system was an empty gesture. The Erethizon would hold the population hostage. The fleet would be powerless to stop them from slaughtering millions. They might even kill a few hundred thousand just to prove they were willing to do it.

It was hard to imagine how I might have screwed up any worse than I already had.

Escorted through the Justice Building, I glared at my mother's back. It made a twisted kind of sense why my sister and my Dad had kept the truth about my mother from me. Whatever else she may have been, she was crazy and morally bankrupt. Now I'd be living with her basically under house arrest. What would that look like? I might be able to escape, but to what end? Who could I get to help me? Almost everyone I cared about was about to be dead. Anyone captured, would be brainwashed to serve the Theocracy.

We didn't go out the front entrance. I'd long known about the secure garage at the Justice Building. This was the first time I'd been inside it.

Two men worked around a crate at the far end of the space. Four more stood at the ready on the loading dock.

"Where's my armored aircar?" my doppelganger demanded.

"It'll be here in a moment Your Highness," explained an armored guard on the docks.

Confusion clouded my doppelganger's face. "It's late?"

"Got it!" yelled the man next to the crate.

The doppelganger dropped to its knees like someone had cut its strings. It stared up at me with a vacant smile. "Do you want to play with me?"

The bodyguard on the right drew his weapon and in one swift motion shot the bodyguard on the left. His head jerked then the rest of his body followed the motion as he crumpled to the floor. The assassin then took careful aim at the doppelganger and ended its pathetic life.

Winny screamed.

My mom scowled, "Damn. Now, I have to make another one."

The bodyguard pulled off his faceplate. "Two hundred thousand credits," he demanded over Winny's hysterics.

Bound, I shrugged my shoulders. "Done. And might I add, worth every credit, Aziz."

"Hey, what about me?" protested Westley, pulling his facemask off.

"You get parole," I said.

"You were already gonna give me parole."

I grinned, "Then the deal hasn't changed."

"You son of a Dru," growled Westley. "After all that work I put into trainin' those brats."

"What?" I exclaimed. I didn't want Westley anywhere near the Dodgers.

Aziz held up a key. "Captain Martin."

I turned around and presented my wrists. Armored officers ambled towards us. The man from the loading dock approached and stood nearby.

My wrists came free and I took off the Steal-a-Face and rubbed my wrists to get the blood flowing again.

The police officer raised his visor. Ted Voorhees ducked his head, "I apologize for trying to kill you earlier." He nodded in the direction of the STP. "I thought you were him."

"You more than made up for it." I put out my hand.

He took it and pulled me into a quick hug.

I jerked a thumb over my shoulder, "You and Aziz?"

"We were both following this asshat," he pointed at the dead clone. "After running into each other a couple of times we joined up. Common goals and all."

"You idiots!" screamed Winny. "Do you have any idea what you've done?" Tears streamed down her cheeks. "They'll kill everyone. You've doomed us all to die. They control the skies. They have Disciplinarians everywhere."

I ignored her, but her outburst reminded me that my people were in danger. "Aziz, the ship. They're going to destroy it."

He shook his head, "No, Zaiem. We moved it."

"Thank gods. What day is it?" I asked.

"Third of Hermes," Ted answered automatically.

"No, Terran standard."

"Oh, uh," Ted scratched at the stubble on his chin. "April, twenty-second."

"Farthogs," I cursed, "we have to get those exchange computers down today."

"What happens after that?" asked Voorhees.

"Then the armada of allied systems engages the Erethizon up there." I pointed to the sky. "We have to disrupt the command and control down here. Do that and the Porcubears can't mount an organized resistance. They rely too much on that AI god of theirs to be effective."

Voorhees nodded, "Yeah. It might work. The Theocracy moved a lot of their tanks and fighters off world. It won't be easy, and someone will have to do something about the space station. I can contact a few other resistance cells."

"Are you listening to yourselves?" Winny punched me in the chest. Hard. "They control the gate. They'll pull ships from a dozen systems and decimate everything."

I grabbed Winny by the shoulders. "Which is why we're going to blow the gate. In a little over a day, it'll be gone."

"You're insane!"

I glanced at my mother. She seemed content to see how everything played out.

I returned my attention to Winny. "No, I'm just sick and tired of our people serving the Theocracy. My Father and the exile Senate put this crazy plan together. And yeah, a bunch of things have to go right, or it'll all fall apart. But I'll be damned if don't do everything in my power to make it work. A lot of people are putting their lives on the line. Many of my friends and allies are going to die over the next week fighting for what they believe in. I'm sure as hell going to make sure it isn't for nothing."

"The... the King?" stammered Winny.

I glared down at her. "Yeah, the King."

"Sir?" The man next to the crate signaled to Voorhees.

"What the hell is it?" he growled back.

"The jammer, it's overheating. We need to move soon."

"By the bouncing balls of Zeus," Voorhees swore, "where the Hades are my aircars? Lenz, see what's taking them so sluggin' long."

One of his men ran off.

A loud knock sounded the metal door leading to the street.

We all looked at each other and then back at the door. Voorhees signaled two of his men to check it out.

"The aircars have to knock?" I asked.

Voorhees shook his head, "No, we've tuned our comms to a range the jammer isn't jamming."

The knock sounded again.

The two men took up positions on either side of the door. One opened the door while the other aimed his rifle at the other side.

Outside in the rain were two kids in comedy and tragedy ponchos. One of them squeaked as a rifle was thrust into her face.

"What do you want," the rifleman demanded.

The girl took off her mask. "Uh... Is Captain Martin he-here?"

"Holly?" I jogged to the door. "What are you doing? You're supposed to be back on the ship."

The men pulled them inside and slammed the door shut.

"Ow!" one soldier exclaimed, "she shocked me."

I shook my head. "Pythia? You two are in such big trouble."

Pythia pulled off her mask and faced toward Holly. "Told ya, he'd be here."

"We were doin' what we were told," Holly insisted. "Honest."

"You're off the ship," I pointed out. "In danger. Exactly what we tried to avoid. How is this doing what you were told?"

Holly held the wet mask in her fingers fidgeting. "Mr. Brady and Mr. Westley said too much time had passed. That something went wrong. They said it was time for plan B."

I glared daggers at Westley. "Plan B?" I asked.

"Yeah, send us in to plant the bombs," Holly explained.

"You, as in the Dodgers," I confirmed.

She nodded.

I pointed at Westley. "I'm going to kill you, then I'm going to kill Brady."

"Whoa, there Cap," Westley held up his hands and backed up a couple of steps. "To you, they're just brats, but they're smart. Give 'em a few years an' they'll be great pirates."

"Not helping your case," I ground out through clenched teeth.

Holly pulled on my sleeve. "Don't be mad at him. We got it done."

"The Central Exchanges?" I asked.

Holly nodded.

"How did you get to them?"

"The same way the other teams did," said Holly. "There are public shuttles between every capital city every hour. It wasn't hard."

I scrubbed my face. What's done is done. No use yelling. Clean it up.

I took a large breath and let it out. "Fine, and did you plant the bomb?"

"Yes," they answered in unison.

"Pithy, you can't even see. What in the galaxy made you think this was a good idea?"

The blind mystic held up her arm. "I'm not totally blind, I have Racy's wrist things. Besides, I told you, you were going to need our help."

"Pithy..."

"No, you listen," her sightless eyes pleaded at me. "You risked your life to save Mom and me. All the Dodgers, too. Whenever things get weird or bad, or whatever, I always ask myself, what would Cap' Martin do, and I do that. You needed my help, even though you couldn't see it. I couldn't just let you go get killed. I had to do something."

There was silence for a few seconds before Voorhees commented, "Damn. Where'd you find her?"

"Later," then to the girls, "When is the bomb supposed to go off?"

Holly looked up like the answer would be found on the ceiling, "Oh, uh-"

A peal of thunder echoed through the garage followed by a resounding boom. Emergency lights flashed.

"Please find shelter immediately," said a calm female voice from a nearby speaker. "There has been a terrorist attack on a nearby building. Please follow emergency protocols and find the nearest bomb shelter. Your safety and well-being are Urson's highest priority." The message repeated in Erethizon.

Holly grinned weakly, "I think... now."

CHAPTER 25 – NEED A RIDE?

"Bus incoming!" yelled a grunt. The big door trundling up.

It was half-open when two armored air-limos executed a power slide into the garage. Gull winged doors opened before the limousines came to a stop.

The first driver gave me a smile and a wink. "Hey, Uncle Mark. Need a ride?"

"Alexis?" I glowered at Voorhees, "You're recruiting kids?"

"Teenagers, and yeah. The Hedgehogs don't see them as a threat. They can get into places and do things my men and I can't," he explained.

"Told ya I knew the right people," crowed Alexis.

A pop sounded across the garage.

"Jammer's blown!"

"You heard the man," shouted Voorhees. "Pile in. Things are about to get hot. Go. Go. Go."

I grabbed Pythia who squeaked as I picked her up.

Aziz snagged Mom's arm and she attempted to shake loose.

"Let go cur! I'm not going anywhere with you."

Aziz gave her a nasty smile. "The bounty on you, Dr. Martin, will make me a very wealthy man. You are coming with me."

He dragged her to the second armored vehicle. She punched and kicked at him the whole way. Westley laughed and climbed in after them.

I sat behind the cockpit, putting me right behind Alexis with Pythia in my arms.

Three seconds later, Voorhees pounded on the overhead, "All in. Punch it."

"Wahooo!" Alexis yelled as acceleration threatened to throw me from my seat.

We shot out of the garage and into the street. The limousine wove through traffic as if the cars were sitting still. The whine of the limo's turbines filled the compartment. I glanced over my shoulder and saw a huge grin plastered on our teen pilot's face.

My heart jumped to my throat. Too fast. We'd hit a building for sure. But time and again, she pulled it off. We came within centimeters, but never quite touched the surrounding buildings. The little girl I'd watched grow up, had the makings of a first-rate fighter pilot.

I felt a sense of kinship and pride as she executed a perfect slalom turn. She put the limo on its side as she powered into an alley slightly wider than the vehicle.

Glancing to the rear, the second armored vehicle followed but over-corrected. It suffered some minor damage as it scraped a wall.

Pythia sat bolt upright in my lap. "Turn left!"

Winny and the marines regarded her strangely.

"Turn left, turn left, turn left!" she hyperventilated.

"Alexis, hard to port," I called to the cockpit.

"Uh, okay."

We slewed and pavement erupted to our right.

"Whoa! Four bogies. I didn't even see them. Thanks, Uncle Mark."

The other limo flashed through the intersection followed by two patrol craft. I recognized the patrol car number. It was the same one that had followed me a few days ago. Two other patrol craft chased us.

Voorhees grunted, "Just like old times, eh?"

I grinned back at him, "This time I'm a passenger."

The armored car shuddered as rounds bounced off its armored hide. Alexis swerved left then right. Rounds peppered the street and surrounding buildings. Traffic evaporated.

"We weren't prepared then." He gave me a predatory smile. "This time we are. Strap in!"

I took a moment to belt Pythia in and make sure Holly was secure.

A marine pulled out an IMPAS with two rockets.

The limo bucked and jerked to the right.

"Rrrraaa!" growled Alexis.

"Problems?" asked Voorhees.

"Lost some power in the number one turbine. We're good."

The marine stood next to the right rear door and gave a thumbs up.

Voorhees called up to the cockpit, "Alexis stand left."

She rolled the armored car up on the left side. The marine threw open the hatch. He popped through like a whack a gopher and fired the IMPAS.

His aim was true. The aircar exploded. Unfortunately, they also tagged the marine. The smoking IMPAS fell into the limo followed by the grunt, missing his right arm.

Winny screamed. Holly threw up.

"Medic!" Voorhees called, but the corpsman was already beside him. Ted unstrapped and scooped up the IMPAS.

Voorhees loaded the last round. "Cartoon stop," he called up to the cockpit.

"Got it," Alexis called back.

The marine Major climbed up to the hatch. Alexis rounded a corner and reversed thrust. My back pressed into the seat as we braked hard. Half a second later was the snap-hiss of the IMPAS firing. A puff of smoke came through the door.

Voorhees ducked back in and loud cracks reverberated through the armored car.

"Go. Go. Go!" he yelled and the restraints bit into my shoulders as we accelerated. Alexis righted the limo.

Voorhees crawled back to his seat around the corpsman and wounded marine.

"That's it?" I asked.

"You got an IMPAS hidden in your shorts somewhere?"

"Yeah, let me unzip my fly so you can grab it."

Voorhees chuckled.

My head hit something, and I saw stars. A grinding noise filled the car. We'd dragged a control surface on the ground.

"Squats!" Alexis swore. "Number one's down to ten percent."

We wove left sluggishly. Craning my neck, I saw the patrol craft through spiderwebbed armor glass.

It exploded.

The second aircar passed over the fireball. A marine aimed at the final pursuer.

The patrol car braked as the IMPAS fired. The shot went wide hitting a building. This put the remaining police aircar behind both limos.

Pythia shocked my knee. "Tell her to go straight up."

"Really?"

Pithy nodded, "Yeah, trust me."

"Alexis, go up," I called over my shoulder.

"He's right on top of us!"

"I know, do it," I insisted.

Alexis grunted as she yanked on the controls. My stomach fell through my bowels and the G forces piled on.

Then my head slammed into Pythia's as the armored car twisted violently.

I swallowed hard to keep from losing my lunch. Two marines weren't as fortunate.

The patrol car swerved into a building. A fireball erupted into the street.

"Ow!" Pythia held her head.

Winny panted and I cringed as she vomited down the front of her suit.

Alexis righted the limo.

A marine cracked a window to let in fresh air. The corpsman performed CPR on the wounded marine. I could tell it was too late. He wouldn't make it.

CHAPTER 26 - ESCAPE

The limousines used ID switches like J-Dee's aircar had. When I pointed out to Voorhees that they'd still be searching for armored aircars, he waved it off.

"Computers believe what you tell 'em. If we tell 'em this is a flower van, then that's what they'll sluggin' well see."

I was skeptical, but no new patrol cars found us.

Somewhere along the way, the second limo peeled off. Voorhees didn't say anything, so I assumed it was part of the plan.

We entered the mountains and hugged the canyon walls. I approved since it would foil any spy satellites. We left the main road and landed in a steep valley.

Queen Nephanie looked better than I'd ever seen her. There was even a stream running underneath her landing struts.

The gull-wing doors opened and we clambered out of the aircar.

Winny's mouth dropped open as she stared at the gauss cannons. "You brought a whole fleet of these?"

"What? No," I waved in the direction of the ship. "This a freighter with stealth armor. If everyone we expect to show up does, we'll have two battleships, with three dozen cruisers, battlecruisers, frigates, and destroyers."

"Battleships?" she asked.

I spread my hands. "Think of a ship four times as long as this, and five times as tall and wide. And it'll be bristling with weapons, not just a couple of gauss cannons."

The airlock cycled as we approached. War 'n Pace came out followed by Brovis.

"Slugin' Porcu-bears!" Voorhees raised his rifle.

"Easy there, Captain." I pushed the muzzle of his weapon down. "Brovis and his men are with us."

"You trust them?" he said through gritted teeth.

"Yes. I'd be dead or worse if he and his men hadn't saved my ass."

Voorhees didn't look like he believed me.

"It's true," I assured him. "Moreover, he's done as much or more than any other member of my team."

That seemed to mollify him somewhat.

"Besides," I continued. "There are eighteen of them. There are seven thousand Terran marines on board."

"I've fought them. Seven thousand may not be enough."

"Fotom Martin," Brovis lumbered forward, "Introduce me to your tiny friend."

"Major Theodore Voorhees, please meet Brovis of Vengaua."

They shook hands. The marine Major only hesitated a fraction of a second.

"Come aboard," I said. "Let's iron out the details to take back the planet."

Tracy and Sophie met me inside the airlock. Sophie wrapped me in a fierce hug, while Tracy wrapped herself around my leg.

"Ow," I whined.

"Are you injured?" asked Sophie.

"Sunburn. Plasma rifle," I explained through gritted teeth.

"Oh." Sophie pulled a hypo out of her pocket and injected me with it. She hugged me again as the drugs slowly made the pain more bearable. I continued to groan, but neither of them seemed to care.

I gave in and accepted that love hurt. "Tracy, how'd you get out?"

"Brady and Brovis. Brady discovered that they were moving me to one of their bases. Brovis attacked the convoy.

"I have a serious bone to pick with Brady, but it'll keep," I said. "How's he doing?"

Sophie frowned, "He keeps trying to leave the med bay. Not as bad as you, but close."

"I'm glad you're back," I said to Tracy.

She smiled, "I'm glad to be back."

Inside the conference room, my command team situated themselves. Voorhees found a seat. Winny followed us in and leaned against the far wall. I didn't trust Winny, but I could assign someone to keep an eye on her. She wouldn't be able to tell the Porcu-bears what we were up to.

I glanced at the ceiling, "Nephie, how have the Erethizon responded to the loss of the Central Exchanges?"

Her melodious tones echoed through the conference room. "As expected, Urson switched to a more distributed network. He's using wrist AIs, personal computers, and intelligent buildings. He's also relying heavily on computing power from the space station and the ships in near orbit. Patrol of urban areas has increased, but the bulk of the planetary assets remain on the bases. The Erethizon have one base located outside of each capital. More than half the planetside equipment and personnel are there."

Voorhees grimaced at the overhead, "That's creepy. Your AI sounds like a live person."

"Thank you, Captain Voorhees. I aim to please." Nephie answered cheerily.

His jaw dropped.

I laughed. Nephie hadn't missed the slight. The fact that she'd decided to clarify, respond positively yet snarkily was a clear sign of how much she was growing as a person. "Thanks, Nephie. Will you be able to track troop movements?"

"Yes, Captain," the AI replied. "Racy's solution to have me pretend to be one of Urson's nodes appears to be working."

"Isn't that dangerous?" I asked Racy.

"A little," admitted Racy, "but we have a very good understanding of how the Erethizon AI infects other systems. He's evolved to the point where we can't dig him out of an infected system without a wipe and reboot. That said the AI is very trusting when it comes to receiving information from his various nodes. We're taking full advantage of that flaw. Any information that comes back is read-only. Nephie can recognize what his code looks like and will ignore anything that even vaguely resembles it. We've reprogramed all our gear to work differently. The chance isn't zero, but it's low.

"After you take out the battlestation and the ships in orbit, we'll blanket global wireless communications with white noise. That will isolate the nodes. They won't be able to contact each other, so the overall intelligence of the system will be diminished.

"Excellent," I turned back to Voorhees. "Can you contact the various resistance cells? Once we take out the space station, we'll have to mop up the peacekeepers. I'm hoping to get additional troops for you, but it's far from a sure thing."

He gave me a quizzical look. "*You* are going to take out the space station?"

I waved indicating the ship.

He took a deep breath. "I don't know how to break this to you, but this is a freighter."

I nodded. "Nephie, what are our chances of taking on the space station in orbit?"

"Chance of successful destruction of the space station is eighty percent," said Nephie.

I shrugged, "We've got some non-standard weapons and stealth. The space station won't be a problem."

"Mission success decreases to fifty percent if any mobile units remain in orbit," the AI amended.

Voorhees frowned, "Okay assuming you can pull that off, that still leaves a dozen bases and a hundred thousand troops. Even if we get every resistance cell to help with the ground force you brought with you, it's not enough."

He was right, of course. "We'll use kinetic strikes on the bases. That should reduce the number of Disciplinarians and supporting equipment you'll have to deal with."

He let out a long breath and shook his head, "That'll help. We'll find some way to make it work. If they start using human shields, we'll be in a world of hurt though. If they hit us with puppy rushes..." He let the statement trail off.

I hadn't heard of the Porcu-bears using waves of innocents as a weapon, but I guess Voorhees had. "I'll give you as many plasma rifles as I can spare. You'll be able to knock them out instead of killing civilians."

"How many plasma rifles?"

"About eight hundred."

Voorhees rubbed his face. "We'll prioritize the units near where they've used those tactics before."

"Take out as many cathedrals as you can. The Erethizon put AI cores in them, so each one is a loci of resistance," I pointed out.

"We know," said Voorhees. "Trust me, every one of us wants those buildings razed."

"Speaking of razed, where are the Dodgers?" I asked.

"They've all reported in," said Mimi. "None of them were caught. All of them took out their targets. Half of them are still flying in. A few are already at an ice cream shop in Aurora waiting for pick up."

I gaped at her. "They all succeeded?"

Voorhees chuckled, "I told ya. Kids. It's their blind spot."

The conference went on for another hour as everyone went over every aspect of the plan for taking back the planet and the system. Each stage had at least two backup options in case the primary ones failed.

The session broke up as the department heads briefed their people.

Voorhees stayed behind and scowled at his wrist AI.

"Something wrong?" I asked.

"Yeah, the other aircar. It's overdue. I need to send some drones out to look for it."

He left the conference room leaving just me and Winny.

She abandoned her wall and sat on the table next to me. She stared at me for a long time before she spoke. "You're not the boy I knew in high school."

"Not even remotely," I acknowledged.

"What happened? How did you become..." she waved indicating me, "this?"

"Porcu-bears," I shrugged. "They invaded. I did what I had to."

She sniffed, "No. You followed the rules. Sure, you could follow a plan, but you were never the one *coming up* with the plan. Something happened to you out there."

Her eyes bored into mine, searching for something I couldn't fathom.

I chewed my lip, "I ran. The Porcu-bears had Dad. We know what they do. I couldn't let them use me or my sister against him. So, we joined a bunch of gun runners, pirates really, and left the planet.

"I learned a different way of doing things. I learned how to attack from the shadows and disappear back into them. I made new friends. And... enemies. I lost a lot of those friends." I remembered Captain Houston, Randy, Boldrini, and Trent. A lot of people had died because of me. Because of the Erethizon. "There's something in me. A drive. A need. Save my father. Save Yale."

Winny searched my face, searching for something. "You've... killed people?"

I sighed, "A lot of people. Most were bad. Some of them were in the wrong place at the wrong time. Others died because I sent them to their deaths." My heart ached. So much suffering at my hands.

The edges of her lips twitched up in the ghost of a smile. She put her palm against my cheek. "Let me help you."

I snorted, "I don't trust you."

She blinked, "Why not?"

"Because you're Winny. You do what's best for you."

She leaned in and her lips pressed to mine. This time I didn't return the kiss. Her breath smelled of rosemary. I let it go on for too long before I reached up and took her hands in mine breaking the moment.

Her crystal blue eyes searched for something in my own. "But there's something else..."

"There's... someone else."

She frowned. "Where is she? I want to meet her."

I shook my head, "Not here. She was... injured. We had to leave her behind."

"But that's why you don't trust me?"

"Winny, I... You worked with *them* for muse's sake."

She lowered her gaze, "Yes. I wanted a good life for our people. I thought the best way to do that was to work within the system. If I could get the Theocracy to ease up on the laws, give more freedoms to Yale, then our people wouldn't suffer as much." Her chin came up. Her face came level with mine. "If I could get them to make me the regional governor, let me direct their puppets for them, I could make life bearable for the planet."

"And now?" I prompted.

"And now I'm not sure. You have a plan that has a reasonable chance of success. It may bring the wrath of GGS down on us and the Erethizon will show back up. I worry that your actions are going to get a lot more people killed. You can't keep them out. Drive them off and they'll show up with more force than we can possibly stand against."

"If we can drive them off, they will never be able to take the system again. That I can promise you," I squeezed her hands. "And as for Gilstrap Gate Systems, the Erethizon already control the board. Destroying the gate won't make us any worse off except that trade between systems will take longer."

"How are you going to keep them out?"

"Self-replicating mines."

She tilted her head, "You're serious?"

"Yes."

Voorhees knocked on the door behind me.

"There's something I have to show you," he said.

"I'll be right back, Winny."

Voorhees walked briskly up the passage as I followed. After three turns he spoke, "You can't trust her."

"I don't."

"Then why did you let her stay for the whole briefing?" he growled.

"She thought appeasing the Theocracy was the best path for our people. We have to dissuade her of that illusion. We're taking back the system. She knows things. She's been the right hand of that puppet thing for over a year. She'll know what they've done and the best way to undo it."

He looked at me skeptically.

"She can't go anywhere or talk to anyone," I pointed out. "Taking back the system is just the beginning. The planet is screwed. We'll need her to help fix it."

We went into the marine combat ops room. I didn't get down here often. It was a training room that doubled as a Combat Operations Center if something happened to the bridge. The screen showed a video of the other aircar taken from a drone. The hatches were open and bodies littered the ground around the vehicle.

"Farthogs," I breathed. "Ambushed?"

"No, only the driver was shot." Voorhees used the controls to zoom in on one of the bodies. Dried blood was caked around his eyes, ears, nose, and mouth. It had pooled beneath his head in a reddish-brown stain a few centimeters wide.

I swallowed hard to keep from throwing up. As soon as I could control myself, I stated the obvious, "Biological weapon."

The marine Major nodded, "Three people aren't accounted for."

I gritted my teeth. "Who?"

Tracy stepped in from the hatch and wrapped her arms around my leg, "I'd let you guess, but you've already figured it out."

I pinched the bridge of my nose. "Aziz, Westley, and my Mom."

CHAPTER 27 – THE PLAN

"Okay team, I've got a very important mission for you." I caught the eyes of all the Dodgers, to make sure they were paying attention. They sat in a semi-circle in a clearing near where we'd hidden the ship. The look of earnestness on their pre-teen faces matched any squad of marines I'd ever addressed.

"We're going up there," I pointed to the sky, "to bombard the Porcu-bear bases from orbit. The slugs we'll be raining down on them are small but will be moving incredibly fast. Faster than the eye can follow. The bases will be shielded, so it will take three or four hits to take one out. When that happens, you don't want to be anywhere nearby. Anyone within a kilometer will be killed instantly. Anyone within three kilometers will likely be hit by falling rocks. High winds, dust, and debris out to ten kilometers. Earthquakes for hundreds of kilometers. In short, don't be anywhere near the bases after we take off."

There were wide eyes, as they realized how big the destruction zone would be.

"Those bases aren't your concern. What is your concern are the Porcu-bears that won't be caught on those bases. I want you to tell Brady about every Porcu-bear you can find. How many there are, what equipment they have, where they're holed up, or which way they're moving. He'll pass that on to Captain Voorhees and the Resistance fighters who will deal with them."

Holly raised her hand and I nodded to her.

"What if we can swipe a data pad or wrist AI?" she asked.

"Good question. Erethizon tech is a low priority. Most of it we can't use. While the Resistance does have the ability to break the encryption, they can't afford to risk the viral AI the Porcu-bears use infecting our systems."

"What about tarring their equipment?" asked another Dodger.

"Explain," I prompted.

The boy stood up, "Mr. Westley taught us a command string that freezes up their computers and stuff."

"Really?" I received a number of nods in response. "Then yes, if you can sneak in and cause their equipment to stop working, without getting caught, do it. They'll be able to reset it, but that'll take time. If it's not working at a critical moment, so much the better. I can't stress it enough though, don't get caught."

The questions wound down after a while and I retreated to a nearby tree Brady was resting under. "You doin' alright buddy?"

"Uzai," he cursed. "Stop asking me that."

"Don't mind him Uncle Mark," said Alexis with a wink. "He's just bitchy because he can't be on the ground with them."

Brady gave her a half-hearted glare.

"What about you Alexis?" I asked. "Are you okay playing taxi for these miscreants?"

She shrugged with one shoulder, "It's not a YF16, but I'll make do."

I blinked. "The resistance has a starfighter?"

She grinned. "We have three. We just don't have the armaments for them."

I briefly reminisced about flying a YF16. The thrill of flying at Mach five. The excitement and terror of combat. Now my niece was following in my footsteps.

"Safe travels, Alexis." We clasped forearms.

"Safe travels, Uncle Mark."

***

Eight hours later, Voorhees and his people were away and getting ready for the main event. Alexis had taken the Dodgers to a safehouse. Mimi, Tracy, Winny, and I were on the bridge staring at the holo-tank. A timer ran down at the bottom of the tank.

"Mimi, are you looking at that pic again?" I asked.

"Sorry, sir. I'll put it away."

"I don't mind, it's just a bit ghoulish."

Mimi cracked her knuckles, "I wish I'd been there. I'd have loved to kick Aziz's ass to the system's edge and back again. I'm going to transmit the vid to Sandy when it's all over. No way she'll take that bastard back after that."

"If you'd been there, you'd be dead," I pointed out.

She pulled up the picture of the dead bodies again. "It would've been worth it. Admit it. You'd be glad if he died, too."

I'd hated the assassin, but he'd been a potent tool. Pay him, point him at a problem, and he'd take care of it with ruthless efficiency. Circumstances suggested he and Westley had signed on with my mother. I didn't remember enough about her to know whether they'd be a threat or not.

Winny regarded my first officer oddly but didn't ask.

The timer reached zero.

Nothing happened.

I wasn't concerned yet. This close to the planet, mass sensors were useless. We tapped Clyde's feed, so we saw what he saw.

Five minutes. Ten minutes.

I started to worry. It was possible, however unlikely, that the missile platform we'd dropped coming in had been discovered. Stealthed, powered down, and ten thousand clicks from the gate the chances of it being discovered were remote.

But not zero.

"Nephie, bring up the system-wide tactical map on the main screen."

"Of course, Captain."

As the image appeared, the cause of the delay became apparent. Orbital mechanics. The gate was not in direct line with Yale. The sun was in the way. Also, the gate was five point two light hours away. The max distance for faster than light comms was four light hours.

"This is a developed system. Don't they have comm relay satellites?" asked Mimi.

"Yeah," I answered, "they should be just inside the orbit of Euryale."

"Status change," said Nephie.

The image in the holo-tank zoomed onto the battleship. Its ion engines glowed as they started thrusting to break orbit.

"Status change," intoned Nephie a second time.

The image switched to the battlestation. Hoses and power lines retracted. Shuttles raced toward landing bays. Two of the three destroyers hadn't detached yet, but it was obvious that they were in the process of leaving the station.

"What about the other destroyer in orbit?" I asked.

The holo-tank refocused. "The destroyer has fired attitude jets but has not brought main engines online. Analysis indicates it is preparing to enter a semi-synchronous orbit opposite that of the battlestation," said Nephie

"Well, that's disappointing," said Tracy.

"At least we won't have to take them on at the same time," said Mimi.

"Okay, we need to let the local defense clear out." I adjusted the main screen to show local space. "Let them build up enough acceleration so that it will be untenable for them to come back and engage us."

Mimi studied the orbital dynamics, then moved the time slider forward. "We should launch here."

"Not bad," I observed. "We'd be between the station and the tin can and the station would be coming to us. I'm a little worried about the timing. Not the battleship, mind you, after two hours, it'll be committed."

"What then?" asked Mimi.

"Nephie," said Tracy, "adjust the plot for standard tactical doctrine." The plot changed and the two destroyers assumed positions on either side of the battleship. "Nephie assumed that the Porcu-bears would rush out to the ring. The danger is there, and the Erethizon thought the system was safe. But we've blown up buildings on the ground and the gate ring. Now they'll assume the system is no longer safe. They might assume, correctly, that these attacks are a prelude for a large-scale invasion. Clyde or the task force Commander may play it smart and use the destroyers as screening elements."

"Which means when we hit the station," I took up the line of reasoning, "the Commodore may not peel off the destroyers to deal with us. It all depends on how aggressive or conservative his thinking is. We can take on one destroyer after the station. Three?" I shook my head.

Mimi nodded, "Okay, what's the alternative?"

"We wait ten hours and launch from the other side of the station," said Tracy. "We'll be playing catch up, trying to match velocities with the station, but the Commodore won't send the destroyers back. Everything will be decided well before they could get even a sniff of the planet."

I held a finger in the air, "but the invasion vanguard will be in the system by then. The Porcu-bears will deploy their ground forces out of the bases. They haven't put up a new planet shield. They know they can't do anything against orbital bombardment. So, they will disperse their forces so we can't get them without endangering civilians. Voorhees' job will go from difficult to impossible. He doesn't have the manpower to do it."

Tracy's ears flattened against her head. "So, we're stuck between a frequa and a cliff." She wrinkled her nose. "Nephie how accurately can you hit a target on the other side of Yale from orbit?"

"Under normal conditions, I'd be able to hit a target within five kilometers," she answered.

"But..." prompted Tracy.

"But at the moment I have access to Urson's feeds for airspeed and atmospheric density," Nephie replied with confidence. "With this data, I can hit a target within a hundred meters, even on the far side of the planet."

Tracy grinned ferally.

"You want to reverse the next two phases of the plan," I guessed.

She rolled her nose, "Take off sooner, time the bombardment to have the impacts happen as close together as possible, then hit the station."

I rubbed my face, "Farthogs. It'll pretty much guarantee that we'll be facing three destroyers, but it'll give the ground forces the best chance of success."

"Isn't this a stealth ship?" asked Winny. "Can't we disappear after the attack?"

I shook my head, "We can hide as long as our armor plates aren't damaged. Any chink in the armor ruins it. The more damage we take the easier we are to see. We're a powerful little package, but that's a battlestation. We're not getting away from that thing unscathed."

I scanned my bridge crew. Zane had been quiet for the whole exchange. He nodded with conviction. Tracy and Mimi smiled. They were behind the plan as well. Winny...

I beckoned to her. "Winny come with me."

She followed me off the bridge and into my cabin.

I closed the door then leaned against my desk.

Winny examined the floor and didn't seem to know what to do with her hands.

"I'm going to put you off the ship."

Her eyes widened, "What? Why?"

"You didn't sign up for this. These people are my crew. Fighting is what they do. It's unfair of me to put you into harm's way."

"You can't!" she protested.

"I'll leave a couple of marines with you. You can wait this out somewhere safe. My father will need people like you when this is all done."

"You don't expect to survive, do you?"

I rubbed the coin in my pocket. "It's not a suicide mission, but optimistically I give us a thirty percent chance."

Winny stepped to me and pulled my hand out of my pocket. "You still have it."

I gazed down at the coin. My grandfather's profile, the last king of Yale. He'd thought he'd be the last king. Might have been if the war hadn't reached us.

"He was a good man," murmured Winny. "Personally, I thought your grandma, was wiser."

I barked a laugh.

She smiled up at me, "You must have thought so. You named your ship after her."

"I named the ship after her because she had an iron will and a vengeful streak a kilometer wide."

Winny closed my fingers around the token. "And yet she could be subtle. My Father used to cuss like a sailor whenever she outmaneuvered him in parliament."

Her hands warmed against mine. Her eyes bored into me. "Winny, I-"

"Shhhh," she put a finger to my lips. "Your heart belongs to another. I know. I'm not asking you to betray her. But she's not here right now, and right now, you need me. For now, let me be your Nephanie, the velvet fist behind the wise benevolent king." Winny wrapped her arms around me and burrowed her head into my chest.

"Winny, I want you to stay safe."

"No. Stop it. I'm staying with you." She squeezed me tighter. "You can have your men drag me out of here kicking and screaming, but you won't. You know I'm right. My place is here with you. I won't let you face this alone."

I felt my resolve crumbling, but I wasn't ready to give in. "This is a warship. Your skills aren't suited for the dangers we'll find out there."

"You're the Prince," she countered. "When you beat these hedgehogs into submission, you're going to need someone like me to convince them to surrender. Otherwise, they'll fight to the last man. More people will die. I'll help you save lives."

I leaned back and saw her jaw was set. "You believe that."

"No one understands them better than I do."

"There's a good chance we'll all die."

There was steel in her gaze. "I'm willing to take that chance. You've changed. Matured. I believe in you."

I searched her face and her body language for any hint that she was trying to deceive me. None of the signs were there. "Alright, let's get you a suit."

"What?"

"We're going into combat. The ship will get holed. Air will rush out. You'll need an airtight suit."

Now she looked uncertain.

"Don't worry. I'll teach you how to use it."

***

"Okay Zane, take us out."

The ship lurched upward, and my stomach did a couple of somersaults before the artificial gravity kicked in.

"Mr. Zane?"

His head ducked down, "Sorry, sir. I'm a little nervous."

"And you have every reason to be," I said. "Steady as she goes."

"Aye, sir."

We lifted smoothly after that. The ground fell away as we rose higher and higher. I watched the screens, waiting for some indication that we'd been noticed. Tracy or Nephie would see anything wrong before I did, but an extra pair of eyes never hurt.

Ten minutes later we were in orbit. This time the counter at the bottom of the tank was for Nephie. We'd be engaging the battlestation shortly. We needed to take out as many of the ground bases beforehand.

The counter hit zero and Nephie, began her programmed firing sequence.

"The station is scanning in our direction. Still below threshold." Tracy showed her teeth. "Feradit! The EM from the gauss cannon. They're detecting it."

CHAPTER 248- SITTING DUCKS

I clutched the coin until the edges hurt my palm. "Nothing to be done about it. Continue firing." If Voorhees was to have any chance on the ground assault, we had to take out the bases.

In the holo-tank, gold icons indicated the approximate locations of our shots. Nephie controlled both the dorsal and ventral cannons, firing at trajectories and precise velocities. Any maneuvering might cause our shots to miss.

"Focused scanning. Above threshold. They've seen us." Tracy paused, "Shots away for half our targets." Then louder, "Missile separation!"

"Go active," I ordered. "Zane, prepare for evasive maneuvers, but do not, I repeat, do not execute them until all ground shots are away. Launch countermeasures at two and a half clicks."

"Why are you waiting to use the countermeasures?" asked Winny.

"Because the missiles will be here before we can move," answered Tracy. "We'll have to take the first volley. Waiting gives us the best chance of evading."

"Oh, so we won't get hit?" asked Winny.

"No," I said, "they're going to ring us like a bell." No sense lying to her. She'd see the results in twenty seconds.

"Countermeasures away, brace for impact," Tracy gripped the console.

I held on to my armrests. Half a second later I was thrown forward. My combat harness bit into my waist and shoulders. Ignoring the pain, I called up the ship's status. Bow and starboard shields were down. Two forward compartments showed pressure loss. I resisted the urge to ask Rowdy for a damage report. He'd tell me as soon as he knew.

"Nephie?" I asked.

"Two shots are off-target. Follow up shots are away. Ten seconds to complete ground offensive. Another volley is incoming."

Rowdy appeared in a display on my left.

"Give me the bad news my friend."

"Forward sensors and missiles tubes are destroyed," he growled, "We're holed, but not badly. The shield node is repairable, five minutes on that. Starboard shield will have to be replaced, sensors suite will be fine after a reset, two tubes down, but I'll have one working again in ten minutes."

"Do what you can my friend. With a little luck that'll be the worst hit we take." I didn't believe that for a second, but a captain's optimism was contagious.

"Shots away," announced Nephie.

"Zane, go evasive. Tracy, gauss cannons to defensive fire."

Zane executed a picture-perfect Split-S placing our port shield to the battlestation.

"Any movement on the task force?"

"None," Tracy tapped at her console. "And the destroyer on the far side hasn't poked its head around the planet yet."

"Thank the muses for small favors."

Our maneuvering combined with defensive fire was effective against the incoming missiles.

"Two hits," announced Tracy, "Port shields at forty percent. Calculated offensive window is forty seconds."

"Use it or miss it. Make us a new hatch, Tracy."

Tracy used the gauss cannon offensively, pounding away at the battlestation's shields. Rowdy's shield bashing rounds spat toward the battlestation at speeds impossible to see with the naked eye. Space stations can't move out of the way. Every shot hit.

The effect wasn't as devastating as it had been for us. The shields didn't go down after the first volley. They did go down by over a third.

"It's not enough," said Tracy. She switched us back to defensive fire "They'll tear us apart before we can get a good shot in."

She was right. We needed to do more damage to the shield. We carried gravity missiles. They did great against armor but were less effective against shields.

"New contact," yelled Tracy. "The destroyer is visible around the edge of the planet.

"Farthogs," I swore.

"If I may, sir," said Nephie. "I believe I have a solution."

I watched as Tracy with Nephie's help used flares, decoys, and defensive fire to whittle down the incoming volley. The battlestation wasn't using gauss cannons yet. We were still a little too far out for them to use them on us effectively.

"What've you got Nephie?"

"If you're willing to allow me to control a volley of our missiles, I believe I can bring down the battlestation's shields."

Winny's eyes widened in horror. As Terrans, we'd all grown up with horror stories of AI's going rogue and killing thousands of Terrans. Mimi, more familiar with Nephie, shrugged with her hands up. Tracy gave me a nod. Muscat had trusted their AI's for centuries.

I took a deep breath and let it out as I wrestled with my bone-deep fears of letting an AI, any AI, have complete control of a weapons system.

"Brace!" warned Tracy and the shields flared as one missile impacted. Two others detonated close enough to do serious damage. The shield gauge dropped to two before crawling back up to three. Another hit and we'd be holed or worse.

I closed my eyes. I either trusted the AI or I didn't. Either she was my friend, or she wasn't. I rubbed my grandfather's coin. "Do it," I ordered.

"Missiles away," confirmed Tracy. She'd already switched to offensive fire. Our estimate of their shield strength edged downward.

Our missiles sped toward the space station. I watched as they seemed to dance as a group. They wove around each other passing above, below, behind, and in front of each other as they juked up, down, and side to side.

Defensive fire from the station sought them out, seeking to put rounds where the incoming threat would be. They missed. The station fired, then hesitated, as the station targeting computer realized that the missiles had drastically altered course.

Oddly, the station didn't fire another volley at us.

When our missiles were within five hundred kilometers of the station, defensive gauss cannons fired continuously to box in the incoming ordinance. A tried and true tactic we used as well. Except the Nephie controlled missiles sacrificed one of their number so the others could get through.

The gravitic missiles struck. A small section of battlestation hull deformed. The station shield went down. And not just the section facing us. All the station's shields went down at once.

"Fire at will!" I ordered.

Tracy took immediate advantage of the situation. Gauss rounds and gravitic missiles streaked toward the station.

The station altered tactics, using all weapons defensively. They even detonated missiles in our line of sight to blind us with light and radiation.

I studied the tactical display noting the station's shields flickering on and off. "Nephie, what did you do?"

"Something Sin'dani taught me," the AI admitted. "When Nemo was being built, I asked her about her design decisions.

She explained her overlapping shield strategy. In scanning the battlestation, I found the flaw she attempted to correct."

I returned my attention to the holo-tank. The station changed tactics again and devoted a trio of missiles to us. Tracy nailed them, but our shield strength dropped to ten percent.

I remembered a similar conversation I'd had with Cindy. "You found a place along the hull where power and data lines could be destroyed and cause a critical failure."

"Yes, Captain. The area was a meter wide, so precise targeting was required."

Our second volley of gravitic missiles hit the station. Micro-singularities crushed entire sections of hull. The result resembled swiss cheese. Moments later fire burst from the station and quickly died in the vacuum of space. Deck and running lights extinguished.

"Scans indicate a missile magazine has suffered catastrophic failure." Nephie brought up a scan of the battlestation showing the extent of the damage. "Secondary detonations have disabled main power. Radiation is above survivable levels for anyone not in an engineering hardsuit."

"Time to intercept with the closer destroyer?" I asked.

"About half an hour for zero intercept. Half that for a flyby." said Mimi. "Also, the two destroyers from the task force have split off from the battleship."

"Nephie, is that a destroyer in dry dock?"

"On the far side of the station? Yes, Captain."

"Tracy, get some recon drones out. Zane take us to the far side of the station. We'll be out of sight of incoming forces and we can use it for cover."

"Aye, aye," they replied in unison.

"What are you thinking?" asked Mimi.

"Ever hotwire a destroyer?"

***

The closer enemy ship declined to engage. It sent its own recon drones, but they weren't stealthed. We shot them down, and they stopped wasting them. It stood off five thousand klicks away and waited for the escorts. That suited me just fine.

I sent War 'n Pace to secure the destroyer in drydock. Some station personnel had taken refuge there. War 'n Pace offered them a choice: use the escape pods or die. There were no fanatics in these Porcu-bears. They all chose to take escape pods to the planet below.

The destroyer hadn't left port because it was being overhauled. It didn't have armaments or an AI. Rowdy hotwired the engines and Mimi put the ship, its name translated as Thorin's Peak, into a ballistic trajectory before they returned on a shuttle.

"The shuttle is back," confirmed Nephie.

"Great, Zane, take us out. Follow that ship."

We caught up quickly. The course put the station between us and the returning destroyers. It worked for longer than I had any right to expect.

"Quills has seen us," Tracy's ears twitched. "They're powering main drives. Feradit, that ship has legs."

I glanced at navigation, "Mimi?"

"At their current acceleration, they'll be within firing range in three hours." She punched a couple of keys and her display changed. "Cocheck's Rock and Prophet's Cliff have the acceleration advantage but are further out. They'll catch us in four."

"Okay, the chase is on. Rotate the watch. I want everyone rested." I stood. "I'm going to try to take a nap. I suggest first section do the same. Be back in two."

The relief crew took over and I retreated to my cabin. I'd laid down on my couch when there was a soft knock at my door.

Sitting back up, I sighed in resignation. "Come."

Winny stepped through the hatch and closed it behind her. "Do you have a minute?"

"Only just. I meant what I said about getting some rest. I'm following my own advice."

She sat down next to me, and I adjusted to put some distance between us.

A tear formed on her cheek. "I'm scared."

"You should be."

"I'm serious."

"So am I."

Winny grabbed at the legs of her suit clenching and unclenching it in her fists. "Right. Thirty percent."

I gave her a half-smile, "If it makes you feel any better, I think our chances are slightly better than fifty-fifty now."

She frowned, "One ship against three has you giving us better odds?"

"Actually, it's two ships against three, and yes."

She snorted, "I heard what Rowdy said. Peak has no weapons. It's just an engine with enough thruster control to keep it on course. It's started to spin, did you know that?"

"Yep. Up and down don't mean much out here. Trust me, the slow roll doesn't matter. In fact, that might help."

"How are you so sure?"

I shrugged, "There are a lot of things they might do. No plan survives contact with the enemy, and I'm not going to jinx us by saying what I want to do will work. Something will go wrong."

Winny inched closer, and I inched an equal distance away.

"I'm going to take a nap now. We'll talk later," I assured her.

She let out a breath. "I don't have quarters."

Farthogs. And I couldn't assign quarters without taking time away from my much-needed rest.

I cleared my throat, "Fine. You can rest on my couch. I have a bed over there." I jerked a thumb toward the door to my bunk. "Just don't disturb me for the next couple of hours."

She chewed on her lip for a handful of seconds before she said, "Okay."

CHAPTER 29 - BATTLE

My personal AI pinged me awake about ten minutes before I needed to report back to the bridge. I rolled off my bed and nearly stepped on Winny. I hadn't heard her come in. I have an area rug, I couldn't imagine it was comfortable to sleep on.

Oh well, her choice. I left quietly and went to the bridge.

Mimi and Tracy were already there. "What's the sitrep?" I asked.

Mimi brought up the near system in the holo. "Quills has reduced accel. Rock and Cliff unchanged. They're trying to enter engagement range together."

"Keep us at forty thousand klicks," I ordered. "Nephie is my math correct?""

"Yes, Captain," confirmed the AI. "We will be out of their powered envelope. However, if the flotilla continues to accelerate, they will move into our envelope shortly."

"Does that mean what I think it means?" yawned Winny as she walked onto the bridge.

"It means we'll probably get three good volleys before they can even hope to hit us," I clarified.

"Three?"

"Every time we fire, we stop accelerating and turn side on to them. When we do that, they get a little closer. They don't have to slow down. They might, depending on how aggressively they want to evade our shots, but they don't have to. We might get only two, or as many as five. My bet is on three."

The distance to the flotilla dwindled. "Winny, you'll want to put your pressure suit on now."

She bolted from the bridge.

"Mr. Zane, increase speed if you will," I ordered. "Keep that forty K distance."

"Sir, we're leaving Peak behind," he pointed out.

"That's okay, Mr. Zane."

He tilted his head away from me with a frown.

I gave him a conspiratorial wink. "What? You thought we were going to keep her? Were you expecting some prize money?"

"Uh, yes sir."

"Sorry to disappoint. Peak is a distraction." In the holo-tank, the destroyers crossed a yellow line. They'd crossed into our range. "Sound battle stations. Come about. Give 'em both sides."

Battle stations sounded, but Nephie kept the noise on the bridge to a minimum.

Zane pulled us broadside to the flotilla. Tracy fired all eight tubes. We rolled and then fired eight more.

"Fish are away," reported Tracy.

"Tracy, give 'em a few gauss rounds. Keep them honest."

"Aye, aye." Tracy matched actions to words and fired controlled bursts at the approaching Erethizon.

The missiles flew past Peak and into the oncoming Porcu-bears. They did not evade, instead they coordinated their defensive fire. It proved effective. None of our missiles made it to them. The last was intercepted two-hundred and fifty klicks from Cliff.

"Again. This is our last freebie, so make it count."

Zane and Tracy used the same maneuver and sixteen more missiles sped toward our targets. They passed Peak as they entered our effective fire range. Two missiles impacted

Rock's bow. The shield there fell. The bow deformed, but Rock didn't slow.

They figured out Peak was unmanned. Quills pulled alongside, using the runaway ship as partial cover from our gauss fire. Cliff wasn't as close. It passed on the other side of Peak a mere hundred kilometers from the hull.

"Rowdy, blow it."

He didn't acknowledge, but the aft end of Peak disintegrated in nuclear fire as its engine went critical. The explosion appeared as a flash of light. Up close, I knew that expanding gas, radiation, and debris pummeled both nearby ships. Rock far enough away to be affected.

Quill lost starboard shields and careened bow to bow with the remains of Peak. She vented air.

Cliff lost port shields but didn't look as damaged as Quills. It did have a gaping hole amidships.

"Hard about. Attack pattern Delta. Focus fire on Rock."

Stars spun as we adjusted course to pass the destroyers on our starboard. Gauss cannons ripped into Rock's nose. Missiles closed the gap. Rock created a web of steel around itself as it fought to fend off the incoming threat. It wasn't enough. Without supporting fire from Cliff and Quills, two missiles bypassed the shields and tore into the tin can.

The front half of the ship crushed into a shape resembling a hawk's bill. Main engines still appeared to be functioning, but the Erethizon destroyer lost its line and broke formation.

Quills did not immediately return fire. With its damaged side facing us, it may not have been able to. Facing Cliff's undamaged starboard, it spat six missiles at us and rained gauss rounds into our shields.

Tracy picked off the incoming ordinance, but only twenty thousand kilometers separated us. Too close. Two missiles impacted our starboard shields taking them down to thirty percent.

"Roll and return fire." I gritted my teeth. Knife fight range. Our tech advantage would erode quickly under heavy fire.

Quills and Cliff both rolled, and twelve missiles screamed towards us.

It was too much. Five of them slammed into us. The fourth took out the port shields and the fifth hit the bridge.

CHAPTER 30 - HOLES

Our hull armor is pretty good against gauss cannons. Not as good against nuclear missiles.

Hull breach alarms sounded and died as a hole opened right behind Tracy. Winny's scream echoed in my ears as she flew off her feet. I reached and missed. Winny slammed into a rail.

Tracy grunted as her harness yanked her to a stop. I watched in horror as it started to rip.

The Muscat threw an emergency seal kit at the breach. It hit at the same moment her harness tore loose. The canister exploded around Tracy.

The wind stopped and Winny dropped to the floor, unmoving.

I slapped my quick release and threw myself toward the tactical station. "Medical Emergency to the bridge. Zane, roll us. Mimi check Winny and Tracy."

I stabbed the gauss cannon controls, targeting Quills and fired four missiles at each destroyer. Quills' shields dropped.

Cliff didn't react. Perhaps because the gauss cannons focused on Quills. They'd shot at us with their unshielded port side. They attempted to roll too late. Two missiles hit the starboard shield, two impacted aft. The gravitic missiles deformed the aft section making the ship look like a giant fishhook.

Quills' shields succumbed to the onslaught. They had enough protection for the first missile. The remaining three hit amidships. Quills resembled a barbell.

I scanned local space. Rock accelerated out of the engagement zone. With its bow crushed, they might have gone dutchman. Either way, they were out of the fight.

I spun and crouched next to Tracy. "You okay?"

"Leg... broke. Hurts," she growled out through gritted teeth.

Everything from her hip down was encased in sealant. "Medical is on their way."

She nodded jerkily.

Mimi was next to Winny. I crossed and knelt on the other side. I held Winny's hand. She squeezed back. I linked to her suit. The biomonitor showed damage to her lower back, but not what was damaged. Her breathing and heart rate had spiked and were crashing. She was going into shock. I instructed her suit to keep her warm.

I nodded to Mimi and she bolted to the back of the bridge to the medkit.

"Hey, Win-win, you got a little banged up there," I said. "Didn't I tell you to belt yourself in?"

"Uh... yeah. I forgot." Her eyelids drooped.

I squeezed her hand, "Come on Win-win. Stay with me."

"Ow. Tired. Need a nap."

"Not right now." I knocked on her helmet. "Yale is depending on you. We can't rebuild a planet overnight."

Her eyes rolled in their sockets.

Mimi prepped hypo shots of stim and medi-nano.

"Nephie, what's the story with medical?" I asked.

"Battle damage has cut off Medical from internal sensors and data."

"What? What about the backups?"

"Wireless nodes in that section of the hull are also offline."

My heart sank. My sister was in there. If it had decompressed, did she get a suit on? Had she died of asphyxiation as her blood boiled in her veins?

I swallowed hard and I willed myself to focus. I tried to tell myself that if she was dead, there wasn't anything I could do about it now. My friends on the bridge were here. I could help them.

Mimi opened the port in the arm of Winny's suit and jammed the first hypo home. Winny winced then groaned. Then Mimi switched hypos as I held her down.

Winny screamed, "Squats, squats, squats!"

"Sorry, Win-win. You have to stay awake. Try not to move," I cautioned.

She nodded vigorously.

I glanced around. "Zane, we need a backboard. Find one."

He tapped a couple of keys on the helm then sprinted for the open cabinet. I was confused for a moment. There wasn't a backboard in there. But he pulled out the power drill from the repair kit and used it to pull up a deck plate.

He dragged it over and together we carefully lifted Winny onto it.

"One, two, three," Together we lifted the deck plate with Winny on it.

Mimi ran to the hatch and keyed it open for us. Air whooshed as the pressure equalized.

"Thanks. Mimi, you have the bridge. Keep Tracy company."

"Aye, aye."

Zane and I carted our passenger down to medical. My suit sensors showed the air pressure was about two-thirds normal but increasing.

Outside of medical, the glow of emergency lights revealed a passage filled with wounded. We set Winny down. A marine recognized me and shouted, "Make way!" into the suit coms.

I found Racy at the hatch to medical. The panel was open but none of the lights were on. If this section was without power, more of my people were going to die. Winny might be among them.

"How bad is it?"

Racy jumped. Then realizing it was me, she gave my leg a quick hug before returning her attention to the panel. "Main power is out in this entire section. The battery backups too." She slapped the space above the panel where the wire was taped. "I'm stealing power from the emergency lights. Maybe we can get the hatch to work."

"And check if there's air on the other side," I added. We could use the crank to open the hatch, but without power, we couldn't tell if the compartment on the other side had pressure. We didn't want to decompress the passage.

The panel lit up and Racy yipped with delight. Five seconds later it showed that the pressure on the other side was half an atmosphere. Hard to breathe, but survivable. How low it had gotten? We might open the hatch to a room full of corpses.

Steeling myself against the possibility, I nodded to Racy.

The hatch opened two centimeters. A whine echoed up the passage as the pressure equalized. I motioned two marines over, and together we muscled the hatch open.

Medical looked like it had been hit by a tornado. Paper and equipment were everywhere. A body with half its neck missing was face down in a pool of frozen blood. A gash at the back of the compartment looked like someone had squeezed syrup through it where the sealant had hardened. To my right, a body was pinned to the wall by a piece of shrapnel. My stomach rebelled and my heart spasmed as I recognized the hair color. I couldn't breathe. I forced myself to lift her head.

It wasn't Sophie.

I let out a shuddering breath.

Racy startled me when she touched my leg. "That poor woman." She pointed, "That's what's keeping the power out. Emergency power feeds are to the right of her."

War entered with marine slung over his shoulder. "Hey War, set him down and give me a hand."

He did and trotted over to me. Together we pulled the shrapnel, body and all, out of the wall.

Racy wrinkled her nose and started cutting the wall.

I found the hatch to my sister's office sealed. I held my breath and knocked 'shave and a haircut.'

Wild pounding sounded back.

I sighed in relief. Several people were in there. Hopefully, one of them was my sister. With the network down, they'd have had no way to contact anyone outside the room.

Minutes later, Racy gave a shout and the room lights came on. Screens flickered to life. Marines and crew cheered.

The hatch popped open. Two doctors and five nurses ran past. Sophie wrapped me in a hug.

"I thought I was going to die in there. Thought everyone else was dead."

I removed my helmet and returned the hug. "Never. I'll always be here for you."

"Idiot. You sure as Hades took your sweet time."

"You know how it is. Rush hour traffic. The skyways were clogged. It took forever." I stroked her back. "Winny's out there. She has a back injury."

She frowned up at me, "That girl who dumped you in high school?"

I'd dumped her, but I didn't bother correcting Sophie. "Yeah, she's a collaborator. Helping the Porcu-bears run things. Says she was trying to help people. Not sure if I believe it, but she does."

She gave me one last squeeze. "Get out of my way moron. I've got people to save."

I kissed the top of her head as she slid past me.

"Him, him, and her. Put them in the ICU beds. Kevin, prep that one for surgery. Mark and Angie, triage. Put everyone on the to-do list." Zane had found a marine to help him move Winny.

I squeezed Winny's hand. As she tried to sit up, I put my palm on her chest. "No. Lie still." I kissed her forehead. "I've got a ship to run, but I'll be back down later to check on you."

"Was that your bitchy sister?"

"Yep."

Winny groaned, "Farthogs. This day just keeps getting better and better."

***

Zane and I returned to the bridge. The air pressure was almost back to normal. The air smelled acrid as a smoky haze filled the bridge. Rowdy cut Tracy free from the deck.

"Watch it. Watch it!" Tracy's gaze fixated on the plasma torch. "You're going to cut my leg off."

"I'm not going to cut your leg off," Rowdy assured her. "I took detailed scans. Trust me. I know exactly where your suit is. I'm more concerned about thermal induction."

"Therma-what?"

Rowdy sighed, "Tell me if it gets too hot."

Tracy rolled her nose.

In minutes, he had her loose. A pair of marines carted her off to medical on a stretcher. I received a message from Sophie. She'd commandeered a cargo bay. I approved it, belatedly. We had a lot of injured, and we weren't done yet.

"Rowdy, what's our status?"

He set down the plasma drill and stabbed at his tablet, "Multiple hull breaches. Stealth is gone, obviously. All shields except stern are non-functional. Both gauss cannons are operational, but about half our missile tubes are offline. Most secondary and support systems are fine, but a lot of power and data lines were sheared."

I pinched the bridge of my nose. "I know it's too early for repair estimates. When you can, let me know what you can get working again and how long it will take. "

"Of course, Captain."

I swiveled in my chair to face Mimi. "Okay, what are we looking at?"

She punched up the local area in the holo-tank, "We own near space. The space station, Quill, and Cliff are junk. Rock is dutchman. No indication her crew has been able to regain control. Even if they do, they've got a lot of V to delta. If they regained control right now, it'd still be half a day to come back to us."

"That doesn't seem right," I sneezed as the smell of burnt plastic assailed my nose. "Even if the bridge and COC are toast someone in engineering should be able to hit the big red button."

Rowdy wrinkled his nose. "I can think of a dozen things that could cause the emergency shutdown to not work. A dozen more of why you might not want to shut the engines down. Fuel port stuck open, containment leak killed the crew, hardware damage..."

I shook my head. "They're not our problem yet. What about the outer system?"

Mimi zoomed out. The warp gate was a cloud of debris.

"Thank the muses, at least there won't be any reinforcements for a month."

Mimi pointed, "The Erethizon won't need reinforcements."

The Alliance fleet and the Erethizon fleet formed battle lines. We were too far out to get visuals, but mass sensors could pick out ships by tonnage. The Alliance fleet had two battleships, five cruisers, and five destroyers. The Erethizon had three full battle groups. Three battleships, twelve cruisers, and fifteen destroyers. Twenty-seven Porcu-bear ships to our twelve.

In fleet actions, tonnage matters. In almost every engagement, the force with the higher weight in ships usually wins. The Erethizon had more than twice the ships than the Alliance.

This was going to get bloody. The Alliance would likely lose.

If there was a bright spot, it was that an Erethizon battleship was out of position. The one from the inner system was still steaming for the engagement zone. It would take two days to get there. The battle would probably start in about six hours.

"Zane, Mimi, set course for the outer system," I ordered. "We won't be able to do much, but maybe we'll draw some fire. Hell, maybe we'll get lucky and take out a pair of destroyers."

CHAPTER 31 - DISTRACTION

"Rowdy, give me good news."

My Muscat engineer looked up from his screens, "Just a moment Mark." He typed in a number of commands and then turned to me. "Do you want the bad news, or the worse news?"

I pulled the coin out of my pocket and rubbed it. "Worse news first."

"The port shield node, it isn't coming back until I have time to print a new one."

"Ugh, what else ya got."

He pulled on his ears, "That last salvo of missiles you fired, it's the last one for a while. The feed system is toast. Engines down to a third of their output. The keel gauss cannon is fixable, the dorsal one is fine by the way." He sighed, "I can get the starboard and bow shield generators working. We're running out of replacement air. If we stay out of combat long enough, I can have the damaged attitude thrusters replaced."

"We'll keep our speed down. I have zero desire to tangle with anything for a couple of days. Can we empty the cargo bays and just pressurize the passages and workspaces?

Rowdy wrinkled his nose, "And everyone will sleep in their work areas?"

"You're right, that won't work."

"Humph, but we can install a temporary airlock in the spine at each end. Another for Sophie's cargo bay full of patients. Turn conference rooms into bunks."

That was a more workable solution. We had a few spare temporary airlocks for repair work while underway. That wouldn't leave us critically short but should allow us to conserve air. "Let's do that. Let the crew know. We may end up confined to our suits, but I'd like to put that off as long as possible."

"Rowdy, what if we only had to deal with two missile systems?"

"What do you mean?"

"I mean what if we repaired the feed systems on the bow and then on the port or starboard side?"

He scratched under his chin, "I can cannibalize one broadside and the aft system. We can make that work. Give you two tubes in the bow and say four to port?"

"That's workable."

Rowdy cocked his head to the side, "How attached are you to the aft shield nodes?"

I saw where he's going with it. "You want to give us bow, port, and starboard coverage if we take the nodes from the aft section. Won't that expose the engineering section to too much radiation?"

Rowdy shook his head, "No, we've still got enough of the stealth shielding back here to protect us from solar or missile radiation."

The more I thought about it, the better I liked the idea. I'd have to adjust tactics to protect the aft, but it wouldn't be obvious to our enemies.

"Good idea Rowdy."

I left engineering and worked my way forward. A repair crew saw me coming and moved to clear the passage, but I waved them back to work. A quartet of repair drones followed in their wake. Right now, every minute that could be spared to repair the ship was worth its weight in diamonds.

Our lives would hang in the balance of how much they could get done between now and the next engagement.

I dropped by medical. Sophie was hard at work saving lives. I gave her a wave but didn't disturb her.

Arriving at the bridge, I saw Racy's tail sticking out from the tactical console. I realized I had a big problem.

"Mimi, I'm moving you to tactical."

"What? I can't do that."

"Your scores from the academy say differently. It isn't your usual duty station, but you know how to run the systems. Tracy is injured and her suit won't be repaired in time. All the spare suits are Terran sized."

She sighed, "Skipper, as much as I appreciate your confidence, I'm not the best person for the job. I overthink. In the heat of battle, I might hesitate. I couldn't live with myself if someone died because I didn't act fast enough. You should take over tactical."

I shook my head, "I can't. As Captain, I have to balance the needs of the ship and crew. I'll be focused on the big picture. The tactical officer has to have their head in the game. Completely focused on weapons, ship position, enemy disposition, appropriate firepower, and a thousand other things. I'd be pulled in too many directions to do it effectively. I'm only human."

Racy backed out from underneath the tactical console. She wiped an arm across her brow smearing grease on her forehead. She had a suit on, but her helmet and gloves were off. "I have an idea, but I don't know how practical it is."

"What?" I asked.

She rolled her nose at me. "Let Nephie take over tactical."

I laughed, "Nothing against Nephie, but she's a computer, an AI. How is she supposed to balance priorities in combat? What ships are a bigger threat? A bigger threat to us or the fleet? What risks are acceptable? She doesn't have a firm grasp on mortality, hers or ours. We can't depend on that calculus when people's lives are at stake."

Racy frowned and crossed her arms over her chest.

"Captain?" Nephie's voice came over the speakers tentatively.

"Yes, Nephie?"

"I understand what you're saying, but I believe you're wrong."

"Go on." I prompted. I'd come to respect the AI's opinion and I wasn't going to dismiss her out of hand. I could hold my own in a philosophical discussion with her.

"That opinion was correct for the formative months of my life, but I don't believe it's relevant now." She paused for the benefit of the organic life forms. "We've been through a lot of battles together. You've balanced the lives of the crew versus the lives of countless other people we're out here protecting. Do you know how many people are living on Yale right now?"

That was an odd Segway. "No."

"Seven hundred million, two hundred and fifty thousand, six hundred and thirty-two give or take any births or deaths since we left orbit. Many of them have no clear understanding of the threat we face for them out here. A small percentage even feel that fighting the Erethizon is wrong. I've learned that all life is precious, even mine. Not everyone gets the chance to live out a full life. The actions we take up here cost lives. Not only on this ship, but also on the planet. What really matters is the quality of life for those that come after us. In the last year, I've seen friends and crew die. Some were tortured by the worst scum this universe has to offer. I also gave birth to a new life. Nemo is me, but not me in so many new and fascinating ways. Our actions here will affect her future as well. Am I alive? I don't know. I think so. I want to live, but not at the expense of the people I care about. My family. Some of it is my programming, of course, but more of it is who you are and what you mean to me. I want to protect you all and keep you safe, but I can't have what I want. You're out there trying to make the galaxy a better place for people you don't even know. I love you and I want to support you even though it pains me. I've found that balance.

Nephie paused before continuing, "I'm veering off-topic and getting long-winded. That is the correct phrase, yes? Long-winded? Anyway, I'm your friend and I'm your crew, Captain Martin. Where you go, I'll follow. It isn't blind trust or Racy's programming. It's faith. I have faith in you to make the right choices. There have been incidents in the past. Previous generation AI's have turned on their Terran charges. I need you to trust me when I say that I will never betray you, this ship, or its crew."

I wanted to believe her. I really did, but how could I know if it was just an equation for her. What if she'd absorbed everything in the ship's library on political science and was trying to manipulate me? Free of constraints, would she be a better tactician than Sara or Tracy? If we gave her that much power and autonomy, would she kill innocents? If I got in a disagreement with another ship Captain, would she overreact and fire on that ship?

"Thank you, Nephie," I said finally. "You've given me a lot to think about. I'll give you my decision later." Maybe there was a marine on board that could fill the role.

I took care of a few ship's business things: Rowdy wanting additional input on repair priority. War 'n Pace wanting to help the repair teams. Yes, if the marines wanted to help out the repair crews, by all means. And an update on the relative positions of friendly and hostile ships in the system.

I pulled them up in the holo-tank. "Mimi, what are these new contacts in the outer system?"

She glanced over, "Not sure. They came in on stealth. Mass sensors say these seven are probably freighters. We have a positive classification on the three destroyers riding escort." She adjusted the controls and zoomed in. Details were sketchy, so the icons showed the relative size and velocity of the incoming ships. "They're in formation. Troop transports?"

I nodded, "I believe you're right. The original plan called for a battalion of ground troops. I didn't think the Senate could come up with enough men. It looks like they found them."

Mimi zoomed out, "That's good placement. None of the battleships or cruisers can intercept. They'd have to send..."

The icons at the battle line changed.

"Yep," Mimi confirmed, "send in the wolves. The Porcu-bears are splitting off seven destroyers to intercept."

I rubbed my eyes. "Farthogs. That's what I would have done in the Erethizon's quills. The Porcu-bears have the tonnage. They can get the destroyers to intercept the transports a few hours short of the planet. Three escorts probably aren't enough to tie up that force."

I stifled a yawn.

"Sir," asked Mimi, "when was your last rack time."

"Uh..."

"Un-huh. Go. I'll man the bridge a while longer. Hit the rack and then you can break me. If we're going to harass the Porcu-bears on the outside of the coming engagement, we'll need to be sharp."

I opened my mouth to disagree, to insist that she take a break first. Mimi stamped her foot hard on the deck startling me.

"This isn't a debate. If you don't go now, I'll call your sister. She'll declare you unfit for command until you've gotten eight hours. Don't push me. You know I'll do it and she'll back me up."

My mouth opened, but my complaint died in my throat. Her look said she'd follow through. I held up a hand in defeat. "Okay, I know when I've been outmaneuvered. I'm off to bed. Call me if-"

"Go!"

Racy chuckled. I saluted and left the bridge for my quarters.

I stopped inside the hatch to my quarters. Something was wrong, but my fatigued brain couldn't parse what it was.

CHAPTER 32 - WINNY

In place of the usual pile of unfinished paperwork was a sandwich on a plate. My stomach growled reminding me that I hadn't eaten in at least eight hours.

There was a note from Winny. *Nephie gave me directions to the galley. I met Inga. She said that you hadn't been in and was concerned you hadn't eaten anything since breakfast.*

Winny must have left it before she'd gotten hurt. Amazingly, the grav plate in my desktop kept it in place. I eyed the sandwich and wondered if it was okay to eat it or if I'd betray Sara if I accepted food from Winny. My stomach growled again. I decided, for the moment, eating outweighed right or wrong by my girlfriend. It wasn't a date.

I crossed to my desk and started in on the sandwich. Biting into it, I realized it tasted different but in a good way.

I opened a comm to Winny half expecting her to be in surgery, but she accepted the request. The vid window popped up.

"How are you feeling?"

"Better. Your sister may be a queen bitch, but she's a fantastic surgeon."

"What kind of sandwich is it?" I asked.

"Saggitan ham and moly. I remembered that you liked ham and cheese sandwiches. Inga had good ham, but only that crappy Terran processed cheese. She had moly from Cassini, which tastes almost the same as real Swiss cheese, I asked her to substitute it."

I had to admit it was the best ham and cheese sandwich I'd had since I'd turned smuggler three years earlier. "Thanks, this is great."

I ate the sandwich and washed it down with a glass of juice. We made small talk catching up on some of our mutual friends. She suggested we have a dinner party with them.

"Winny, that's really nice, but…"

"I know, you've got a girlfriend and she wouldn't approve." She sighed, "We were good friends before we ever dated. I know that ended badly and that I was at least partly to blame."

Wholly to blame, but I didn't say it.

She continued, "But we can still be friends. I want to be friends. When we take back Yale, I want to work with you to put the planet back together." She pouted. "So how about it, can we be friends?"

I needed friends and she would be a great one to have in my corner. I grinned, "On one condition."

She groaned in frustration, "What?"

"You give me puppy dog Winny whenever I ask."

She smirked and wiggled around like an excited dog with her tongue hanging out and her hands flapping up and down. Then winced a little as it tweaked her newly mended back.

I felt a little bad, but grinned at her antics. "Okay, we can be friends."

***

"Captain?"

I awoke with a start. I blinked in confusion trying to determine where the voice had come from. I was in my bunk. I half expected to see Winny sacked out on the floor again. No Winny. She was in the med bay. It wasn't her.

"Captain?"

The sound was in my head. Nephie was using my implant to talk to me.

"Yeah, Nephie?"

"The situation has changed. Mimi asked me to call you to the bridge."

"On my way."

I fumbled around in the dark and pulled on my skinsuit. Then I picked up my armored helmet and it banged against the bunk frame.

I stepped out into the main room and pulled my armor on. Five minutes later, I was on the bridge.

"What's up?"

Mimi pointed to the holo-tank. "We've been talking with the Alliance. The freighters are carrying troops. The escorts have peeled off to engage the Erethizon flotilla."

"Farthogs, how long was I out?"

"Twelve hours. Anyway, the battle is about to begin. I figured you'd want to be up for it."

Not that we could do anything about it. We were way too far away. Also, something felt wrong.

Mimi saw my confusion. "The engines are offline. Rowdy took them down for repairs."

I nodded. We would still be on a ballistic trajectory toward the outer system, just not accelerating for a few hours.

Sitting in my command chair I called up the whole system in the holo-tank, then I narrowed in on the outer system battle. The Alliance forces had made their initial attack run. It hadn't gone well. Of the initial battle group, five ships remained. Two battleships, two cruisers, and a destroyer. The Erethizon appeared to have lost four cruisers and five destroyers. The Alliance forces headed into the inner system, and straight toward the battleship heading out to meet them.

"That will be an epic engagement," I commented wryly. "When those battleships meet, anything caught between them will be pasted like magnapple jam."

"Oh yeah," said Mimi. "I wouldn't want to be on the cruisers or destroyers. As the screening elements, they'll be in the thick of it."

I changed the focus and pulled up the main Erethizon battle fleet. They were chasing the Alliance in system. The Alliance had the acceleration advantage and the Porcu-bears wouldn't be able to catch them anytime soon. I studied the plot and gave a whoop of excitement.

"I know, right?" Mimi had seen it as well.

"What?" asked Zane.

I pointed to the asteroid field. "That's where we dropped the self-replicating mines on our way in. The Porcu-bear fleet will be running into them any minute." Then to Mimi, "Do we have any way of telling how big the minefield is?"

Mimi shook her head, "No, that's kinda the point of a minefield. You're not supposed to see it until it's too late. Good thing our forces knew it was somewhere in system. They went straight through it. Now we bring on the pain."

"Bring it!" We were still dreadfully outmatched, but anything that decreased their combat effectiveness would help us.

The lead ships, destroyers, entered where the field should be… and nothing happened. The minutes dragged on and still, the Erethizon kept coming.

"The recognition code!" exclaimed Mimi.

Maybe, I thought. "Nephie, send a message to the Alliance fleet. Let them know where the mines should be and tell them to turn off the recognition code."

"Done, Captain."

It shouldn't have been effective beyond a thousand kilometers, but maybe it was interfering with the mines. Had they swept the asteroids while we were busy on the planet? Conventional wisdom held that commercial traffic avoided asteroid belts. Not that there was any real danger, the asteroids were plenty far apart to make navigation a non-event, but why risk having to adjust your vector when going above or below was easier. Or maybe they discovered it right away when they were looking for us. Or maybe the mines saw them as friendly.

The Erethizon flotilla was now fully inside where the minefield should be. None showed any sign of distress. We were a long way away. Visual confirmation would be half a light day, but mass detectors would show changes right away.

"Farthogs," said Mimi. "What went wrong?"

A cruiser jerked. Then two more. Then the mass detectors indicated two ships breaking apart.

"Yes!" We all exclaimed together.

The fleet altered course. It tried to move above the asteroid field to get clear of the mines. An hour later any damage that was going to be done had been. The butcher's bill: four cruisers. Of the cruisers that had made it out, two were moving at half acceleration. If the battleships had taken any damage, we didn't see it from this distance.

"That was better than expected," said Mimi.

I laughed darkly, "Yeah, now instead of being dreadfully outclassed, we're only badly outclassed. The battle for the outer system is now three battleships and four cruisers to two battleships and two cruisers."

"And two destroyers," amended Mimi.

I nodded, but I knew that the two tin cans wouldn't last ten minutes when the weapons started flying.

"We're being hailed, Captain," said the AI.

"Thanks, Nephie," I responded. "By whom?"

"The George Washington."

"Farthogs, really?" I turned to Mimi whose mouth hung open. "Put him on."

Admiral McCormick's face filled my screen. "Martin? Holy farthogs on a stick. You're still alive."

I grinned at him. "It'll take more than a handful of hedgehogs to do me in, McCormick."

He snorted, "It's war, all it takes is one lucky SOB with a rock."

"Flying Aphrodite colors? Aren't you from Earth?"

"Do I sound like I'm from Earth?"

I snorted, "Yeah, pompous attitude, guttural butchering of Terran. I pegged you for North American."

He barked a laugh, "Then I fooled you too. No, I'm Aphrodite born and bred. I learned to sound like a core worlder. The only way to climb ranks in the Confederate Navy."

"You fooled me. For what it's worth, I'm glad we're on the same side this time."

"Don't thank me. I argued against coming, but that slimy snake you sent conned enough of my senators to swing the vote."

I snorted, "I resent that, slimy snakes everywhere will take offense. Wayne is far worse."

"Ha!" Then he grew more serious. "You think we can pull this off?"

He knew the numbers. We had a better chance of stopping a comet with a survey probe, but we'd already damaged them far more than we had any right to expect.

"I believe that my crew and I will do our best. Win or lose, we'll take a lot more of them than they will of us. If I end the day at the river Styx, Chiron better have a goddamn cruise liner, cause it's going to be one hell of a party."

McCormick nodded in understanding. "What shape are you in?"

I sighed, "Running out of air and spares. I've got more holes in my ship than a colander and not enough missile tubes to threaten a sand kitten."

"So, Freyan wolf pack."

"You know it," I admitted, "hit and retreat. Keep them off-balance."

"Look me up when this is over." He gave me a wan smile. "I'll buy you a beer."

"I'll hold you to that," I said and terminated the comm.

I didn't say anything and no one else spoke for long moments. I tried to imagine what it had been like for McCormick. He'd essentially stolen a battleship. Granted, Aphrodite had been a member of the Confederacy, but what had it taken to convince the crew to abandon the core worlds and follow him there. I hope he hadn't had to kill anyone. Maybe he put some off in a neutral port somewhere?

"Captain," Mimi interrupted my thoughts, "The Erethizon are about to engage the escort ships."

She'd already directed the holo-tank to focus on the battle. The main Erethizon armada was a half a light day away. This battle was only twelve light minutes away. We'd have a detailed visual confirmation almost right away.

Three destroyers against seven. I had to admire the courage of their captains. They had to know they weren't going to survive the confrontation. That they were willing to sacrifice themselves to let their transports make it to ground filled me with a mix of emotions that was hard to describe. Respect, gratitude, and admiration for sure. They were spending their lives and the lives of their crews to help free my world.

I stood and saluted. Mimi and Zane followed my lead.

"Nephie, get crew roster of those Alliance ships. Those men and women are heroes and deserve to be honored."

The missiles flew as soon as they were within range. The gap between the opposing forces filled with fast-moving icons. Neither force decelerated. The combined relative velocity was impressive. Explosions tore into ships on both sides. It was horrific and strangely beautiful. A sickening loss of life that might have been mistaken for a fireworks display at this distance.

Then it was over. The carnage a matter for the history books. The Alliance destroyers were wrecks. Pieces spun wildly in the Erethizon's wake. Two Erethizon ships veered from formation, their drives silent, bits of flotsam and jetsam coming loose in showers of metal.

"They didn't slow down," observed Mimi.

"They did, but not much. Some of their ships must not be able to make full acceleration."

"The transports?" I asked.

Mimi punched it up in the tank. My heart sank as intercept numbers appeared. The transports were slowing down to land on the planet. The destroyers were doing a flyby. The lightly armed and armored freighters would be skrit in a barrel. Easy targets.

The destroyers had the acceleration advantage in spades. If the transports tried to run, the destroyers would still catch them. They'd have even more time to turn them into space junk. Their only hope was to continue with the landing and pray that enough of them survived the engagement. It was going to be a slaughter. Hundreds of thousands of marines would die without an opportunity to fire a shot in their defense.

Five destroyers versus seven freighters. I punched up the math even though my brain already had the estimate. The Porcu-bear destroyers would have enough time to fire three salvos of missiles. Two hundred and forty warheads. Twenty-four for each freighter.

I buried my face in my hands. All those people. If they had landed, Yale would have a chance. The Erethizon would be forced to send troops if they wanted any hope of retaking the planet. It would take months with the gate gone. Months they could have used to dig in. Fortify the planet. Retaking it would be costly. Perhaps more than the Erethizon would be willing to pay.

My chest hurt. Tears streamed down my face. My vision blurred as I stared at the holo-tank willing it to change. There had to be something, anything anyone could do to get them to stop…

Something I could do to get them to stop…

The realization hit me like a gut punch.

CHAPTER 33 – IT HAS TO BE ME

There was something I could do. It was crazy. Suicide even.

I activated internal comms. "Rowdy, how long before the engines come up."

"They're coming back online now," he growled.

"How much power will they have?"

"They weren't badly damaged. You'll have full power."

I wiped my eyes. "Mimi, sound abandon ship."

"What?!" exclaimed Mimi.

"Assuming we stuck with the original plan," I pointed at the freighter icons. "That's seven freighters of fourteen thousand men each. A hundred thousand people counting crews. They're all going to die… Unless we do something completely unexpected and a little nuts."

"You're going to do a suicide run." It was a statement, not a question.

I let that percolate through my head for a few moments before answering. "Yes."

Mimi took a deep breath and let it out. "Well, farthogs. It's been a good go. Let's do it."

"You're leaving too." Mimi had to live for Pythia and Sandy. She couldn't stay.

"Fuck that!"

"But Sandy-"

"Cowan droppings," Mimi slammed a fist into her palm. "You can't run the whole ship by yourself even with Nephie's help. I'm staying. I knew I might not come back from this. If you're going to take on five to one odds in a half wrecked ship, I'm going to be right there with you."

I recognized that look. I wasn't going to change her mind. I turned to my helmsman. "Mr. Zane-"

"I'm staying, too."

"We're not coming back from this Will," I said.

"My parents died on Butcher's World. Orphaned when I was sixteen," Zane admitted. "I traveled from place to place searching for any way I could strike back at those Hedgehog bastards. I ended up on Eureka and volunteered to go to Isura. If we're going to kill Porcu-bears, I'm staying here."

I nodded accepting his choice. "Nephie, I uh…"

"I agree with your assessment of the situation," said the AI. "I have a child. My legacy will live on in Nemo. I would follow you even if I had a choice. I only ask one thing in return."

"What's that?"

"Let me off my leash. Our chance of success goes from twelve percent to twenty-four percent if I'm allowed to use my full capabilities. It's my life and the lives of my crew, please don't let your prejudices hinder my ability to keep us alive as long as possible."

Prejudices, that was a bit harsh. "Um…"

The AI sighed, "You'll still retain the ability to shut me off if I do something wrong."

I thought about it. If I waited until right before combat to turn her safeties off, she couldn't try to save the crew by running away. She'd already demonstrated that she could override her safeties at least twice in the past six months. In each instance, she'd acted in the best interests of the ship and crew and hadn't countermanded my orders in any way. Farthogs, we'd all be dead in a few hours anyway.

I shrugged, "Okay, right before we go into combat, I'll remove all the safeties."

"Thank you, Captain."

***

We'd reversed course and headed into the jaws of the enemy. I was in the airlock to Engineering. One of the Muscat marines, Trippy, was with me. I often argued with them that I didn't need a bodyguard while on my own ship. I sometimes won that argument, but I didn't bother making it this time. It was reassuring to have him at my back.

This was going to be a hard conversation. I needed Rowdy, but I didn't need Racy. *Protect the family* was hardwired into the Muscat psyche. How would they take it when I ordered one to go and one to stay? What would this do to Racy? The pair of them were devastated when Randy died.

McBeth came to mind. "If it must be done, best it be done quickly," I paraphrased and cycled the hatch.

I stood at the top of the ladder and found the entire Engineering crew waiting for me. Rowdy and Racy were front and center with arms crossed over their chests.

"We're staying," growled Rowdy. "So, before you start getting all noble, trying to get us into an escape pod or shuttle, save your breath."

I descended the ladder without speaking. Maybe one of Rowdy's Engineering assistants could take charge. I knelt in front of them and gave the Muscat a hard stare. "Everyone who stays is going to die. You're my best friends in all the galaxy. Don't come with me. Do me a favor and live."

Rowdy and Racy wrapped me in a hug. I should have expected it, but it caught me off guard. They'd become much better with personal space since they'd been around so many Terrans, but it was difficult for them. Muscat needed physical closeness. Their noses nestled on either side of my head.

Racy spoke into my ear. "Stupid Terran. You're not our friend. You're our family." Her long snout rubbed against my jaw and her breath warmed my neck. "What kind of family would we be if we didn't stand by you when you needed us."

Tears leaked across my cheeks. "I can't watch you die. I can't be responsible for your deaths."

Rowdy hugged me tighter, "And we can't let you face danger alone. We can't make your choices for you, but you can't make our choices for us either. We'll face this challenge together. It's what family does."

My gaze fell on the eight Terran and Muscat Engineering crew gathered around us. They smiled with calm determination.

I sighed, "Fine. If I'm to ride into Hades, at least I'll have good company."

I stood and turned to Trippy, who'd stopped halfway down the ladder.

He rolled his nose at me. "Don't look at me. You're a great guy and all, but my brothers and sister are getting on a shuttle."

"But not you," I said, catching the implied non-statement.

He gave a very Terran like shrug. "I'm the designated dead guy. I'll be here trying to keep you alive as long as possible."

"Are you sure there's no way I can convince you to leave?"

"No, Sir. If I thought there was a way to convince you not to go through with this, I would do it in a heartbeat. We both know that won't happen. Since you're committed, I'm committed to being here with you. There's nothing you can say to make me leave."

I smiled wanly, "Hades, who knows. Miracles happen every day, right?"

"Yes Sir, they do."

***

"I'm going to kill you."

I gave my sister a lop-sided grin, "Not a threat. I'm going to die anyway."

"Then I'll bring you back," Sophie glared at me, "and kill you again."

"I love you too, Sophie."

She held me tight. Earlier, she'd railed at me for an hour. When she realized she couldn't change my mind, she beat on my chest and cried. It was in her office. No one else saw.

A single tear rolled down her cheek, "I know why. I know it's something you have to do, but don't do it. When this is over, the Kingdom will need you. There is no one to take your place."

"That's not true. You're better at all the political stuff than I am."

Sophie frowned up at me, "People need heroes. Living heroes. War heroes. They need people they can look up to and give them hope. That's you."

"I can't be an inspiration from the grave?"

"Living heroes are better than dead martyrs every day of the week."

"That's why they'll have you, Florence Nightingale. Get these patients, nonessential crew, and marines off my ship. Save their lives. Be their hero. I can't be a hero. I'd just let them down. Reality is a bitch that way."

Sophie huffed then spun around to take charge of the evacuation.

Someone tapped my shoulder. I turned to find Winny on a hover stretcher with a marine guiding it along. Winny grabbed my hand with hers.

It made me uncomfortable, but I thought better of it. In a few hours, I'd be dead, if it made her happy, then I'd hold her hand.

"I said I wouldn't leave you."

"You can't follow where I'm going. Help my father bring our people back from the dark," I replied.

"Our people will remember you as the Prince who gave his life for them. I have the whole speech worked out."

"With you begging me not to go." I said.

"Well," she shrugged, "can't let you talk all the credit."

The marine guided her stretcher onto the shuttle. I stared after her. She was planning on using my death to her political advantage. I should be upset, but after I died, whatever she did probably wouldn't matter to me.

A pair of orderlies stopped next to me, and Tracy was on this stretcher, the non-powered kind that people just carried. I knelt and held her hand. "I feel bad about sending you off like this."

"Not as bad as I feel leaving you here."

"At least you'll live to see tomorrow."

"And face the wrath of the Queen. I'd rather charge a thousand Porcu-bears."

I smiled at her, "She wouldn't approve."

"No, she wouldn't." Tracy's mouth opened and closed but no more words came out. I touched her shoulder and gave her a gentle squeeze.

"Good luck out there, Gran'osida," she said finally.

"You too, Tren'scadi."

***

I watched the shuttles depart, knowing I wouldn't see my friends again. "Muses keep them safe," I murmured.

Returning to the bridge, I reviewed the tactical situation in the hollow tank. The five Erethizon destroyers had closed in on the Alliance transports. The enemy wasn't in range of us or them yet. We'd been accelerating 4 hours. In two more hours, we'd be within firing range. Rowdy's repairs were great. The engines exceeded expectations. The Porcu-bears had slowed, so they must have taken some damage from engagement with the Alliance destroyers.

We had two working missile tubes in the bow and two missile tubes to port. Bow and starboard shields were working at peak efficiency. The port shield was at 70%. Given a choice, I wouldn't be going into battle with the ship this damaged. The thousands of people who would die if I didn't intervene kept me going. I didn't want to die. Giving my life and the lives of my people for those transports was the right call. It was the sort of thing Sara would do too. I tried to imagine Winny doing something selfless, but I couldn't imagine her sacrificing herself for the greater good.

We'd catch the Erethizon just before they were in range of the transports but not by much.

"Captain, the Erethizon fleet is reacting to us."

"Show me Nephie," I said.

The holo-tank zoomed in on the destroyers. Two of the destroyers were decelerating hard. The time to engagement shrank from two hours to twenty minutes. "Everyone buttoned up?" I asked.

Mimi, Zane, and Trippy responded in unison. "Yes, sir."

"Nephie, sound battle stations." The alarm sounded in every compartment with air and over the comm in every pressure suit.

CHAPTER 34 - SACRIFICES

"Nephie you are weapons-free." In for a penny, in for a credit. If I was going to trust Nephie, I might as well go all the way.

"Fire at will," I ordered

The bow missile tubes spat out two missiles. The Porcubear destroyers turned their broadsides to us and spat out sixteen missiles then rolled and spat out sixteen more.

"They aren't taking any chances," said Mimi.

"They can't let us get close," I explained, "or we'll do enough damage to them to make intercepting the transports impossible. They'll catch them if those three Erethizon destroyers can continue to accelerate. If we force them to alter course, then we win."

"I hate to break it to you Sir, but we're not going to survive thirty-two missiles," said Mimi.

"Oh ye of little faith," I remarked with a lop-sided grin.

"Captain," Zane cocked his head at his console. "Nephie is giving me some odd navigation instructions."

"Nephie, what are you thinking?" I asked.

"Captain, we can make it through this barrage, if Zane does exactly what I ask him to."

"It's important for the tactical officer and the helm officer to work together, Nephie." I reminded her.

"I agree captain," intoned the AI, "I haven't taken control over the helm. I'm just informing Zane of the maneuvers I need for him to perform for the strategy to work."

"You can get us through this?" I asked.

"Twenty-two percent chance of success. Can you do better?" she asked.

I laughed darkly. "No," then to Zane, "do as she asks. It's her ass on the line, too."

Zane eyed the instructions suspiciously. "Ooookay."

We slewed hard to port. The incoming missiles were outside our defensive envelope. Nephie fired two missiles from the starboard tubes then two more. The missiles veered off on odd trajectories not heading directly at the Porcu-bear destroyers.

We went well off our line and the incoming salvo altered course to intercept. The first missile cluster bunched up. Then the first two missiles from our port salvo intersected the cluster.

Nuclear fire blinded every sensor.

Even blind, Zane altered course. Main engines cut out, thrusters fired, then the main engine screamed back to life. We cut to starboard and down relative to where the destroyers anticipated our position would be. Starboard missile tubes spat out four more missiles in rapid succession.

Sensors resolved the battlespace. Of the first enemy salvo of sixteen missiles, two remained. They were off target, heading toward where we would have been if we hadn't altered course.

Mimi whistled, "Farthogs, thirty-two to eighteen. We're less screwed, but-"

The second salvo of missiles reacquired us and altered course… Into the path of two more of our missiles. Again, cascading detonations blinded everyone.

Our gauss cannons opened up. The starboard shield dropped from a hundred percent to sixty-five percent.

"Sorry, Captain. I missed one," apologized Nephie.

I blinked. "You're doing great Nephie. Keep up the good work."

"Thank you, sir."

The sensors cleared. It was less effective this time. Perhaps a tac officer on the Erethizon destroyer or the missile AI figured something out. Whatever the reason, six of the missiles in the second salvo survived.

Our gauss cannons sought out the cylindrical death machines.

Alarms sounded as the restraints bit painfully in my chest.

"Bow shields are down," reported Nephie, "starboard shields are at twenty percent. Bow armor is damaged, but missile systems are functional. The shield node overheated but will be up in five minutes."

"Not fast enough," I said. "Zane, bring us to starboard twelve degrees and up sixty. Nephie arm and drop four missiles from the starboard tubes."

"They'll never hit the destroyer without guidance Captain," said Nephie. "They will see them."

"Not if they're in our wake," I responded.

"For this to work, I won't be able to get out of the way," said Nephie. She dropped four missiles staggered from the port tubes.

"They're maneuvering," warned Mimi. "They're presenting broadsides for another salvo."

I saw the second salvo Nephie fired earlier approach the destroyers. Two for each one. I knew Porcu-bear defensive fire would take them all out.

The destroyers presented broadsides again and each fired eight missiles and rolled to fire eight more. To my surprise, the first missile of each pair detonated early. Five hundred kilometers away, they wouldn't do any damage to the enemy ships… But it blinded the enemy ships and enemy missiles.

The second missile of each pair exploded in the midst of each of the Porcu-bear salvos. This wasn't as spectacular as the first, but the missiles hadn't yet armed themselves.

Instead of sixteen missiles, we faced seven. Gauss cannons filled the space between us and the enemy missiles. Two missiles made it through.

The ship bucked under me, slamming my head against my chair. I groaned and reached to the back of my head, which didn't work since I was in my combat armor.

"Bow shield is down. We have one missile tube up front. Starboard shield is also gone. We're holed in cargo bays two and three. No critical systems damaged," reported Nephie.

Neither Erethizon destroyer had fired another volley. This close, missiles were too risky.

"Gauss cannons to offensive fire," I ordered. "Fire all tubes. Keep the port side toward those bastards as much as possible."

"Aye, aye, sir!" Nephie and Zane shouted.

We raked the two destroyers. They returned the favor. Our shield busting rounds tore into their shields and they failed, while our port shield still had sixty percent left.

Shrapnel spewed forth from the aft end of the second destroyer. The drive plume from its engines flickered once, twice, then the whole aft end of the destroyer erupted in atomic fire.

Our victory was short-lived. We could only keep the port shield toward one target. As a result, the first destroyer got an unobstructed shot at us.

The bridge disintegrated around me. The holo-tank evaporated in a ball of fire. Consoles and screens shattered.

CHAPTER 35 - DESTRUCTION

Metal bits exploded away from me as decompression carried much of the debris into space.

"Aw, squats. Oh hell. Farthogs that hurts."

"Zane?" I called out. "Are you okay?" A stupid question. Of course, he wasn't okay.

I activated my mag-boots and unlatched myself and ran to his side. There was a hole in his chest plate right of center. The suit had sealed itself. I checked him over but didn't find any other holes. Tears streaked his face.

"What hurts?"

"Chest. It's wet on my stomach. Ughhhh." He grimaced. "I can breathe though."

Good news. I checked the datapad. His heart rate had spiked and was now crashing. I instructed his suit to give him a stimulant and a pain reliever. Shock would kill him if I didn't act fast. "I'm getting you some medi-nano. Hold tight."

He groaned, "I'm not going anywhere."

I picked my way to the medkit at the back of the bridge. Mimi was there but not moving. Trippy lay next to her. I didn't see any holes in either of them. Their arms floated in the microgravity. Right now my priority was Zane.

I grabbed the medkit and returned. Opening the port on Zane's arm I shoved the medi-nano hypo home.

"Ow… Oh yeah." His eyes unfocused and he passed out.

Checking his suit readout, I saw the nano working to seal the wound, and stabilize his condition.

I turned my attention to Mimi. Steeling myself for the bad news, I tapped the datapad on her arm. It showed her unconscious with a mild concussion. I administered a stimulant.

She whimpered as she came awake. "Ugh. What hit me?"

"The list of what didn't hit you is shorter."

She tried to focus on me. "Captain?"

I decided that she needed some medi-nano too and slammed one into the port.

Her focus sharpened, "Woah. Gimmie more."

I smiled, "You'll be fine with that. What hurts?"

She blinked a few times. "Uh, headache. Going away now." She shook her head to clear it, then winced. "What about you?"

What about me? I checked my suit for holes and didn't find any. A lot of gouges in the armor though. I checked my datapad and to be sure. "Yeah, I'm fine."

I checked Trippy's datapad. It showed trauma to his back and neck. I gave him some nano as well. He'd hurt himself if he came to, so I gave him a sedative.

The comms station had a hole through it. I swapped out two cards with the undamaged console next to it and powered it up. "Nephie?"

"Captain? Thank the Muses. I feared the worst."

"What's our status, Nephie?" Please let the rest of my crew be okay.

"I don't know Captain. Most internal and external sensors are offline. I have a few repair drones on the hull, but their sensor capabilities are limited. I can tell we're still accelerating, but I can't determine the course. We don't appear to be under fire. What internal sensors I have suggest that everything in the forward compartments has lost pressure. I have no data for the aft section."

"Thanks, Nephie." I went over to Zane and unlatched him from his seat. "Mimi, help me with Zane and Trippy. We'll take them with us to the COC." I hoped that the Combat Operations Center, our backup bridge, was still intact.

The hatch at the back of the bridge didn't have power, so we used the manual release on the inner and outer airtight doors.

Our suit lights made odd shadows in the unlit passageway. Halfway to the ladder I stopped mid-step as I saw open space past my foot. The breach was just outside the hatch to Nephie's closet.

"Nephie, there's a hole through the ship right outside your room. Watch out for it if you bring any repair drones this way." I didn't want to think how close we came to losing the priceless AI.

"Of course, Captain."

Mimi and I pulled Zane across the breach, then Trippy. We made our way to the spine passage that led back to Engineering. A suit light danced up the passage.

"Hey," I called, "who's in the spine with us?"

"Mark?"

Relief flooded through me. "Racy!"

Racy ran up the passage and hugged my legs. "I'm so happy your safe."

Mimi snorted, "What am I, chopped skrit?"

Racy patted Mimi's leg. "I'm happy you're okay, too."

"How's Engineering?" I asked.

Racy ran a hand over her helmet. "We're all fine back there, but none of the systems in the bow are talking to us. We thought the ship had been torn in half."

"Thankfully no, but the bridge is toast. We're heading to the COC."

Racy sucked in a breath, "There is no COC. There's a breach where it used to be."

I let out an exasperated breath and leaned against the wall, "Well, farthogs. But Engineering is okay?"

She nodded, "Yeah, Dad and everyone are fine. All the systems are working, just no data from the forward sections."

"What's about outside?"

She shrugged, "We don't know. None of the external sensors are working."

I shook my head in frustration. "At least Nephie's okay."

Racy brightened, "Really?"

"Yeah, she just can't see anything and can control only one gauss cannon."

Racy's eyes went wide, "Oh, poor thing! She must be going crazy with so little input." She motioned to us, "Follow me."

We followed her to the Engineering airlock. In short order, we were all through.

Rowdy hugged my legs. "Mark, I'm happy you're okay."

"I'm glad you're okay too. Is it true, everything is okay back here?" I studied the space. It looked fine.

He nodded, "Yeah, reactors and engines are fine." He glanced right and I followed his gaze. Racy headed into the airlock with two spools of data cable. "Where are you going sisha?"

"To Nephie! She's all alone up there. I'll hook her into Engineering."

He pulled on his ears, "Okay, don't take too long. We don't know how bad it is yet."

That statement brought me back to reality. Or the reality outside the ship, rather. Three destroyers, possibly four bearing down on ten defenseless freighters. I took in the Engineering space with a critical eye.

Rowdy shook my leg. "Mark?"

"Do we have a sensor suite?" A plan formed in my head. We needed to give the Porcu-bears something else to worry about. If they had to respond to us, they couldn't attack the transports.

Rowdy pointed to a corner, "I have most of the parts for one, but the parts printer in cargo bay two is damaged. I don't have the rest of what I need to put it together. Specifically, I don't have servos or a control interface."

"What about a tablet?" I asked.

Rowdy blinked once. "You mean as a control interface?" He ran a finger along his jaw. "Uh, yeah. We can download the control software, but someone will have to point the sensors in the direction of what you want to scan."

My head bobbed as I put it all together. "Mimi, how do you feel about a spacewalk?"

CHAPTER 36 – LET'S TAKE A WALK

Mimi and I were on the hull ninety degrees from each other, slowing moving our cobbled together sensors back and forth across the space in front of us.

"Captain, can you move your tablet twenty degrees more to the left," asked Nephie, "I can't see all the transports."

I complied and the plot updated in my head's up display.

"This is never going to work," groused Mimi.

"What do you mean? It's already working," I countered.

"You and me, lashed to the hull, where any stray micro-meteorite can end us in a second, heading toward three destroyers which will be shooting missiles and gauss rounds at us. Oh, yeah. This will be great fun."

"We've got shields on the port section of the hull. Nothing's going to hit us. And besides, it could be worse, we could have been facing four destroyers."

I heard the eyeroll in her voice. "Total luck that those missiles you dropped took out that second destroyer."

I grinned, "And yet, here we are, living to tell the tale."

"Yes," she said in an overly enthusiastic voice, "alive for at least the next twenty minutes. Joy, oh joy."

"You didn't have to come."

"And now I'm wishing I hadn't."

"You can wait it out inside. I can get one of the Engineering techs out here."

"Nope," she said with exaggerated certainty, "I wouldn't miss this for the world. And might I add that I'm so glad no one will ever know we attempted to do something this mind-bogglingly stupid."

I chuckled, "Nephie, how are we looking?"

"Like someone took an aircar to be recycled, then decided it was worth taking out for one last spin after it was half shredded," she answered.

Privately I agreed with her assessment. "Can you be more specific?"

"Oh god, oh god, we're all going to die." She deadpanned.

"Nephie?"

She sighed, "We have half our maneuverability, bow and port shields thanks to Rowdy's forethought in replicating enough parts before the printer died, linkages to the dorsal gauss cannon have been restored, I have three missiles tubes, and I'm being commanded by a madman."

"Excellent, may Athena guide us."

"Captain," said Nephie, "my libraries indicate that Athena is the goddess of wisdom in combat, may I suggest a different deity be invoked?"

"What did you have in mind?"

"There appear to be no deities of certain failure in Greek mythology. Perhaps Atlas, the titan forced to hold up the weight of the world?"

"Have I ever mentioned that I love your optimism Nephie?"

She didn't respond.

In my HUD, the bubbles of powered missile range intersected.

The Erethizon did not turn side on to deliver a broadside. Instead, they shot two volleys from their stern missile tubes. That gave us twelve incoming threats.

As Nephie and I had discussed, she spat out five missiles from each of her three tubes. As each missile exited, instead of racing toward our targets, they kept pace with us. When all were out, they screamed toward the enemy. That gave them fifteen threats to worry about.

That also meant that their missiles were halfway to us before ours took off in pursuit of our quarry.

"Rowdy," I yelled, "come thirty-five degrees to starboard."

We angled so that enemy missiles would impact the port side. Nephie detailed three missiles to take some out.

"Captain," said Nephie, "shield your eyes… now."

Mimi and I put our heads down and flipped our sensor tablet combinations. We hoped to be able to retain the ability to use them while the enemy was blinded. Even with my eyes closed faced away from the blast the endless night of deep space seemed to light up like the sun had just gone nova.

"Okay, you can look now."

Mimi and I flipped our sensors around and scanned the sky in sweeping motions.

The frozen image in my HUD refreshed. Three missiles from the initial salvos still bore down on us.

Even better, four missiles streaked toward each of our targets. As I expected, it was too much for the destroyers to ignore. The one on the far left tried to copy our tactic and shoot down the incoming missiles with her own. Nephie accounted for this and sent the four missiles wide. The defensive fire found one, but the remaining three impacted the aft section of the Porcu-bear ship. I saw the shields flare as the first two missiles hit home. The third went straight through and exploded in the ship's engine room. It opened up like a metal flower and began to spin.

The other two destroyers held to traditional doctrine and turned side on to meet the threat. Better able to bring their gauss cannons to bear, they were more successful. One missile impacted the shields of one destroyer the other got two.

Unfortunately, it wasn't enough to damage either ship. It helped us. They couldn't accelerate while turned sideways to provide maximum defensive fire. However, calculations showed that the Erethizon would still catch the transports short of the planet.

"Okay Nephie, hit them again," I ordered.

We repeated our maneuver firing a new volley of fifteen missiles at the Erethizon. The Porcu-bears, for their part, fired four volleys of two missiles each at us. Sixteen missiles, one-upping our salvo. They were learning though, each salvo was spread out, so we wouldn't be able to catch more than four missiles in any salvo we targeted.

In my HUD, I saw the spinning derelict pull ahead of the other destroyers. Force of the blast having imparted some momentum. Oddly enough, it stayed on the same course had been on before it had been hit.

"Nephie, can you route two missiles to give that derelict a nudge?"

"What? Why?" she asked.

"To give them something else to think about."

She split two missiles off from the volley. Our volleys came abreast of theirs.

Nephie being able to direct the missiles in flight was a real advantage. She took out all of the first volley, three of the second. That left nine missiles for the Porcu-bears and five for us.

The Porcu-bears turned side on to shoot down the incoming missiles. They shot down all but one. That one impacted the rightmost destroyer's shields but did no further damage.

We'd done it though. Nephie confirmed what I suspected. "Captain, the transports will make the planet. The Erethizon will be unable to make intercept."

Mimi whooped and pumped the tablet sensor above her head.

Gauss cannons fired continuously from their position amidships, reminding me that we were not out of danger.

"Captain, Mimi?" Nephie said with some urgency.

"Yes?"

"Duck."

There was no cover on the hull. I held my tablet to my chest and couched as low as I could. The world lit up around me. Unlike before, I was baked alive in my suit. My magboots came loose but the safety line yanked me painfully to a stop. I was flat on my back.

I tried to push myself up, but my left arm screamed at me. There was a big gouge, but my suit was still sealed. My arm bent at an unnatural angle.

Gritting my teeth, I punched my suit's datapad. Relief spread through my arm and then through the rest of my body.

"Captain, I'm coming," yelled Mimi.

"Belay that," I ground out. "I've lost my tablet. You're the only eyes we have. Stay put. I'm crawling back inside." I reached for the line securing me to the deck but used my injured arm. It reminded me of my mistake immediately. "Ow."

The gauss cannons fired, hitting the enemy destroyers. The port and aft shields on the left-most destroyer winked out. It rotated its starboard shield to us.

Then the impossible happened.

The spinning derelict swung into the destroyer. The captain or helmsman must have seen it too late. Thrusters fired in vain, trying to get out of the way. The laws of physics weren't having any of it. The Erethizon ship couldn't apply enough force fast enough. The bow of the derelict impacted the unshielded stern of the destroyer, sheering the entire section off. Both ships spun off in different trajectories.

The remaining destroyer altered course to get clear of the derelicts. The two dead Porcu-bear destroyers spun away, the remaining uninjured destroyer swung wide. The new course would put the planet between us and them. The freighters were on the near side and would land safely.

"They're running," said Mimi. "Wahoo! Let's chase 'em down!"

"Let them go," I ordered.

"Are you sure, Captain? I'm pretty sure we can take them," said Nephie.

I felt lightheaded. "Yeah, I'm sure. Fire on it if fires at us, but otherwise, let it go." I couldn't catch my breath. What was happening to me? "We aren't in any shape to chase them down… anyway."

My stomach rebelled. I hadn't thrown up in my suit since the academy. I tried to ask Mimi for help, but my ears rang and my vision went grey around the edges. Then the stars went away.

CHAPTER 37 – NO REST FOR THE LIVING

Stabbing pain in my arm brought me awake. I groaned and tried to sit up.

"Whoa there, Skipper," Mimi put a hand on my chest. "Don't get up yet."

I was on the deck in Engineering. My helmet was off and the section was pressurized.

Rowdy walked over to me and sat on my chest. His face was centimeters from my own. "Nephie says you need to rest. Don't even try to get up."

I struggled to take a breath, "Okay, okay. I won't try to move. I promise... Rowdy, I'm having trouble breathing."

His head cocked to the side, "But you don't have a chest wound?" Then realization dawned, "Oh, sorry." He moved beside me.

"I can't move my left arm."

"Neural blocker," answered Mimi. "You've got a compound fracture. Nephie told me how to set the bones, but you have to keep it immobile until the nano has a chance to knit your bones back together."

I nodded, "But nothing's wrong with my back or ribs or anything?"

"No," said Rowdy.

"Okay, then help me sit, and can someone get me some water?"

"But Nephie said-"

I held up a hand, "Nephie, it's okay if I sit, right?"

"Yes, Captain," the disembodied voice responded, "but don't jostle your arm. The medical texts in my library are very firm on that point."

Reluctantly, Mimi helped me lean against an air recycler. Rowdy got me a glass of water. Zane and Trippy slept on the deck nearby.

I regarded Mimi, "So, we're blind?"

She shook her head, "No, Rowdy got the parts printer working a couple of hours ago. We've got three sensor packages on the hull."

"But the aft section is still the only part of the ship that has pressure?"

Rowdy shrugged, "We're putting Queen Nephanie back together slowly but surely. That's the Terran phrase, right? Slowly but surely? At this point, any yard would write her off though."

"Yeah. The transports make it down okay?"

"Yes," said Mimi. "The captains couldn't say enough nice things about us. They've hooked up with Voorhees and are fortifying the cities. He says they have enough force to take back the remaining contested areas."

I sighed, "At least there's that. We're in orbit above Yale?"

"Oh, yeah," said Mimi, "stable and chugging along at three kps." Mimi activated a large screen on the forward bulkhead with her wrist AI. It showed a global map of Yale. Most of it was red. "The latest data shows that we control thirty percent of the planet, but that thirty percent is the major population centers." The view expanded to encompass half of the solar system. Things in the outer system are looking grim though." She narrowed the focus to the Alliance and Erethizon ships. She highlighted the friendly forces. "We've still got both battleships and one cruiser. They're attempting to flee." Mimi highlighted the Porcu-bears. "The Hedgehogs have three battleships, four cruisers, and the one destroyer. From a numbers perspective, we've won all but the last engagement. But it's a losing game. We just don't have the tonnage to win."

I saw the timestamps in the bottom right corner, "We're getting this in real-time?"

"Yes, sir," said Mimi. "The Alliance has been dropping recon drones throughout the battle. We requested their encryption, so we can see their telemetry."

It also showed each ship's status. "George Washington has engine damage," she continued. "It's slowed by a third. Star Shark and Firecat aren't willing to leave it behind, and the Erethizon fleet is catching up. It'll be the end of them."

Mimi tapped her wrist AI and the intercept appeared on the screen. They wouldn't be able to reach the grav limit and jump clear. We were watching their last stand.

"Farthogs, so close." I lamented. Kane, McCormick, all the people I knew on those ships would soon be dead. How many of my friends had died already?

Rowdy, Mimi, and I observed in silence as the bubbles indicating powered missile envelopes converged.

Then as one, the entire Erethizon fleet veered away from the retreating Alliance forces…

"What the…" wondered Mimi aloud.

"New contacts," said Nephie. "Ten, eighteen, now twenty-three unknown ships are at the grav limit." She paused. "We are being hailed."

"Us, specifically?" I asked.

"No, sir," said Nephie. "They are asking for Gran'osida Martin. That is one of your names correct?"

My jaw dropped and I felt as if a huge weight lifted from my shoulders. "Yes. Holy Muses, yes. Nephie please put them through."

A familiar image filled the screen, "Gran'osida Martin, on behalf of the Muscat Matriarchy and the house of Gran, we would like to formally accept the terms of your proposed

Alliance. We apologize for our tardiness. Cassini refused to let us use their warp gate, so we had to go the long way around."

I bowed my head to the Queen's only son. "Your Highness, we are honored to fight beside our brothers and sisters of the house of Gran. The kingdom of Yale and the house of Martin welcome you."

The Prince bowed and then his ears folded back and his eyes softened. "Clan brother, you are injured. Do you require medical assistance?"

"I am injured, but not seriously. I'm more concerned about by my brothers and sisters in arms near your position."

"We've transmitted surrender orders to the Erethizon fleet in your system." The Muscat Prince's grin turned feral. "They haven't responded."

I smiled in relief, "Then I leave their fate to you, my brother."

"Attack the brother, expect the clan." The Prince quoted the Muscat proverb. "Vengeance is mine." He ended the comm.

The Muscat fleet winked out then reappeared in the path of the Erethizon fleet. Both sides launched missiles.

"How did they do that?" asked Mimi.

I shook my head in disbelief, "I have no idea. Theoretically, it isn't possible to form an R-drive bubble so close to another mass, but they sure as Hades just did it. And they did it in formation."

"Did you know they were coming?" asked Rowdy.

"I sent a message to the Queen before leaving Isura requesting assistance. I didn't run it through the senate," I explained. "I expected her to turn me down. She'd be committing her Empire to a war with the Erethizon. I'm just one knight. She's responsible for hundreds of billions of people."

"War is coming to the Empire anyway," Rowdy pointed out.

"But was it the right time," I added. "The Erethizon engineered the collapse of the Confederacy. They're poised to conquer it piecemeal. She could put off entering the war for ten or even fifteen years."

In the outer system, missiles from both sides converged on their targets. The battle was short, brutal, and almost completely one-sided. Three Porcu-bear ships managed to transmit their surrender. The rest of the Erethizon fleet was gutted.

CHAPTER 38 - POLITICS

"Muses, I hate these things," I mumbled.

"Shut up," admonished my sister quietly, "You've never been in a royal receiving line before." Then to the next ambassador, "Judy, I'm so glad you came. I have that recipe you wanted for magnapple pie. Get with me later and I'll forward it to your wrist AI."

I shook the ambassador from Aphrodite's hand. "Good to see you again Judy. Has it really been seven years? You haven't aged a day."

The ambassador moved on to my Dad and I whispered through my teeth to Sophie. "You know what I mean. Saying nice things to people you barely know. I never got the whole receiving line thing. Can't we just mingle around the room like normal people."

"Smile," Sophie prompted.

We stood to either side of James Bartlemay, as our picture was taken. The lead delegate from the Butcher's World Senate in exile grinned. "We still on for pod ball in two days?" he asked.

"Oh yeah," I assured him, "You and Brian are going down."

He punched me in my injured arm and moved onto my Father.

"Ow," I whimpered so that he couldn't hear.

"Pod ball?" Sophie spat through a fake smile and gritted teeth. "Mark, your arm needs time to heal. That wasn't a simple break."

"I planned on canceling at the last minute," I admitted. She rolled her eyes. "Yeah, sure you were."

The end of the line approached, and I was horrified by who was there. Sophie and I both knelt.

"Your Highness," I protested, "I humbly apologize for the affront. I had no idea they put you at the back of the line."

The Muscat Prince gave a quick hug to my sister then to me. "I requested it. I hoped to steal you away for a few minutes." I let go, but Gran'ziti held me firm. "What? So quick to end our meeting?"

I chuckled, "Terran customs," I explained. Ignoring convention, I wrapped the Muscat Prince in the full embrace he expected.

"Ah. Much better." He patted my back. "Let me say hello to The King. There's a place nearby we can talk privately?"

"Yes," I signaled to Tracy and her brother Trippy.

We were in the royal audience chamber. The space was large enough to host a football game but built with diplomacy in mind. The chamber had several small sitting rooms located behind heavy velvet curtains and clever secret doors. I made a polite apology to a few waiting dignitaries and let Tracy and Trippy lead me to one of them.

For most of my life, this building had been a museum. My doppelganger had lived here, as part of the illusion of being a Prince of Yale. I'd always thought the building was gaudy and ostentatious. Now I'd be expected to live here. I hoped to get a budget to redecorate my apartment.

We entered a small sitting room hidden behind a tapestry commemorating some event I'd never bothered to look up. The Prince came in not long after. I knelt and gave him a proper hug. I sat in a velvet armchair and The Prince settled on a suttee.

"How's your Mother?" I asked.

"Fine, fine," he grinned up at me. "She wanted to come, but as the queen, she's pretty much stuck on the homeworld. He paused and squinted at me. "So, the Treaty, it wasn't approved by the Senate before you transmitted it." It wasn't a question.

I shook my head, "No, I pulled a page from Senator Wayne's playbook and put it together without their input. I didn't involve the Senate but had approval from my Dad and Sophie." I cocked my head at him. "That doesn't disappoint you, I hope. I couldn't be sure your people would approve it or come to our aid. It was a gamble. Your Mom or the nobility might not view it as the right time."

He rolled his nose at me. "If the King approved, I'm sure the Senate will approve it as well."

I wasn't so sure, but that was a battle for another day.

The Prince continued, "The Queen has been following your activities closely. She's very taken with you. She's been searching for the right moment for a while now. The Erethizon numbers advantage isn't something we'll be able to overcome on our own. As tough as our ships are, we can't overcome ten to one odds."

"It's important to me that The Muscat be paid for any patents going forward. I wanted to provide reparations, but I didn't think I could get the Senate to agree to that." To be fair, I didn't think we could come up with the money to pay for licensing either, but that was a job for the Senate.

He snorted, "Right now, your war-torn planet needs all the resources it can muster to rebuild." Gratzi pulled at his ears absently. It was obvious he wanted to say something but couldn't bring himself to do so.

I put a hand on his shoulder, "Racy is fine. She thinks of you often and misses you every day."

The Prince crawled into my lap and hugged me, "Thank you," he whispered into my ear.

I held him as long as he wanted, then he sat on the arm of the chair. It was a little uncomfortable with him so close, but normal social distance for me was uncomfortable for him.

"Has your Father and the Senate arranged your life-mate?"

I let out a long breath, "Not yet. I'm engaged to Sara, and her father is a high-ranking admiral on Shoshing. Shoshing isn't part of the Alliance. Mr. Wayne and the conservatives are making noises about marrying me to an ex-girlfriend of mine. So far my Father has held firm that it's my choice."

"And he's not pressuring you?"

"Oh, no," I assured him. "He is. He's pointed out on several occasions that if Winny and I were married, he'd be able to push anything he wanted through the Senate. He's asked me repeatedly to reconsider, especially since..." Since Sara was still recovering from her ordeal with the pirates and the sabotage attempt.

Gratzi held my hand in his, "She's still in the hospital."

"Yes. Sophie says she's getting better. Memory Blurring has been partially effective."

He grinned with teeth, "From what I hear, she's a strong woman. She'll make it through. I hope I can call her clan sister someday."

I smiled with more confidence than I felt. "She'll pull through. In the meantime, we have a war to fight. It's time we took the battle to the Porcu-bears."

The Prince held a fist high, "Qualpida favora Muscat."

I held up my fist and gave my planet's rally cry, "Yale forever!"

The End

About the Author

TH Leatherman is a writer from Firestone, Colorado. He enjoys science fiction, fantasy, wine making, and the Rocky Mountain lifestyle. When not busy writing his next book, he can be found hiking with his wife and two sons, or walking his rescued dogs. He graduated Summa Cum Laude from Regis University with a degree in Business Management and a minor in Psychology.

Connect with Mr. Leatherman

Check out his blog and links to other books

https://thleatherman.com/

https://www.facebook.com/TH-Leatherman

@thleatherman on Twitter

Can't get enough stories by TH Leatherman? New chapters of exclusive stories are posted every other week on his Patreon page.

https://www.patreon.com/THLeatherman

Check out TH Leatherman's YouTube Channel for weekly videos. Author interviews, book reviews, and tips for writers.

https://www.youtube.com/channel/UCpB5ygo4EBYzt3V8XXyyrHQ

Reviews!

Authors (especially me) love reviews. Good, bad, or indifferent tell me what you think. You can do it easily on Amazon and Goodreads, but anywhere book lovers congregate is appreciated.